Three wo
mother
Three me
they k
Can they agree?

THE *Secret* BABY BARGAIN

Three brand-new stories from reader favourites
Barbara Hannay, Meredith Webber
and Mary Nichols

THE *Secret* BABY BARGAIN

BARBARA HANNAY
MEREDITH WEBBER
MARY NICHOLS

Harlequin Mills & Boon Limited, Eton House, 18-24 Paradise Road, Richmond, Surrey TW9 1SR

ISBN: 978 0 263 86756 5

009-0309

Printed and bound in Spain by Litografia Rosés S.A., Barcelona

The Billionaire's Baby Surprise

BARBARA HANNAY

Barbara Hannay was born in Sydney, educated in Brisbane, and has spent most of her adult life living in tropical North Queensland, where she and her husband have raised four children. While she has enjoyed many happy times camping and canoeing in the bush, she also delights in an urban lifestyle – chamber music, contemporary dance, movies and dining out. An English teacher, she has always loved writing, and now, by having her stories published, she is living her most cherished fantasy. Visit www.barbarahannay.com

Dear Reader,

You may think it's strange that babies and violent cyclones are somehow connected in my mind, but it's a reflection of my real-life experience.

Soon after my husband and I were married, we moved away from temperate climates to tropical North Queensland. Our first home was a bargain, having been damaged by Cyclone Althea, which had practically flattened Townsville a few months before we arrived.

The summers that followed were punctuated by the wailing of cyclone warnings on the radio and TV. I can remember wading through floodwaters that reached mid-thigh when I was pregnant with my first baby. With baby number two, I bought a clothes-dryer after we had twenty inches of rain in twenty-four hours.

But my impulse to connect the arrival of babies with extreme weather goes deeper...

Both events – births and cyclones – change lives. They also bring unexpected happy surprises. When my children were little, I discovered wonderful, generous friends. Other young mothers, who like me lived a long way from their families in the south and together we formed sanity-saving support networks.

And I can attest that during and after natural disasters, people always reach out to help each other. People in homes with electricity and water offer their washing machines and hot showers to their less fortunate neighbours. Meals cooked on gas burners are shared and neighbours help each other to clear debris.

When babies are born, parents and families rapidly adjust to the challenges and joys of raising them. And after cyclones, forests often recover more quickly than we expect. In both scenarios, the cycle of life continues...

It was fun writing a secret-baby story within the setting of a cyclone and I hope you enjoy Claire and Jack's journey to happiness.

Happy Mother's Day!!!!

Barbara Hannay

For my dear mum, Beryl Dow.
You're the best!
Happy Mother's Day.

PROLOGUE

CLAIRE EDEN leapt from the airport taxi, thanked the driver as she thrust the fare into his hand, and hurried through the bewildering maze of hospital corridors to the maternity ward.

By then the drama was over. Her sister Flora was sitting in bed with her newborn son in her arms.

'Come and look at him,' Flora called, grinning madly.

Claire came and looked. The baby was tiny and red-faced, wrinkled and bald, and he looked like an old man in a bunny rug.

Her sister's eyes shone. 'Isn't he perfect? Isn't he gorgeous?'

'Gorgeous,' Claire repeated, but she was looking at Flora rather than the baby.

Her sister's wild dark hair tumbled over the pillows and her pretty face, though paler than usual, was luminous. She was gazing at her infant son with damp, bright eyes, and with a look that was at once awestruck and wondering, fearful and courageous.

She had never looked more beautiful.

* * *

'Does Harry's father have fair hair?' Claire asked later, after the baby had been bathed and dried and his neat cap of fine red-gold hair had become visible.

Flora closed her eyes and sank back against the pillows. Despite Claire's advice to the contrary, she'd refused to inform the baby's father about her pregnancy and she still hadn't told Claire the man's name.

'No, the father's not fair,' Flora said now, in a clipped, let's-drop-that-subject voice.

But Claire felt a need to persist. 'Our family has always been dark.'

Flora's eyes flashed open, and Claire recognised her sister's stubborn look. 'Lots of babies start out fair and go dark later. Like chickens and ducklings.'

'So you can't even confide in me?'

'Leave me alone, Claire, and stop being the bossy big sister.'

Flora was tired, so Claire let the prickly subject of Harry's father drop. She gave her sister a kiss and a hug, and went off to find a motel room for the night.

The next morning she returned, with a massive bunch of roses and lilies.

Flora beamed at her. 'Harry's a brilliant feeder. You should see the way he latches on. Like a little tiger shark.'

'Does he hurt you?' Claire asked, flinching.

'No, but funnily enough my leg's a bit sore.' Pushing the bed sheet aside, Flora reached down to massage her shapely calf. 'I think I must have bruised it. Probably banged it when I was in labour and didn't even notice.'

'Tell the doctor about it,' Claire said.

Dismissing this suggestion with a shrug, Flora smiled. 'All my friends from the island are coming over on the ferry to see Harry today.'

Claire suppressed her sigh, but secretly she envied her sister's idyllic lifestyle as an artist on a tropical island. Claire's life in Brisbane, much further south, was madly hectic. As the co-owner of a company that managed special corporate events, she mostly felt like a hamster on a wheel—on call twenty-four hours a day, seven days a week, continually stressed.

In fact, Harry couldn't have chosen a worse possible time to arrive. This very day Claire's company, C&C Events, was overseeing their biggest gig yet—a massive launch for Brisbane's Inner City Traders, designed to lure shoppers out of suburban malls and back into the city heart..

All the clothing shops had come together to put on a huge fashion parade. Restaurants were hosting a gourmet food fair out in the street. Rock bands, a youth orchestra and school bands were to perform on a central stage. Buskers, fire eaters and sidewalk artists had been hired, and radio stations had set up outdoor studios.

The success of an event of this scale rested on meticulous planning and attention to detail, and yesterday afternoon Claire had been halfway through her last-minute checklist when she'd received Flora's text message.

My labour's started and I'm frightened. Can you come? Now???

Ever since their parents' death, Claire had been weighed down by a motherly concern for her baby sister, so she'd dropped everything in the hands of her business partner and hopped on the first plane north.

Claire knew Flora didn't hold with working to deadlines. She claimed that her creativity couldn't be forced inside timetables and she couldn't understand why Claire let her clients rule her life. It was impossible for her to appreciate the sacrifice Claire had made to be here.

Perhaps that was why Claire blurted out the thought that had been bothering her all night. 'What are you going to do about Harry's father?'

Flora rolled her eyes to the ceiling.

'Flora, you have to tell him. Any man deserves to know he has a son.'

'I can't tell him.'

'Why ever not?'

'I don't know where he is. He's gone away—sailing around the world, climbing mountains, jumping out of planes. Anything he can find that's extreme and reckless.'

Claire wouldn't let this distract her. 'Is he Australian?'

Flora nodded.

'Then he's bound to come back eventually.'

'But he won't want to know about the baby.'

'How can you be certain?'

Flora's fingers plucked anxiously at the bedsheets. 'He made it clear his life was all about fun. He's irresponsible and selfish. He certainly wouldn't want to settle down. Besides, if I tell him his family will find out, and I don't want that.'

'What's wrong with his family?'

'They're filthy rich.'

'Excuse me? And that's a crime?'

This was not making sense. Claire and Flora had inherited quite tidy sums from their parents. Claire had used her share to go into business with an old school friend. Flora had bought a cottage on Sapphire Island, with world-class views across the Bay.

'You're not exactly poverty stricken, Floss.'

'But I like to live simply,' Flora protested. 'You know that. I want to be close to nature, and I want Harry to have a healthy, stress-free childhood, out of the public eye. On the island.' She heaved another exaggerated sigh. 'If the father's family knew about Harry, they'd have him in a private prep school in Sydney before he was out of nappies. He'd have a nanny or three, his own chauffeur—the whole circus.'

'Good grief. Who have you slept with? A royal prince?'

Her sister had the grace to blush. 'Near enough.'

'Oh, for heaven's sake, Flora, you've got to tell me now.'

Flora's eyes flashed to Harry, tucked innocently asleep in his blue and white blanket, and then she swept her gaze to a bland painting of lavender orchids on the wall and sighed theatrically. 'All right. If you must know, his name is Jack Dysart.'

At first this meant nothing to Claire.

But then the penny dropped.

'Not *the* Dysarts? You don't mean—' Claire gulped when she saw the telltale wariness in her sister's eyes. 'Don't tell me—he can't be one of Theodore Dysart's sons?'

Flora nodded sadly.

Good grief. A Dysart has bedded my sister.

Claire recalled the many photographs she'd seen in newspapers and magazines of this famous Australian dynasty. 'I thought the Dysart sons were married. I seem to remember they're called Joseph and—and Nick?'

'Jack's the third son, and he's not married. He prefers to let his older brothers have the limelight. I guess he's a bit of a black sheep.'

'But—but—he's still a Dysart. Wow!'

It was the only thing Claire could say. She stared at baby Harry with renewed respect. Today he looked pink, rather than red, and his tiny lips were making cute sucking movements in his sleep. His ears were incredibly neat and sweet, and so were his pink fingers as they curled over the rim of his blanket.

Claire was rather relieved she could say in all honesty that he *was* gorgeous after all, but she found it impossible to accept his connection to his father's powerful family. The Dysarts' wealth was massive! And so was their power.

And the very mention of them had turned Flora into a lioness, fighting to protect her precious cub.

Claire's day at the hospital was punctuated by calls to and from her business partner.

'Everything's going really well,' she was assured.

'As usual, your nitpicky attention to detail has paid off, Claire. We haven't had a single hitch.'

'Great. Have a glass of bubbles for me,' Claire replied. 'Better still, have more bubbles ready for when I get back. I'll be home by Friday evening.'

Wrong.

Very early on Thursday morning, Claire received another phone call.

'Miss Eden?'

'Yes?'

'This is Jonathan Bryce, your sister's obstetrician.' His voice was deep and solemn, and Claire knew immediately that something was wrong. Then she heard terrible words.

'I'm very sorry, Miss Eden. I have bad news.'

CHAPTER ONE

PALM trees, white sands, latticed verandas… A crystal-clear aquamarine sea…

The sweet scent of frangipani…balmy tropical nights…and a dark-eyed girl called Flora Eden…

These were the temptations that had lured Jack Dysart back to Sapphire Island after a restless eighteen months of adventuring around the globe. Today, however, as he boarded the ferry bound for the island, the tropical waters were a dull, sullen grey. Heavy metal clouds clustered and brooded on the sunless horizon and the air was thick and oppressive.

A cyclone with the innocuous title "Fred" had been brewing for days out in the Coral Sea. Overnight it had changed direction and turned west, and now a hurricane-force gale was heading straight for the North Australian Coast. It was expected to make landfall near Sapphire Island within the next twenty-four hours, and tourists had rapidly cancelled bookings and scrambled onto planes or buses heading south.

The ferry was almost empty, and Jack was more than

happy to sit alone on the top deck, one arm flung casually over the railing, while waves chopped at the sides of the boat and salty wind lifted his shirt collar and buffeted his face.

He'd sailed the Atlantic in a force nine gale, he'd spent three days trapped in a blizzard in the Andes, but he'd never experienced a tropical cyclone. Now, while others were running away from the danger, Jack was happily heading towards it.

What better way to celebrate his return to Australia than a weekend alone with a lovely girl while a savage storm raged and rattled outside her cottage?

Claire Eden stood in the queue at the tiny supermarket on Sapphire Island's beachfront esplanade and rechecked her list against the contents in her shopping cart. Batteries for the torch, the lantern and the transistor radio. Tinned food. A small gas bottle for the primus stove. Baby formula, nappies, extra water.

Today her habitual attention to detail was warranted. With a cyclone coming, the island's few shops were fast running out of emergency supplies.

She smiled down at her baby nephew, Harry, strapped in his seat in the shopping cart, and he giggled up at her.

At nine months, he was a chubby, bonny boy, with a perfectly delicious glowing complexion, a cap of honey-blond hair and bright blue eyes. Almost every day Claire was newly astonished by how deeply she adored him. She only prayed that she could keep him safe during this cyclone.

If they'd been given more warning she would have left the island and taken him south to Brisbane and safety. But the direction of the cyclone had changed very suddenly. By the time Claire had heard the news at six o'clock this morning the phone links and websites to all the airlines had been jammed. When she'd finally got through all flights south had been fully booked.

The supermarket queue shuffled closer to the checkout, and Claire cast an anxious glance outside. It was hard to guess that a dangerous storm was heading this way. The palm trees fringing the beach still swayed gently, but the air was very hot and muggy, and clouds pressed low.

She saw the ferry coming from the mainland, chugging into its berth at the end of the long, old-fashioned wooden jetty.

'I hope they've brought more kerosene,' said the woman beside Claire.

'And let's hope they brought plenty of beer,' added a male voice further down the queue. 'Can't sit out a cyclone without beer.'

There was a ripple of laughter and mutters of agreement, and for a moment the nerve-tingling tension in the small shop lightened.

As far as Claire could tell the general attitude to impending danger among the islanders seemed to consist of little flurries of fear amidst an almost casual excitement.

No one wanted their homes to be damaged, but the islanders spoke about "Fred" with a kind of fascinated awe, as if the threat of a cyclone had injected a sense of adventure into their quiet lives. They seemed impressed that their little island would play host to a major event.

Claire preferred events she could spend weeks planning for, with outcomes she could control, but she'd given up that life nine months ago. Since then her world had morphed into a completely different, not unhappy routine of quiet domesticity and caring for a baby.

Little Harry looked up at her and grizzled, impatient with waiting in the queue. She gave him her keyring to play with and he laughed at her, showing three tiny white teeth, then he shook the keys and rattled them against the wire sides of the shopping cart. Claire dropped a swift kiss on his silky hair. He was such a sweetheart.

While the baby investigated each key in turn, she amused herself by watching the handful of passengers alight from the ferry. Most of them were locals, but her attention was drawn to a tall, dark stranger.

Babe alert…

Flora's cheeky voice sounded in Claire's head, and just like that she was caught by an agonising slug of grief. After nine long months her heartache over Flora's death could still leap out of the blue and catch her as if she'd been harpooned.

Pressing her lips together to hold back a wave of sorrow, she tried to distract herself by concentrating on her shopping list. No use. She knew it off by heart and she'd checked it twice already. Her eyes flashed back to the hot-looking stranger.

He was exceptionally handsome, and he strode from

the ferry with his head high—as if he owned the island and half the Pacific. Even though he seemed in no hurry, his long legs allowed him to overtake everyone else easily, as the passengers made their way along the weathered planks of the jetty.

He was dressed in light coloured trousers and a pale blue shirt, with long sleeves rolled back to his elbows. His hair was short and dark, his longish jaw shadowed by designer stubble, and he carried a duffle bag over one shoulder. Gold glinted at his wrist.

Claire was intrigued. His clothes might have been considered causal if he'd been arriving in a big city, but here on the island he was almost overdressed. Most tourists arrived in shorts and T-shirts and sandals. She wondered if this man had come on business, and amused herself by considering the possibilities.

Could he be a journalist, hoping to cover the cyclone firsthand? An insurance assessor, getting in early? Or perhaps he owned business here on the island—a hotel or a guest house—and wanted to make sure it was secure?

He strode past the supermarket and someone jogged Claire's elbow. She jumped, then realised it was her turn at the checkout.

'He's a regular hottie, isn't he?' Lily, the checkout girl, grinned at Claire and sent a wistful smile in the man's direction.

'I suppose he's OK,' Claire agreed briskly. 'As eye candy.' Hastily she unloaded her shopping trolley, and hoped no one could see the rush of colour in her cheeks. How annoying. She might have been suffering a date drought for over a year now, but she was not desperate.

To be honest, she was not particularly interested in men any more. She only had room for one man in her life—little Harry. She'd woven such happy dreams for the two of them. By next year Harry would be running on the beach and learning to swim. Soon he would be making friends with other island children. She would form a playgroup with their mothers.

She looked forward to buying him fat crayons to draw with, little trucks to push around in the sand, a tricycle, his first school uniform, a soccer ball. OK, maybe part of that dream held a misty, man-sized shape—a vague possibility for the distant future. But she was in no hurry to find him.

She paid for her groceries and wrestled the keys from Harry's firm grasp before unbuckling him from the shopping cart. Her heart turned over when she lifted him up and he gave a joyful little kick, before snuggling in against her hip. No great looking man could ever make her feel as important or as loved, or as warm and as melting, as this little guy.

Reaching for her shopping bags, she took a moment to adjust her balance, testing the weight of the baby on her hip and the bags in her other hand. She had to climb steep steps cut into a cliff to reach Flora's cottage.

The cottage, however, was incredibly cute—a timber bungalow, with a white-latticed veranda, a red iron roof and a garden, fenced by a low drystone wall and filled with bright tropical shrubs, ferns and flowers. Behind the house, protected from the sea winds, a small flagstone courtyard was bordered by sunny nasturtiums, pots of geraniums and tubs of herbs.

And right now the tall dark stranger from the ferry was standing on the cottage's front doorstep.

Claire came to a startled halt and, ridiculously, her heart began to thump. As she watched, the fellow lifted his hand and rang the doorbell.

'Harry,' she whispered. 'Who on earth is he? What does he want with us?'

Harry merely cooed.

To Jack's annoyance, no one came to answer his ring.

Of course he'd known that Flora Eden might not be home or, worse, that she might not live here any more. But as he'd been coming from Asia he'd flown into Australia via Cairns, and it was only a hop, step and a jump down the coast to reach this island.

He could have phoned ahead, but he'd had the crazy notion that it would be fun to surprise Flora. He should have known that women—even a girl as happy-go-lucky as Flora Eden—rarely liked to be surprised. And now the shoe was on the other foot.

If Flora wasn't here he would have to spend the weekend alone. Jack was in the mood for company.

He tried the doorbell again, shoved his hands into his trouser pockets and leaned against the stair railing, whistling under his breath as he looked out at the choppy waters of the bay and at the ferry, rocking in its moorings at the end of the jetty.

A flutter of blue danced in the corner of his vision, and he turned to see a young woman emerging through the arch of pink bougainvillea at the top of the cliff steps. Relief flooded him.

But the relief was temporary. All too soon Jack realised his mistake—the woman in the blue dress was not Flora.

Her hair was dark, and reached her shoulders, but Flora's hair was a riot of tangled curls and this woman's hair was dead straight. And, despite her graceful bearing, she wasn't as beautiful as Flora. She was taller, slimmer, older and plainer—and, to clinch the widening gap between the two women, this one had a baby.

She fixed Jack with a severe, frowning stare as she hurried along the path and then, to Jack's dismay, turned in at Flora's gate. At the bottom of the short flight of steps she stopped and set down her shopping bags, then stood with her shoulders back, regarding him sternly.

Jack had been lolling against the railing, but he straightened instinctively, almost as if he were a small boy and this adult had corrected him.

'Hello,' she said. 'Can I help you?'

'I'm not sure. Do you live here?'

'Yes,' she said, colouring, even though she eyed him steadily. 'Were you expecting someone else?'

'Yes, I was hoping to find Flora. Flora Eden.'

To Jack's consternation the colour fled from her face. Momentarily she swayed, and then she clutched tightly at the baby in her arms. 'Flora's not here.' Her face twisted unhappily. 'I'm afraid Flora—' She shot him a bewildered look. 'Haven't you heard?'

'I don't think so,' he said carefully. What should he have heard? Not bad news? 'I've been overseas,' he said. 'Out of touch.'

'Are you a friend of Flora's?'

He swallowed uncomfortably. 'Yes, I am.' What else could he say? Now Jack thought about it, this serious-eyed woman looked as if she might be related to Flora. He could scarcely admit to her that he'd turned up here on the strength of a pleasant stop-over a year and a half ago.

'You're not—?' she began, and then she shook her head and closed her lips tightly, as if she needed to prevent herself from saying more.

'I'm Jack Dysart,' he said. 'I met Flora when I sailed through here from the Whitsunday Islands.'

Her sharp intake of breath alarmed Jack. She looked more worried and paler than ever, and she hefted her baby a little higher on her hip.

'Jack Dysart?' she said unhappily. 'Oh, yes, Flora mentioned you. I'm Claire. Claire Eden. Flora's sister. I—I'm sorry you've come all this way for nothing.'

She looked back over her shoulder to the bay, and the passengers boarding the small white ferry boat. 'Perhaps you'd better get away while you can? There's a cyclone coming, and that's the last ferry back to the mainland.'

Jack narrowed his eyes at her. He wasn't going to be dismissed so easily. 'So where's Flora now?'

She wouldn't meet his gaze. Fine hairs lifted on the back of his neck.

Hugging her baby tightly, Flora's sister said, so softly he almost missed it, 'She died.'

No.

The shock of her words caught Jack like a kung-fu kick. Flora—that lively, healthy, glowing girl—dead?

'That—that doesn't seem possible,' he said shakily.

'I know.' Miserably, Flora's sister looked down at the baby in her arms.

'How did it happen?'

She lifted her gaze to him and her eyes were tragic. She studied him in fraught silence, and he could sense conflicting emotions waging war inside her.

With a stab of dismay, Jack knew that she didn't want to trust him.

But she said, 'I—I guess you'd better come inside.'

She bent to pick up her shopping, but he launched into action. 'Here,' he cried, leaping down the three steps. 'Let me get those for you.'

'Thanks.' She looked as if she'd tried for a smile and missed.

CHAPTER TWO

JACK DYSART!

Claire hoped she didn't look as shocked as she felt.

Of course she recognised him now—was surprised she hadn't done so straight away. But her mind had been so fixed on the cyclone.

She took a desperate breath and risked looking at him more closely. She had to admit that he fitted Flora's description of an adventuring playboy. He had the weathered leanness and fitness that came from real-life adventuring rather than mindless slogging in a city gym. And his eyes were the most amazingly clear blue-green, like the tropical sea on a calm, sunny day. A careless girl could drown by simply looking into them.

Claire had no intention of being careless, but she wondered what Jack would say if he knew he'd tormented her conscience for the past nine months.

At first she'd fiercely resented his existence. After all, he'd contributed to her sister's death by making her pregnant and then leaving her to cope alone. From that point it had been easy to take on board Flora's belief that

Jack was a threat to Harry's happiness simply because he was a Dysart.

Claire had studied every media report about the Dysart family. Jack, as the youngest son, was not often in the spotlight, but there were reports of him breaking off an engagement to some society darling, and a mention of him heading overseas on reckless adventures.

And, if the rumours were to be believed, the Dysart men were all tarred with the same brush. They were as arrogant and demanding as they were good-looking. Dangerous in the extreme.

Just the same, there had been times in the past nine months, as Harry had grown more and more adorable, when Claire had been troubled. She still believed—possibly naively—that any father deserved to be notified about his offspring.

But how could she do that when Flora had been so very vocally against it? And what rotten luck that he'd chosen this day of all days to turn up.

She couldn't afford to waste time staring into dreamy blue eyes. She still had a long list of preparations to complete before the cyclone hit.

If she'd thought she could quickly tell Jack about Flora and then send him back onto the ferry, she would have got it over now.

But she feared that a Dysart would not be so easily dismissed. Besides…it was beyond Claire to explain the tragedy of her sister's passing in a throwaway sentence on the front steps. Unhappily, she pushed the key in the lock and nudged the front door open.

Inside, the cottage showed very few signs of Claire's occupancy. After Flora had died she had been too grief-stricken to worry about her fetching own things from Brisbane. Later, after she'd adjusted to the new rhythms of caring for Harry and life on the island, the trappings of her city life had felt irrelevant.

What need had she, on a tropical island, for a dozen business suits? She'd bought copies of her favourite CDs, and novels by her favourite authors, and all sorts of clothes and toys for Harry. But almost everything else in the cottage belonged to Flora.

The floors were pale polished timber, the walls colourful and bold. And, with a typical dash of her artistic panache, Flora had decorated her home with an interesting blend of whatever took her fancy.

Family heirlooms, such as their mother's antique English furniture and porcelain, sat happily beside a Moroccan carpet and a Malaysian wicker birdcage. And scattered everywhere were Flora's whimsical sculptures, made from driftwood and shells and other found objects from the beach.

'You might remember the kitchen's through there,' Claire told Jack, pointing through a doorway fringed with multicoloured wooden beads. 'You can dump everything on the bench for now, thanks.'

Claire sat Harry in the middle of the Moroccan rug, with a basket of toys to keep him happy, and then flopped into one of the deep, squishy armchairs and began to gnaw on her thumbnail. Damn. She hadn't chewed her fingernails in months.

She knew she should at least offer Jack Dysart a cup

of tea—but she was afraid he might settle in, and she wanted to get rid of him quickly. She had cyclone preparations to worry about. But, even without that concern, she was scared that if Jack stayed too long she might eventually blurt out the truth about Harry. And for the time being, at least, she owed it to Flora to stay quiet.

Jack came into the room and the baby cooed and chuckled up at him. Jack smiled politely, but with the distanced, faintly horrified air of a bachelor who habitually avoided babies.

Claire pointed to the other armchair and, as Jack sat, willed herself to stay calm. This was so hard. She wasn't used to entertaining super-attractive wealthy playboys in her living room. And she wasn't used to keeping conscience-troubling secrets.

Jack sat forward, almost on the edge of the chair, not at all relaxed, with his elbows propped on his thighs, hands tightly linked. 'I need to know what happened to Flora.'

He looked and sounded so genuinely concerned that Claire almost felt sorry for him. But then Harry began to crawl across the carpet, chasing a multicoloured ball, and she remembered the fierce battle-light that had glowed in Flora's eyes when she'd spoken about the Dysarts.

'Actually, there's not a lot to tell,' Claire said, speaking quickly to get it over. 'It was one of those terribly sudden things that should never have happened. It came out of nowhere. Deep vein thrombosis. A—a clot.'

Jack glared at her with stark disbelief. 'Surely she was too young to die from something like that?'

Claire sighed, and offered him a small smile of sympathy. For the past nine months she'd been tortured by the same question.

Why? Why? Why?

If only Flora hadn't been so casual about that soreness in her leg.

If only Claire had spoken up. She was the big sister, the sensible one; she'd looked after Flora when their parents had died. She prided herself on her attention to detail. She should have done something—said something. It would have been so simple to alert the medical staff. *Excuse me, could you please check my sister's leg?*

But what could she tell Jack about that now? How could she explain that even young women could die of thrombosis after delivering a baby? One mention of a baby and Jack would, after a couple of questions and a quick calculation, deduce his connection to Harry.

All it would take was a single slip and she'd make Flora's greatest fear come true. Harry would be whisked away by his reckless and selfish father and absorbed into the Dysart dynasty.

Claire hadn't realised she'd been gnawing at her thumbnail again until she felt a jab of pain. Hastily she folded her thumb inside her fist. 'There's no reasonable explanation. It was one of life's cruel twists of fate,' she said unhappily. 'Totally unfair and too awful to believe.'

Jack looked stunned as he nodded. 'That's for sure. It doesn't make sense. I mean…' He paused, gave his thigh an exasperated thump. 'I've been doing crazy things. Some people have accused me of having a death wish—which isn't true. But I've been risking my neck on all kinds of reckless stunts. And Flora stayed safely at home and—'

He couldn't finish the sentence, and Claire stared at him in surprise. He was reacting the same way she had, burdening himself with unreasonable blame. Survivor guilt, the experts called it. But it was the last thing she'd expected from this man. If he knew he'd made Flora pregnant he would probably feel much worse.

She felt a warm ripple of sympathy for him.

Warning flash!

Jack Dysart did not need her sympathy. How could she have forgotten so quickly that his presence here spelled danger?

Good grief. He'd only been in her house for a matter of minutes and her nice fat preconceptions about him were already being ripped up like documents in a paper shredder.

Time to get her head together.

She cast an anxious gaze beyond Jack, through the deep casement windows to the view of the bay, which was so brooding and grey and moody today.

Was it her imagination or were the waves churning more now than they had been five minutes ago?

Jack followed her gaze. 'The wind's picking up.'

'Yes.'

'I'm sorry,' he said, rubbing a hand over his face as if it might ease his shock. 'I'm taking up your time.'

At that moment Harry, who'd been crawling merrily about the room, reached Jack's foot. With a little crow of triumph he grabbed at Jack's trousers and used the fabric as leverage to haul himself upright onto distinctly wobbly legs. He beamed at Jack with a gummy grin.

'Well, hello,' Jack said politely, and then he looked at Claire again and smiled.

His smile sent a high-voltage current scorching through her body. No wonder her sister had fallen for this man. Could any woman resist him?

'Looks like he's almost ready to start walking,' Jack said.

Claire tried to answer, but her tongue was paralysed. How ridiculous. Clearly she'd been living on an island with a small population for too long. In Brisbane she had seen men as good looking as Jack every day—well, on a regular basis, at any rate.

Frantically she dropped her gaze and concentrated on Harry. 'It probably won't be too long before he walks,' she agreed. 'He can get all the way round his cot, hanging on to the rails.'

She usually felt a spurt of motherly pride when people praised Harry's progress. Today she felt nothing but agitation. How annoying to be so nervous of Jack.

Quickly, she rose from her chair and swooped on the baby, lifting him away from Jack's legs and into her arms. He smelled of sunshine and baby powder.

Below, in the bay, the ferry let out a loud blast.

'The ferry's leaving now,' she told Jack reproachfully. 'You're going to miss it.' He wouldn't even make it now if he ran all the way.

He shrugged and smiled. 'That's OK. I was planning to stay. I've never seen a cyclone at first hand.'

How childish, Claire decided, needing a reason to

dislike him. He was as silly as the men at the supermarket, clamouring for beer and planning to sit out the cyclone as if it were some kind of exciting spectator sport.

Somewhat icily, she said, 'Do you have anywhere booked to stay?'

'Not yet, but I'm not too worried. I'm sure I'll find a room at the hotel. Most of the tourists have gone. I'll find somewhere.'

A small silence rode by.

Claire knew this was the point where a warm and generous woman like Flora would say, *You're very welcome to stay here. There's plenty of room, and with a cyclone coming I'd really appreciate having a man about the house.*

Claire imagined herself actually saying those words—throwing out a welcome mat with an easy, casual smile. She opened her mouth but nothing happened. Which was pathetic. Cyclones were frightening, and she really could do with a man about the place, but she had as much chance of offering Jack Dysart a casual invitation to stay with her as she had of swimming to China.

Annoyed with her tension, she cast an unhappy glance to Jack's duffle bag, propped where he'd left it beside the front door. He followed her gaze.

'Right,' he said. 'I'll get out of your hair.'

In two strides he was at the door, swinging the bag over his shoulder. Claire felt an anxious, almost desperate disappointment—which was crazy—but she said nothing to stop him.

He raised a hand in a sharp salute.

'Bye,' chirped Harry. She'd taught him how to say goodbye and to wave, and now he proudly lifted a chubby hand and flapped it madly.

Jack grinned at him. 'You've got a smart kid there.' He went down the steps and looked back over his shoulder. His blue eyes glinted. 'Take care.'

'You, too.'

From the cottage doorway Claire watched him, broad shoulders braced against the buffeting breeze, as he strode along the clifftop. He ducked his head as he entered the bower of bougainvillea, which was already being stripped of its frothy pink flowers by the strengthening winds. Then he gradually disappeared as he descended the steps cut into the face of the cliff.

Claire felt ridiculously lonely. She looked at Harry. 'You were showing off for him, weren't you? Walking and talking and waving goodbye.'

'Da,' Harry answered with a chuckle.

Harry answered every question with 'da', but this time Claire's eyes filled with tears. 'Yes, baby boy, he's your dad,' she whispered.

And suddenly she wished she hadn't whisked Harry so quickly away from Jack. If she hadn't intervened Jack might have actually touched his son. He might have come into contact with Harry's warm, peachy-soft skin and his sturdy, robust little limbs. Jack might even have been rewarded by one of Harry's sweet, wet-mouthed kisses. And they, Claire thought with a fond smile, were something else.

She sagged against the doorjamb, the impending

cyclone forgotten as she thought about her own father and the endlessly patient games of tag he'd played with her and Flora on the beach. She often wondered if her father had wished that one of them had been a son.

And now here was Jack, with a son he didn't know about. Just now he'd been so close to Harry, but he hadn't so much as touched him.

Suddenly she was overtaken by memories of that time, after Flora's death, when Harry had been handed into her arms…

In the hospital…

The nursing sister had approached her. 'Would you like to hold the baby?'

Mutely, Claire had nodded, but she hadn't been sure she could summon the courage to hold such a tiny baby. She'd felt too horrified, too raw and numb—still hadn't been able to believe that the slight pain in Flora's leg had been a blood clot that had moved during the night and lodged in her heart.

Claire's own heart seemed to have stopped. She'd had to remember to breathe.

'It might be best if you sit down,' the sister had told her.

'Right.' Claire had sat, heavily.

'Hold out your arms. Now, relax, dearie. That's it. Use the crook of your elbow to support his little head.'

Claire had barely been able to see Harry through her tears, but she'd felt the warm weight of him in her arms. He'd squirmed a little and turned his head to nuzzle at her breast. 'Sorry,' Claire had sobbed. 'I can't help you, baby.'

'Yes, you can.' The sister's voice was warm and encouraging, and she handed Claire a small bottle of formula. 'Here—tilt this just so, and bump it gently against his cheek.'

Claire's hand trembled as she pressed the rubber teat against the baby's skin. Harry went almost cross-eyed with surprise, and she couldn't help smiling through her tears.

'Pop it in now,' the sister said as he turned to the bottle, his mouth open like a baby bird's beak.

Claire did as she was told. She tipped the bottle up, and just like that her nephew was guzzling hungrily.

Instinctively she had pressed a soft kiss to the top of his head. He smelled…amazing. She drew in a deeper breath, taking in the warm, clean, new-baby scent of his skin. She felt the strong movement of his arms and legs squirming inside his blanket and she saw his eyes, blinking and slightly unfocused, as he gazed up at her.

Her heart had constricted and she had fallen helplessly in love…

'Da,' Harry said again now, patting at Claire's damp cheek.

She cuddled him close. Jack was Harry's father, and she felt terrible denying him the knowledge that he'd given life to such a beautiful little son.

But how much worse would she feel if Jack claimed Harry and took him away from her?

Could she bear that?

Could she risk losing Harry? In the past nine months she'd undergone a startling transformation, living a life on the island that she'd never imagined for herself while her partner Carol had continued to run their business in Brisbane. Carol had been fabulous; C&C Events had gone from strength to strength, while Claire had found a new contentment in this tropical retreat.

The Dysarts, however, could very easily shatter her happiness. Their family dynasty was built on owning everything they could lay their hands on. If they caught wind of a new grandson Harry wouldn't be allowed to live in happy anonymity on Sapphire Island.

She was still wrestling with the rights and wrongs of this when Jack suddenly reappeared at the top of the cliff.

She was so startled she almost dropped Harry.

Jack looked startled, too, as if he hadn't expected to find her still standing in the front doorway.

How long *had* she been here? She felt rather silly, and unreasonably frightened. Why was he coming back? Nervous skitters danced down her spine as he turned in at the gate and approached her.

'Did you forget something?' she asked.

Slowly Jack nodded, without smiling. He came to a halt in the middle of the path. With his hands hitched loosely on his hips, he looked up at the cottage through narrowed eyes. 'It occurred to me that I shouldn't make assumptions.'

What assumptions? What was he talking about? Claire couldn't tamp down her rising panic. She clasped Harry so tightly he squawked.

Jack said, 'Has your husband checked your roof?'

Claire felt her cheeks blanch. 'My—my husband?'

Jack stood patiently enough, waiting for her answer,

but she couldn't think what to say. Her mind had turned to mush.

At last she managed, 'I—I don't have a husband.'

Jack gave a shrug of impatience. 'Your partner, then. The baby's father.'

Was this a trick question? 'There's n-no father. Only Harry and me.'

He scowled at Claire. 'You're not serious?'

Her heart was thumping so hard she needed to sit down. 'Y-yes. I'm perfectly serious.'

'And you're planning to stay here? Alone? A woman and a baby in this cottage on top of a sea cliff in a cyclone?'

*Oh...*how silly she'd been. Jack wasn't interested in Harry's parentage. Of course—he was concerned about the weather.

Weak with relief, Claire said defensively, 'I think we'll be safe enough, don't you?'

He raked a hand through his short dark hair in anguish, and muttered something that might have been a curse.

Upset by the implication that she was reckless, Claire drew her shoulders back. 'I haven't finished my preparations. I still have to fit storm shutters to the windows and clear the garden of potential flying objects.'

'I'm glad to hear you have storm shutters at least.' Stepping over a low, colourful bed of sea daisies and gazanias, he frowned as he examined the timber slats attached to a windowframe.

'I believe it's quite simple to fit the shutters,' Claire said. 'They just slide into place.'

He nodded. 'But you've got the baby. You'll need help, won't you?'

Her eyebrows lifted in surprise. 'Why? Are you offering?'

'Yes.' He was almost smiling. 'You can blame it on a rare attack of do-the-right-thing.'

In the house behind Claire the telephone began to ring.

'That's probably someone offering to help,' she said.

'Tell them there's no need. I'll do whatever's necessary here.'

Her jaw sagged and Jack reached for Harry. 'Here,' he said. 'I'll take the baby. You answer the phone.'

His manner was so commanding that Claire obeyed without question, but as she hurried inside to the phone she couldn't believe she'd actually handed Harry over...to his father. *To the enemy.*

It would serve Jack right if Harry complained loudly about being left with a stranger, but as far as Claire could tell the little traitor hadn't uttered a single whimper.

Her voice sounded thin and shaky as she answered the phone.

It was Dorothy, an elderly friend from down the road. 'Is everything all right, Claire?'

'Oh, Dorothy, I'm sorry you had to call. I haven't forgotten you.' It was a feeble lie. When Claire had been shopping earlier she'd bought extra torch batteries and dog food for Dorothy, and she'd meant to drop them straight up to her. But Jack Dysart's appearance on her doorstep had driven almost everything else from her thoughts.

'I've had a visitor,' she said. 'But I'll bring those things to you as soon as I can.'

'There's no need to hurry, Claire. I didn't want to bother you. But I was just a little worried when you took so long.' Again, she asked, 'Is everything all right?'

'Fine,' Claire said, and then she added rashly, 'What about you, Dorothy? You're all on your own and you must be terrified. Would you like to spend the night here?'

Claire held her breath. The cottage only boasted one spare bed, and her elderly neighbour should have first claim to it. Jack Dysart might have offered to help, but that didn't mean she had to offer him a bed. He could sleep at the hotel. He probably *wanted* to sleep at the hotel.

'Claire, that's terribly kind of you,' Dorothy replied, 'but I couldn't possibly be such a bother. Besides, I don't want to leave my Labradors. Or my home, for that matter. I've lived here all my life. My house and I have been through cyclones before, and I'm sure we'll weather another one.'

'Well, if you're sure. Anyway, I'll call in later.'

After Claire hung up the phone, she went outside. Her heart lurched when she saw Jack on the front lawn, sprawled on his back, with Harry bouncing on his stomach and squealing with joy.

They looked so happy together…so right. Man and boy. Father and son.

The impression was fleeting, however. As soon as Jack saw Claire he was on his feet again, holding Harry out to her as if he was relieved to be free of him.

'OK, where are these shutters?' he asked her brusquely, and he looked so upset that she wondered if he was embarrassed to be caught out playing with a baby.

'They're in a shed out the back.'

He nodded, and immediately began to stride along the path that led around the side of the house to the back garden.

Claire hurried after him. 'If we get the shutters out first,' she called to the back of his head, 'there should be room in the shed for all the pots and anything else that could blow about.'

The door to the gardening shed had rusted hinges, but Jack had only a little difficulty wrestling it open. Inside, the tangle of spades and gardening forks, the rake, the wheelbarrow and the rolled-up lengths of hose, looked more untidy than Claire remembered.

'Sorry about the mess,' she said. 'I'm afraid the shutters are on that shelf at the back. I guess we'll have to clear that gardening gear out first, before we can get at them.' She set Harry down on a patch of lawn. 'I'll help you.'

'Don't bother,' Jack ordered. 'I'll look after these. And if you have a ladder I'll check your roof.'

Again, it was a command, and Claire was wise enough to obey. 'The ladder's in the garage,' she said. 'Thanks very much, Jack.' As she said his name she paused, gave an embarrassed smile. 'This is terribly kind of you.' Then, feeling dismissed, she scooped Harry up again and hurried inside.

CHAPTER THREE

THE wind gusted as Jack stepped onto the roof. He felt the quick riff of excitement that he always felt when there was any hint of danger, but he walked carefully, following the line of the roof trusses, as he checked for rusted nails and screws.

The fact that he was up here, checking out a strange woman's roof, was a situation he didn't want to ponder too deeply. But, weird as it sounded, he'd seen that little baby trying so damn hard to stand on his own two feet and he'd felt an uncanny urge to protect the kid and his mother. Yeah, that urge was really weird. Jack had no idea where it had come from.

Equally puzzling was the anger he felt towards the baby's father. Where the hell *was* that guy? Everyone in Australia must have heard the news reports about the cyclone bearing down on the North Queensland coast. What kind of man abandoned his woman and child to cope alone?

The wind brought a salty smack of sea air as Jack knelt to hammer down a loose section of iron. Truth be told, he liked working with his hands. It was one of the attributes that set him apart from his father and his brothers. They got their thrills from donning Italian suits and scaling the heady heights of business. Jack preferred to be up on a roof, wearing a tool belt and old blue jeans.

He honestly liked this kind of work—and not just when it involved high winds and a whisker of danger. The weather had been perfectly calm when he'd helped to rebuild a school in Nepal, but he'd found it one of the most satisfying projects he'd ever been involved in—even more satisfying than climbing the Himalayas.

Standing again, he moved on to the next section of roof. From up here he had a magnificent view of the entire sweep of the bay, all the way to the rocky headlands of the north and south.

This island was edged by a spectacular frill of scalloped bays which were normally tranquil, thanks to protection from the Great Barrier Reef, but now the seas roiled and seethed darkly.

Behind the cottage a heavily timbered eucalypt forest crowded close to the back fence and scrambled wildly up the sides of a mountain that dominated the island's centre.

It was a sobering thought that by this time tomorrow there might be very little left of that bushland, or the proud hoop pines on the headlands. Trees and their inhabitants were the first victims in a cyclone.

Looking down, Jack could see Claire hurrying about in the garden, collecting pot plants, a watering can, and anything else that might become an airborne missile in a powerful storm. She had tied up her hair somehow, and she moved with a graceful efficiency.

Not that he should be noticing such things.

But during afternoon coffee and cake she'd invited him to stay here. He'd looked across the kitchen table and seen the silver lights in her eyes, the fine delicacy of her face, and he'd stopped thinking about Flora and found instead that he was revising his first impressions of her sister.

Claire Eden had a vulnerable air, but there was something about her that hinted at a deep inner strength, and that intrigued Jack. His original plan when he'd come to the island might have been a lost weekend with Flora, but he'd accepted her sister's invitation to stay for very different reasons—primarily his concern for her safety and that of her baby.

Just the same, Jack was glad that none of his adventuring mates could see him now. A knight-in-shining-armour stunt would put one hell of a dint in his reputation as an international playboy.

A warning for a severe Category 3 cyclone is now current for coastal areas between Innisfail and Mackay. Severe Tropical Cyclone Fred is expected to cross the coast in the vicinity of Sapphire Island and Cape Hunter in the early hours of Saturday.

Gales with gusts up to 125 kilometres per hour are likely in coastal communities. Very destructive wind gusts up to 200 kilometres per hour are likely to develop in the vicinity of Sapphire Island during Saturday morning.

Claire turned away from her computer screen. All afternoon the meteorology bureau's cyclone-tracking map had shown Fred drawing closer and closer to the island. Not that she needed a map to tell her that a savage storm was on its way. She only had to listen to the gathering speed of the wind outside.

From above came the sharp sound of hammering on the roof and she hoped that Jack would be finished soon. He'd be crazy to stay up there much longer.

She looked about her and felt a flush of achievement. The afternoon had passed in a flurry of activity. After hurrying to Dorothy's, to put her mind at rest that her elderly neighbour and her golden Labradors had everything they needed, she'd followed the instructions in the pamphlet about cyclone preparation.

It was more than likely that power lines would come down in the gale-force winds, so she'd organised torches and a transistor radio, fresh batteries, candles, lamps and matches on the kitchen dresser for easy access.

Disruption to water supplies was another possibility, so she'd filled spare buckets and pitchers with water and set them ready in a corner of the kitchen. And she'd made up extra bottles of Harry's formula and put them in the freezer.

She had to admit it was rather terrifying to think that all these precautions might actually be necessary. But she also found the preparations just a little exciting—like in the old days, when she'd been planning for a major corporate event.

For the first time in ages she felt keyed-up and edgy—as if she was back in her office in Brisbane, surrounded by telephones, computers and filing cabinets and lists…endless lists.

Actually, her telephone had been almost as busy this afternoon as it had been in Brisbane. A surprising number of islanders had called to check that she was OK, or to give advice and offers of help. They'd been curious when she told them she was fine, that a 'friend from way back' had turned up to help.

'Not the tall, dark stranger who arrived on this morning's ferry?' her friend Liz had queried. She drove the mobile library around the island's bays.

'He did come on this morning's ferry,' Claire admitted. 'How did you hear about him?'

'Oh, you know what gossip's like on this island.'

Yes, Claire did know. It was the downside of living in a small community.

Liz laughed. 'Lucky you to have an "old friend" to take shelter with.'

Claire had to admit she was pleased she'd finally plucked up the courage to ask Jack to stay. Fatherhood complications aside, she and Harry were much better off in a man's company. The shuttered windows and his work on the roof proved that.

Now, as evening approached, the house was snug and cosy and dark. The fragrant aroma of a beef casserole filled the kitchen. Claire turned on lamps and bathed Harry. She gave him his favourite dinner of beef broth and rice, and then cuddled him in the rocking chair while he had his bottle. His eyes were already at half-mast when she tucked him into his cot.

In the golden glow of his night light, he smiled sleepily up at her.

'Sleep tight, little man,' she whispered. 'Let's hope Cyclone Fred doesn't wake you.'

She looked down at his sweet round face, so innocent and trusting.

I'm putting him to bed, as if everything's fine, when I really don't know what might happen tonight.

She felt a tremor of fear in the pit of her stomach. It quickly spread to her chest and her throat, and for the first time since she'd decided to live on the island she doubted the wisdom of the decision.

It had made perfect sense nine months ago…

Harry had been ten days old when she'd made the huge decision to let go—to become a silent partner in the business and to care for her nephew on Sapphire Island. She'd carried him, bundled in a muslin shawl, and walked along the beach at Breakfast Bay.

It had been a perfect May afternoon and the island had been at its most beautiful. The tide had been coming in, waves gently lapping the sand. Seaweed had floated like green silk scarves in the lacy shallows, and shiny shells had lain scattered where the waves had dropped them.

Above Claire, the sky had been fading, and the tops of the island's hills had been rimmed with the first pink glow of sunset. Two seagulls had chased each other and the softest breeze had played with her hair. She'd drawn in a deep breath of fresh, salty air, and Harry had snuggled closer, and for the first time she had been able to think about Flora without crying.

It had almost been as if Flora were there, talking to her.

See how beautiful it is here? Now you understand what I want for my boy.

In that moment Claire had understood the lesson she'd learned from the past ten days. She'd come face to face with life and death. A precious new life…and a pointless death…

How could she ignore these lessons—these *huge* lessons?

No job could ever be important as family.

And just like that the world she'd left behind in Brisbane had seemed suddenly meaningless. She'd felt almost powerless to do anything but follow this destiny…to live the life that Flora had lost…

But now…

Now, as she watched Harry's thick eyelashes droop, as she listened to the wind rushing and gathering force outside the cottage, she feared that her own life was in danger.

Good grief!

Enough!

With a gasp of shock, Claire stepped away from the cot, horrified that she'd given in to such morbid thinking. The cyclone pamphlet was full of hints on how to stay safe. Of course they'd be OK. She'd always believed that once a situation was carefully examined and a decision was made it was up to her to prove that it was the right decision.

Staying on the island for Harry's sake had been a good decision. Today she'd made another good decision by accepting Jack Dysart's help. Together she and Jack would keep Harry safe.

That settled in her mind, she hurried to the spare room to make up Jack's bed with clean linen.

The rain started just as Jack hammered down the last section of roof. It came at a sharp angle, riding on the teeth of the wind, and the force of it surprised him. In a matter of moments he was drenched to the skin.

He glanced out to the bay again and saw sludge-coloured waves with angry white caps leaping to meet the pelting grey rain. By now the palm trees along the beachfront were bending so low their dark, feathery fronds almost reached the ground. From behind him, a branch broken from a gum tree came spinning past.

Things were hotting up.

'Jack!'

Claire's voice sounded way too close. He spun round to discover her pale face peering over the rim of the guttering. She had climbed the ladder and, like him, was soaking wet. Her dark hair was plastered to her head and her eyes were wide and terrified.

Jack hurried as fast as he could across the wet and slippery corrugated iron. 'What's the matter? What are you doing up here?'

'You should come down now. The roof will have to do as it is. It's too wild up here.'

He couldn't believe she'd climbed all that way just to order him down. Had she any idea how many times he'd risked his neck in circumstances far more dangerous than this? He shook his head at her. 'You crazy woman. I was about to come down anyway.'

Through the sheeting rain, her face lost its certainty.

Wind whipped at him as he crouched beside her, and he gripped the top of the ladder with both hands. 'For God's sake, go back and be careful.'

To Jack's relief she took her time, feeling for each rung and making sure her foothold was secure before she continued down. When she reached the bottom, she waited for him.

'You're soaking wet,' he reproached her again.

They were standing beneath the eaves now, but the slanting rain could easily reach them. It drenched his shoulders, as if a giant bucket had been upended, but at least in the tropics the water wasn't cold.

Lifting her voice to reach him above the roar of the rain, she said defensively, 'I was worried about you.'

'I'm flattered.'

Her mouth tightened. 'Don't be flattered. I didn't want an injured member of the famous Dysart family on my hands.'

Jack couldn't help smiling. He looked deliberately at Claire's hands, which were dainty and capable, like the rest of her. He noticed one badly chewed thumbnail.

Catching the direction of his gaze, she folded her thumb out of sight and asked, 'How's the roof?'

'It's not too bad, actually. I think it should be OK. I put in a few extra nails just to be certain.'

'Thanks.' This time she smiled.

Her grey eyes reminded him of silk shot with silver. Sparkling raindrops clung to her lashes and her lips were pink and lush—surprisingly sensuous.

He asked himself why he was standing out here, raising his voice to be heard, when it would be much more interesting to kiss her. Now, in the driving rain, when they were both as wet as drowned wombats and the wind hurtled and whistled about them.

Oh, yeah…bad idea.

Even if her lover, or partner, or whoever he was, was well out of the scene, this was not *that* sort of weekend.

To remind himself exactly why this would not become *that* sort of weekend, Jack asked, 'Where's Harry?'

'Asleep. He's already had his dinner.'

Claire's chin lifted and, despite the drenching rain, she didn't move away. Something new shimmered in her serious grey eyes—a dazzle of silvery light—and in that moment Jack was quite certain she wouldn't raise any objections if he kissed her.

Normally he was very quick to respond to such clues, but this situation was trickier than most. The threat of the cyclone…the shock of Flora's death…and Claire's baby…

Jack Dysart didn't mix with babies… They awoke bad memories he'd rather forget.

He reached for the ladder. 'I'd better stow this away before it falls and brains one of us.'

Claire paced in the soft glow of her cosy kitchen and chewed at the remnants of her thumbnail. Despite the lamplit warmth of the shuttered cottage, and despite her hasty hot shower and her dry clothes, she still felt shivery and on edge.

Scant minutes ago, when she'd been outside in the rain, she'd experienced a mad urge to fling her arms around Jack Dysart's neck and to kiss him. Senseless.

Where had that come from?

She could blame it on the storm, of course. Wild winds and tempests were supposed to arouse elemental urges. Her year-long date drought could also be a significant contributing factor. And a gorgeous hunk, who was strong and competent and protective, was sure to trigger romantic fantasies.

Thank heavens nothing had happened.

And nothing was going to happen. She couldn't possibly think about Jack in *that* way. He was a playboy, for heaven's sake. He was accustomed to selecting his lovers from the *crème de la crème* of the world's famous beauties, and no doubt equally used to discarding them without a hint of regret.

Claire had never shared her sister's *femme fatale* qualities, or her take-him-and-leave-him attitude to men. She was the sensible, serious sister—the one who always remembered her responsibilities. And right now she should be planning ways to keep Flora's son safe—not only safe from the cyclone, but from the Dysarts.

It was up to her to make sure that Jack Dysart left them tomorrow without a backward glance.

Outside, a fierce gust of rain lashed at the sides of the house and the shutters rattled madly. Claire stared at her distorted reflection in the shiny kettle on the stove and sighed. After the way she'd almost jumped on Jack just now in the rain, her decision to invite him to spend a stormy night in her cottage felt about as sensible and safe as playing with gunpowder.

As if to underline that risk, the fringe of beads in

the doorway parted and Jack came into the kitchen, dressed in well-worn faded jeans that hugged his thighs, and a clean T-shirt that defined his chest muscles to a sinful degree.

His hair was damp from his shower, and his jaw still carried a shadow of stubble. He smelled of the rose-scented handmade soap Claire had bought at the island's craft market.

Folding her arms tightly over her chest, she took a necessary step back and bumped into the kitchen table. Suddenly she felt as nervous as a teenager at her first party.

Jack's smile was lazy and warm.

'I—I hope you had enough hot water?' she said.

'Plenty. Nothing beats a hot shower.'

'If we lose electricity tonight we'll soon run out.'

He shrugged, and she remembered what Flora had told her about his reckless adventures—crossing oceans and scaling mountains and jumping out of planes. No doubt he was as used to hardship and danger as he was to easy living and luxury.

He directed an appreciative glance to the glass window in the oven. 'What's cooking in there? It smells sensational.'

'Just a beef casserole.'

'*Just* a beef casserole? That's fantastic.' He rubbed his flat stomach and grinned. 'I hope there's plenty. I could eat a horse and chase the rider.'

'Well, it's all ready.'

While she extracted the red enamel casserole dish and set it on a trivet in the centre of the table, Jack wandered to the corner of the kitchen and stood looking down at her scantily stocked wine rack.

'Would you like some wine?' she asked, picking up on his rather broad hint.

This time his smile was of the charming, bad-boy variety. 'It seems the night for it, doesn't it?'

Yes and no, Claire thought.

It would certainly be nice to enjoy a glass of wine during a meal shared with an adult, rather than with a baby in his highchair. But would wine make her too mellow? She needed to keep her wits about her.

Jack, however, had already made a selection and was carrying the bottle to the table. 'Where's your corkscrew?'

Claire was tempted to keep the radio playing in the background while they ate, in case important weather announcements were made. But the sound of the cork popping and the picture of Jack standing beside the kitchen table, one hand resting casually on the back of a chair as he poured red wine into two glasses, urged her to stop being Suzy-Sensible and to enjoy this meal. This moment.

It had been too long since she'd enjoyed a man's company. And, unless their world fell apart overnight, he would be gone in the morning.

CHAPTER FOUR

HOME cooking was so much better than the fancy stuff, Jack decided, after just one mouthful of Claire's casserole. The meal was simple and hearty and superb, rich with beef and carrots and a hint of bay leaf and wine. He couldn't remember a meal he'd enjoyed more, and he helped himself to a second serving.

'How did you manage this in the middle of everything else this afternoon?' he asked, with genuine admiration.

'Honestly? It was pot luck. I just threw everything in and hoped for the best.'

She played it down, but he knew she was trying not to look too pleased. And what pleased him even more than her cooking was that she didn't ply him with questions about his family. It made a very pleasant change to be quizzed about his travels, to be treated like Jack Dysart the adventurer, rather than Jack Dysart the Swiss bank account.

Better still, Claire lost her shyness while she questioned him about sailing the Atlantic, or climbing the Andes, or cross-country skiing in Alaska. Her smile deepened, revealing an unexpected dimple. Her grey eyes took on an extra sparkle, especially when he explained that he liked to push himself to the limits, to find harder routes or a purer style—climbing without oxygen, for example, or without support, or without stopping.

'At a guess, I'd say you're a bit like that, too,' he said, watching her over the rim of his wine glass.

Her eyes widened. 'What are you suggesting? That I'm a perfectionist?'

He smiled. 'Perhaps.'

'You're leaping to conclusions on very little evidence. I've hardly told you anything about myself.'

'That's very easy to fix.'

Her cheeks turned pink. Carefully, she said, 'What would you like to know?'

Jack could think of a dozen questions that would turn her cheeks a much deeper shade of pink. Hastily, he rejected them. 'Are you an artist, like Flora?'

She shook her head. 'I'm afraid my sister scored all the artistic genes. At a pinch, I can draw a stick figure.'

'So what do you do, then? Do you stay at home with Harry, or do you have a job?'

'I left my job when Harry was born.' She looked unhappy as she said that, and she picked up her wine glass and took a deep sip. 'Before that I was an events planner.'

The perfect job for her, he decided, casting an amused glance at the lighting equipment and spare batteries lined up on the dresser, the buckets of water standing ready in the corner. 'What kind of events did you plan? Weddings? Parties?'

'No—no.' Pride crept into her voice. 'Our clients are from the corporate world. Groups like chambers of commerce. Business companies. City councils. We organise events like Australia Day, New Year's Eve. Some pretty big gigs.'

'Impressive.'

'You sound surprised.'

'I guess I'm more surprised that you gave all that up to come and live here.'

'Well…yes.' Claire looked suddenly less certain, and she fiddled with the stem of her glass. Then she tucked her hair behind her ear and said, 'It—it seemed the right choice to make after—after Harry was born.'

Why was she so nervous? Jack frowned as she made fists of her hands and set them stiffly in her lap. Then again, he reminded himself, she was a single mum; she might be embarrassed to share aspects of her personal history with a stranger.

'I couldn't have looked after a baby and kept up my Brisbane lifestyle,' she said. 'It was too frenetic. And when Flora died it felt right to bring Harry here. The island's so peaceful, and it seemed the perfect place for a little boy to grow up.'

'Harry's a lucky boy,' Jack commented, and he meant it. But for some reason that he couldn't quite pinpoint he sensed a gap in Claire's story.

Her story sounded rehearsed. And why had her sister's death triggered her decision to come here? The connection didn't quite add up. He felt the same uneasy stirring he'd felt when she'd offered her bare-boned explanation of Flora's death.

He wasn't entirely satisfied. How exactly had Flora developed DVT? What had been the circumstances? Surely Claire could have added a few extra details?

'So when did Flora die? Was it around the same time you had Harry?' He couldn't hold back the questions, even though she might think he was snooping into territory that was none of his business.

Claire nodded, but then she stood rather abruptly. 'Would you like dessert? I haven't made anything, but there's ice cream and fruit. Or there's chocolate we could have with coffee.'

'Left over from Valentine's Day?'

She rolled her eyes. 'I won it in a raffle down at the Breakfast Bay Lifesaving Club.'

'I'd love lifesaving chocolate with my coffee.'

Jack helped by clearing the table, while Claire assembled the chocolate, milk jug and sugar on a pottery serving plate.

She cast a surprised glance at the neatly stacked dishes in the sink, but didn't comment.

He went to the shuttered window and listened. All through their meal the wind's howling had been incessant, bursting every so often into even stronger gusts that lashed the rain and the tree branches against the side of the cottage, each gust wilder than the last.

Claire, with the platter in her hands, turned to him. 'I hate to think it's going to get worse than this.'

'I'm afraid it will.'

Her shoulders lifted in a small shrug. 'We may as well make ourselves comfortable in the lounge room.'

'Great idea.' Jack brought the mugs and the coffee pot.

She set the platter on a low table. 'I'll just check on Harry.'

The baby's room was illuminated softly by a night light, and Jack could see Claire as she bent over the cot. He saw the silky gleam of her dark hair, the cherry-red warmth of her shirt and the pale gracefulness of her arms as she lifted a blue blanket over the sleeping baby.

To his dismay, he found himself remembering his dashed dreams of marriage and fatherhood, and his throat constricted. Quickly he turned his back on the nursery scene, and gritted his teeth as he waited for his habitual bitterness to descend.

'I don't think he's stirred,' Claire said behind him.

As she shut the door, he felt his shoulders relax. 'Harry might be the only guy on the island to sleep through the cyclone.'

'I can't imagine trying to sleep tonight.' Claire looked at her wristwatch and sighed. 'It's only eight o'clock, and the cyclone's not due to cross here till two in the morning.'

She looked at Jack and saw the caustic glint of amusement in his eyes. Damn. He knew she was still fidgety around him, and she hated it that he knew. It set her more on edge than ever.

'We may as well sit back and enjoy the ride,' he said, selecting one of the armchairs.

Claire sat opposite him. She had always liked this room, with its gleaming timber floor and the rich Morocco rug in tones of deep blue, claret and antique gold. The blue of the armchairs looked especially strong against the rich claret walls, and the gold throw cushions tied the colour scheme together beautifully. In this setting, the rose-coloured crockery, the rich brown chocolate on the pottery plate, and the fat blue candle, ready with matches, looked like carefully arranged accessories in a decorating magazine.

Again Claire felt a clutch of fear as she imagined the roof being blown away and the lovely room torn apart and destroyed.

'Are you OK?' Jack asked, watching her keenly.

'Sure.' She pushed the plate towards him. 'Please, help yourself to chocolate.'

As she said this, there was a fearsome crack outside, then a horrible splintering sound and the heavy thud of something falling.

Claire leapt to her feet. 'What was that?'

'At a guess, I'd say it was a tree coming down.'

'I hope it didn't fall on someone's roof.'

Jack shook his head. 'It would have been a bigger bang if it had hit a building.'

She glanced at the door to Harry's room and shuddered.

'Hey,' Jack said with surprising gentleness. 'We'll be OK. There aren't any big trees close to this house.'

'I know you're right. It's just—' She broke off when she heard a new sound, faint and plaintive. 'I think that's Harry crying. The falling tree must have woken him.'

Jack gave a shrug and reached for the coffee pot. 'I suppose he'll go back to sleep?'

'I was hoping he'd sleep through all this.'

Coffee pot in hand, Jack looked at her expectantly. 'Shall I pour?'

But Claire was already on her feet. Harry's wails were growing louder. 'Excuse me. I'd better see to him.'

Harry was standing in the cot, gripping its sides, his little face red and crumpled and tears streaming down his cheeks. 'It's OK,' she soothed. 'Just the nasty wind.'

As soon as Claire picked him up Harry stopped crying as if she'd turned a switch. 'Con-man,' she chided gently. Quickly she changed his nappy and buttoned him back into his sleepsuit, then carried him, blinking at the light, into the lounge room.

'He's normally a good sleeper,' she told Jack defensively. 'But if he wakes he takes a while to settle again.'

Jack's eyebrows rose. 'What do you do?'

'Rock him for a bit. Sometimes he needs more milk.'

Jack set his coffee mug down, and his face reflected sudden embarrassment. 'Perhaps I should leave you two alone? I can start the dishes.'

'No, no—don't get up. Stay comfortable. Finish your coffee and have more chocolate.'

His deep blue gaze lingered briefly on her chest, then darted quickly away. 'But if you need to feed Harry…'

'Oh, no!' Her cheeks burst into flames. 'I'm not breastfeeding.' Quickly she lowered her eyes, self-conscious to be talking about breasts with this man.

By now Harry had discovered Jack's presence, and was smiling cheekily and blowing raspberries at him across the room.

'He's taken a fancy to you,' Claire said, and her blush deepened. She had a dreadful feeling that at any minute now she would make a serious slip and tell Jack that she was Harry's aunt, not his mother.

She had also discovered an amazing likeness between Jack's profile and Harry's, and she was terrified she'd relax her guard and mention it.

Keeping secrets had never been her forte.

'Would you mind holding him while I heat his bottle?' she asked, feeling an urgent need to escape to the kitchen.

'OK. Hand him over.' Jack looked a little troubled, and he spoke without enthusiasm, but he held out his arms for Harry.

'Just keep him away from the coffee pot,' Claire warned.

As they exchanged the baby, her hands met Jack's and she almost jumped. No need for hot coffee pots! Jack's skin burned her. His touch made her heart *thud*. She hurried away to the relative safety of the kitchen.

Jack had always told himself and others that he had no fear of heights but that babies scared him to death. Now, as he looked down at the little guy in his arms, he had to admit the kid was cute. Exceptionally cute—and a real little bruiser, strong and sturdy-looking, with bright blue eyes, glowing skin and shiny golden hair. Bursting with health and curiosity.

Too much curiosity. Harry reached for Jack's nose and squeezed hard. 'Da!'

Jack laughed. 'Da to you!' Gently he squeezed Harry's small button nose.

Harry reacted with a squeal of delight and reached for Jack's nose again.

Jack grabbed a cushion. 'Here. Use this as a

punching bag.' He demonstrated by giving the cushion a thump with his fist, and Harry was easily diverted. With another cry of 'Da,' he bashed happily at the cushion.

Where is your da? Jack wondered. Poor, silly fool doesn't know what he's missing. Cute baby, cute mum. What a waste.

Tiring of the cushion, Harry began to grumble and rub at his eyes. What now? Jack thought. He sent a hasty glance towards the kitchen, but there was no sign of Claire. Remembering his brothers with their youngsters, he stood and began to pace the floor.

To his surprise, Harry liked it. He snuggled in, his head against Jack's shoulder, warm and sleepy, like a cosy koala.

Wind gusted outside, and there was a crash as something smashed against the side of house. The baby stiffened.

'Shoosh,' Jack murmured, stroking the little fellow's back and continuing to pace. 'Shoosh. Mum will be back soon. You'll be OK.'

Jack could feel the amazing softness of the baby's skin against his neck, could feel the tiny puffs of his breath, and out of the blue he was thinking about Marianne again.

He had been young and naive and in love when she had aborted their baby—a tiny dot with the potential to grow into a cute little fellow like Harry.

Her decision, made in secret, had left him devastated, completely gutted.

He'd always had a strong sense of family. He supposed it had been nurtured when he was a very small child by the huge gatherings his grandparents hosted. Christmas had been huge, and for Jack it had been more than the allure of presents and festive food that had excited him. There'd been the fun of hide-and-seek with cousins, while adults dozed after their turkey and pudding. There'd been crazy games in the evening, like charades.

His uncle used to play the guitar, and everyone sang even if they couldn't hold a tune. Family gatherings were the height of simple, unalloyed happiness, and from the age of five he'd planned to be a grandfather just like Pop.

He would never forget the day he'd learned from Marianne's mother that his fiancée had gone to a clinic to terminate a pregnancy.

Their baby.

Jack had stormed into that clinic. Made a terrible scene as he'd marched down corridors till he found the room where Marianne was lying.

He'd been too late. The 'procedure', as they'd called it, had been completed.

Afterwards, when he'd broken off their engagement, Marianne had protested. 'I wasn't ready to have a baby. For God's sake, Jack. Did you expect me to accompany you to the all the parties this season looking like I'd swallowed a watermelon?'

He'd been beyond furious. It had been his baby, too, and she hadn't discussed it with him—hadn't even told him she was pregnant.

'My mother should never have told you,' she'd said. 'I knew you'd make a fuss.'

'Bloody hell, Marianne, don't you think I deserved some say in this? What can I expect from marriage with you when we can't share a decision as important as our child's life?'

He'd walked away from her, and dealt with his intense disappointment by trekking in Nepal. He'd stayed away over Christmas, so he hadn't had to face his brothers with their happy wives and families—three kids apiece.

After that he'd been tagged as an international playboy simply because he hadn't settled down with another woman. Too bad.

'Jack!'

Claire's whispered voice startled him. He turned to find her in the middle of the room, holding the baby's bottle. She came closer, her eyes wide with surprise.

'Has he gone to sleep?' she whispered.

It was only then that Jack realised that Harry had stopped squirming and snuffling. His head was heavy against his shoulder, his body limp and still. He felt a moment's panic. 'Is he still breathing?'

She laughed softly. 'Of course. He's gone to sleep.' She set the unused bottle on the coffee table and smiled up at him. 'You must have the knack.'

He gave a helpless shake of his head. 'I just paced the floor for a bit.'

'Well done. It's worked. Do you think you could put him back in the cot? He might wake if we try another swap-over.'

'I can try.'

Carrying the baby super-carefully, as if he were a box

of explosives, Jack tiptoed across the timber floor. As he entered the doorway to Harry's room he was enveloped by gentle but pleasant smells. What were they? Talcum powder? Soothing lotions?

A night light on a corner shelf glowed in the shape of a mushroom. Beside it sat a teddy bear in a waistcoat, then a blue elephant, a pile of cardboard books and a basket of bright plastic toys.

The floor was carpeted in soft pale green and the cot was white-painted wood. A decorative frieze on the wall depicted Humpty Dumpty, the cat and the fiddle and the cow jumping over the moon. Jack wondered if Harry's father had ever been in this room—this perfect little nursery.

He held his breath as he prepared to set Harry down.

Cradling his little head with one hand and placing another beneath his bottom, Jack carefully…*carefully*…lowered him onto a soft lambskin. As he loosened his hold Harry's arms flew out in a startled gesture, but to Jack's relief he didn't wake and soon settled again.

'Well done,' whispered Claire in a strangely choked voice as she pulled a crocheted blanket over the sleeping baby.

Jack looked down at Harry. His left cheek was brightly flushed from where it had lain against Jack's shoulder. The boy looked so cute, and Jack was cut to the core by a sharp sense of loss…

He turned and saw Claire in the soft light, her eyes luminous and glistening. Not with tears, surely?

Blinking rapidly, she dropped her gaze and gave a

little shake, as if to banish whatever was troubling her. She retreated quickly into the lounge room and Jack followed her thoughtfully. Was she upset about the baby's father? Had the fool deserted her and her boy?

He was still thinking about this as they settled into armchairs again.

Claire leaned forward to test the heat of the coffee pot. 'This is barely warm. I'll make a fresh pot.'

'Don't go to the trouble on my behalf. It's fine.' Jack drained his mug and held it out for a refill, then he selected some chocolate, popped it in his mouth, and smiled at her.

Her answering smile was shy, almost coy, and he wondered why he'd ever thought she was plain. She looked lovely, with her shiny dark hair framing her oval face, and her slim, long legs in beige Capri pants, comfortably crossed.

Outside, the wind began to scream.

Claire tilted her head and fear flickered in her face as she listened to it. 'I checked the radio while I was in the kitchen. A boatshed over in Horseshoe Bay has lost its roof, but no one was hurt.'

'I'm not surprised a roof came off. It must be gusting seventy knots out there already.'

She leaned forward, her expression grave. 'Jack, I know you did a good job on this roof this afternoon, but I think we need a plan. If we start to lose the roof we can't just run screaming into the night. We're supposed to evacuate to the school assembly hall, but it's too far to venture in this wind.'

'You're right.' After a moment's consideration, he

said, 'The roof near the kitchen is in very good condition. I'd say it was replaced a few years ago. If you want to take an extra precaution, my vote would be to get under the kitchen table.'

'Under it?' Claire's jaw dropped.

'It's a very solid timber table.' Jack couldn't help smiling as he watched her expression. He knew she was trying to picture the two of them, plus Harry, bunched up together beneath the table.

'But honestly, I doubt it will come to that,' he reassured her. 'Don't start worrying about it yet. We'll deal with it if and when the time comes.'

'I suppose that's the way you've coped with your hazardous adventures?'

'More or less. It's important to know what needs to be done if the worst happens. But there's no point in getting too frightened about something that may never come to pass.' He smiled. 'Perhaps you should try to sleep?'

Claire rolled her eyes. 'How could I possibly sleep through this?' With an impatient sigh she flounced out of her chair and crossed to the one window they'd left unshuttered, following the instructions in the pamphlet. A window slightly ajar prevented too much pressure from building inside the house.

Jack joined her at the window. It was so dark outside there was little to see, but the beam of a struggling streetlight showed the wild waving arms of ragged trees, palms bowing almost to the ground, and streaks of rain flying horizontally.

Claire turned to him. 'If you're tired, Jack, please feel free to go to bed.'

Her eyes met his.

Bed. *Oh, man.* Had she any idea?

For breathless seconds the air between them seemed to clamour with restless possibilities.

Jack could hardly believe he didn't step closer, reach out and touch her. He'd been growing more interested in Claire Eden by the minute. By the second. He wanted nothing more than to taste her soft, vulnerable mouth, to trace his fingertips over the silky texture of her skin.

She must have sensed this. Like a startled animal, she stiffened. Her eyes grew huge and dark and her distress was obvious.

Hell. His desire for her was shoved rudely aside. What had put that fear in her eyes? Was she frightened of men? Had Harry's father left her emotionally scarred?

'I'm not tired at all,' he said quietly, as he shoved his hands into his pockets and took a deliberate step back.

Her mouth quirked into a quarter-smile. Shyly, she tucked her hair behind her ear. Her eyes met his again, and this time he could see relief and dismay mingled in equal quantities. She dipped her head slightly. No words were exchanged, but they both knew that a possibility had been offered and rejected.

Claire went back to her armchair; Jack to his.

'We have a long night ahead of us,' he said casually as he settled into the chair's deep soft cushions. 'I've told you all about my recent exploits. It must be your turn to tell me all about yourself.'

'Myself?'

'Tell me about your family. Where you grew up.'

'Didn't Flora already tell you most of it?' Claire topped up her coffee and took a sip, held the mug in both hands as she rested it on her knee.

'If she did, I'm afraid I've forgotten.' Jack had no idea how much Claire knew about the time he'd spent in her sister's company, but he didn't think this was the time to enlighten her. 'It was eighteen months ago,' he said. 'Tell me your version.'

She curled her legs beneath her, but she didn't look particularly relaxed. 'Flora and I grew up at Mooloolaba on the Sunshine Coast,' she said. 'We had an idyllic childhood. The best. Our whole family loved the beach lifestyle, and we were all in the Surf Club—even Mum. Flora and I swam every day. We used to pretend we were mermaids.'

Jack could just imagine them as young girls—two dark-haired sea nymphs, one with curls and the other with hair as sleek as a seal's coat.

'Flora was the mischief-maker. She was always getting into trouble.'

Claire looked suddenly upset, as if she wished she could take that last remark back.

She added quickly, 'But then, just as Flora was finishing high school, our parents were killed in a pile-up on the highway.'

'Hell. That's tough.'

She nodded silently, drank more of her coffee.

Jack said, 'Let me guess. After your parents died, you worked to put your little sister through Art College?'

Her eyes widened with surprise. 'Did Flora tell you that?'

He shook his head. 'Lucky guess.'

'Well, you're right. It took ages for Mum and Dad's insurance and everything to be sorted out, and I was terrified Flora and I would be split up, so I got a job to support the two of us.'

He grinned. 'I knew it. It's exactly the sort of thing I can imagine you doing.'

'Why?

'You're capable and practical. And you're kind.'

Her response was a rueful smile. 'In other words I'm wearing a label. *"This woman has a strong sense of responsibility"*.'

'Have I said the wrong thing?'

'No, I don't suppose so.'

'I could have told you you're sexy.'

She rolled her eyes and made some kind of retort, but Jack couldn't hear it. Her words were drowned out by a new, roaring, gut-churning wail from the wind outside.

And then the lights went out.

CHAPTER FIVE

'I HAVE a candle and matches right here.'

Claire was proud of how calm she sounded, but her hands were shaking as she struck a match. The noises outside were horrifying, and the match flame shivered and shook as she held it to the candle wick.

Wind whipped under the doorways, and it took her three attempts to get the candle burning. *'Come on.'*

From somewhere outside there was a terrible, hair-raising screech of ripping metal. And then a loud crash. In the candlelight, Claire's eyes met Jack's. 'Do you think that was someone's roof?'

'Could be,' he said grimly.

Panic ripped through her. 'I hope it wasn't Dorothy's.' Fearfully, she scanned the gloomy interior of the darkened cottage, almost expecting the walls to collapse like a pack of cards. 'We need more light,' she said. 'The torch and lantern are in the kitchen.'

'I'll come with you.'

In the kitchen Jack lit more candles and the old lantern, while Claire tried to phone Dorothy. The phone was dead.

'The lines must be down.'

'What's her mobile number?' Jack reached for his back pocket.

'Dorothy doesn't have a mobile. Says she doesn't need one and they're too modern and newfangled.'

Outside, the wind grew teeth and nails. Tree limbs cracked and fell to the ground with sickening thuds.

'OK. I'll admit it. I'm getting scared.' Claire patted the kitchen table. 'The floor under here is becoming more appealing every minute.'

'It would certainly be safer,' Jack agreed.

'But we'd need to make ourselves comfortable. I'll get quilts and pillows.' She almost ran through the house, grabbing the pillows from her bed, fluffy duvets from the linen cupboard. She was arranging them on the floor beneath the table when the hinges on the back door creaked.

Jack came into the kitchen, her dripping rain jacket draped over his shoulders, a torch in his hand. 'I poked my head outside, but I couldn't see much. The garage over the road has lost part of its roof. That's probably the noise we heard.'

'Thank heavens it wasn't a house.'

His gaze lighted on the nest of quilts and pillows on the floor, and the skin around his eyes crinkled as he smiled at her. 'That looks very cosy.'

It did look cosy indeed, but Claire's heart raced at the thought of getting under there with Jack. It would be like being in bed—and her earlier interest in kissing him had, unfortunately, not gone away.

But how could she cosy up to this man when she was keeping such a terrible secret from him?

She wanted to tell him about Harry. She *should* tell him. This evening he'd been so sweet with Harry, and he'd been incredibly helpful and kind to her. Not at all snooty or arrogant, as she'd expected, but warm and friendly, without any off-putting playboy tendencies to flamboyance.

He was, in fact, a man of singular charm, and he'd made her feel very comfortable—as if she'd known him for ages. And when he'd said she was sexy, and looked at her in that special, smiling way of his, it had torn her in two not to tell him *everything*.

But right now—with this terrible storm raging around them—was hardly the time to reveal a surprise as momentous as a son whose conception been kept secret for eighteen months. Even if she found a very tactful and gentle way to break the news, the consequences would still be dire—Jack's justifiable anger, and the loss of Harry. She couldn't deal with that now as well as the cyclone.

'We'll have to make room for Harry,' Jack was saying, and Claire was relieved to turn her mind to practical details.

'We need something to put him in,' she said. 'I've lent his carry basket to a girl in Breakfast Bay. She had a baby last month.'

'Hang on.' Jack shrugged off the wet jacket and carried it into to the adjoining laundry to hang it up. He returned with her woven cane laundry basket. 'Would this do for Harry?'

Claire smiled. 'We could give it a try.'

The laundry basket was perfect. Claire lined it with a quilt, and Harry didn't wake when Jack gently transferred him out of the cot and into the kitchen.

'I have to say he's a very well-behaved young man,' Jack commented.

Claire smiled and touched her fingertip to the curve of Harry's ear. 'He's on his best behaviour tonight. But then again he always seems to sleep well when there's a background noise. He loves the sound of the vacuum cleaner.'

Jack's eyebrows lifted, turning his smile sceptical. 'I dare say he'll grow out of that.'

Concerned about fire, Claire blew out the candles and set the lantern and the torch on the floor, one on either side of the table.

She and Jack took off their shoes. Jack removed his belt. It was so like getting into bed that Claire became quite breathless.

Across the tabletop, Jack slanted her a wry grin. 'I haven't been under a table since my eighteenth birthday.'

'I haven't been under one since Flora and I played cubby houses when we were little.'

How much harder it would be this time. Truth be told, getting under this particular table was about as difficult as diving into frozen water or leaping out of an aeroplane. The tabletop might protect her from imminent destruction, but beneath it she would face new dangers. Incredibly handsome and charming man-sized dangers.

Perhaps her hesitation was too obvious, for Jack said suddenly, 'Look, there's not much space under there. Why don't I set up camp on the sofa? That way you'll have more room, and I'll still be close by if you need me.'

He was being a perfect gentleman, and Claire couldn't believe her disappointment. What an idiot she was.

'You were all set to get under here. Surely there's room for the two of us?' *Oh, what a nitwit!* How could she have sounded so pathetic?

In the lantern light she saw an odd expression in Jack's eyes—so fleeting she couldn't be sure if it was mirth or impatience, or something else entirely.

Embarrassed, she knelt quickly, while he went through to the lounge room without further comment. She ducked her head beneath the table and stretched out on the quilt until her toes touched Harry's basket. Jack might have been cramped under here, she supposed.

But she was barely settled before another dreadful splintering sound exploded outside, followed by an earth-shattering crash above them—so close that Claire cried out.

She stuck her head out again. 'Wh-what was that? Have we been hit?'

Jack had already grabbed a torch and was heading for the back door. 'I'll take a quick look.'

'No, Jack—don't go out there!'

'Don't worry. I'll be careful!'

Claire heard loud thumping noises, and was surprised they didn't wake Harry. It sounded as if Jack was putting his shoulder to the door to force it open against the pressure of the gale-force wind. He must have been successful, however, for the wind's roar increased to the level of a freight train and the kitchen floor was suddenly flooded with broken twigs, leaves and rain.

In a matter of moments the door had slammed again and Jack was back, his voice raised above the scream and roar of the wind. 'It's bloody wild out there. I only stuck my head out, but I could see a gum tree down. It's fallen across the back fence and onto the garden shed. I'm afraid the shed looks flattened.'

A frightened whimper escaped Claire.

A tree on the garden shed! What would be next? An entire forest started at the cottage's back fence, and the mountain behind the cottage was covered in huge trees. Flying limbs or entire trees could fall on them at any moment.

Panic overtook her inhibitions. 'Jack, get under here. Please!'

'Is that an order?' There was a hint of mockery in his tone.

'Yes, it is. I'm terrified.'

Without further quibble he was beside her, bringing with him the scent of rain and pine-scented wind. His shirt was damp, and his broad shoulders brushed Claire's as he stretched out.

'Do you have enough room there?' she asked, a tad breathlessly.

'Sure. I've camped in far worse places than this.' His eyes gleamed in the soft light of the lantern. 'Have I left enough space for you?'

'Plenty.' Claire lay very still, keeping carefully to her side of the quilt. Rather than looking at Jack, she stared straight up at the underside of the table, where someone, years ago, had scratched initials. She couldn't quite believe she was lying so intimately close to the gorgeous man she'd watched walk off the ferry this morning. Her pulse was galloping like a runaway horse.

'At least we can hear ourselves talk under here.' Jack's voice resonated deeply in the confined space.

Claire felt too overcome to speak. For several minutes they both lay still.

Outside, the rain and wind raged with frightening fury.

She fought down a hot wave of panic. 'I had no idea cyclones were so powerful.'

'I've been in tents in the Andes in a storm,' Jack said, 'but the wind never sounded like this.'

'I've never felt so helpless.' It was true, but she wasn't sure if she was referring to the storm or to the way she felt about Jack.

'If this were a movie,' Jack said in a deliberately calming voice, 'we'd have a deep and meaningful conversation about now.'

Claire closed her eyes. Could she handle a deep and meaningful conversation with this man? There was every chance it would lead to intimate disclosures, and she needed to keep her secret to herself for one last night. It would be too awful to have to cope with Jack's outrage and the fury of the storm at the same time.

Her mouth was dry. She swallowed and ran her tongue over her lips. 'But this isn't a movie,' she said. 'So perhaps we should—um—'

What? *Think, Claire, think.*

'Play a game?' she finished lamely.

Jack groaned. 'Please, no—not games.'

She sent a worried glance his way, saw his bright smile, and decided he was teasing.

'OK, I give in.' Feigning resignation to a gloomy fate, Jack settled himself comfortably with his hands stacked beneath his head. 'What game do you have in mind?'

To Claire's dismay her mind was completely blank. How annoying. Since she'd come to the island she'd been to lots of dinner parties where guests had played all kinds of parlour games. There were no movie theatres and few sources of entertainment here, and the residents were quite adept at amusing themselves. But now, with Jack mere inches away, she struggled to remember a single game.

'Um, we could always ask silly questions,' she said at last.

'Sounds fascinating, Claire. Tell me more.'

Oh, heck. Why did Jack have to suddenly become so arrogant and *Dysart-ish*? Claire closed her eyes and plunged in. 'If you could be any kind of animal, what would you be?'

This was met by a chuckle. 'Sorry. I have absolutely no idea. I've never felt any desire to be any kind of animal.'

'Not even an eagle?'

'An eagle, my dear Claire, is a bird.'

'Now you're splitting hairs.'

'On the other hand, you're probably right,' Jack said,

dropping his bored tone. 'I suppose I *could* quite enjoy being an eagle.'

'It suits you.' She smiled encouragingly. 'Just think. If you were an eagle you'd be lofty and powerful. You'd arrogantly cruise the thermals and pounce, out of the blue, on unsuspecting small creatures.'

'And I would simply fly away from a wild storm like this.'

'A distinct advantage.'

'And what about you?' he asked. 'What animal would you be?'

'A cat,' Claire replied, without hesitation.

Jack turned to her and a faint smile played around his eyes as he studied her. 'That figures. You'd be a sleek little black cat, with a pretty white face and neat white paws.'

'I—I wouldn't care what I looked like. I just want a cat's nine lives.'

'Ah, yes, of course.' His voice was suddenly so gentle she almost missed hearing what he said. 'And why shouldn't you have nine lives when you've lost your entire family?'

The kindness in Jack's voice brought tears to her eyes. She hadn't expected him to be so understanding. Could he sense her aching loss?

At the time of her parents' death she'd known she must be strong for Flora's sake. Her sister's passing, however, had almost destroyed her. If it weren't for Harry, the only other living member of her family, she might have broken down completely. Even so, she'd felt cast adrift on a very lonely sea.

'If I had nine lives, I'd gladly trade them all to have my family back.'

But her current dilemma returned to haunt her, and Jack's kindness only made the problem so much worse. She felt terrible, accepting Jack's comfort while she kept quiet about Harry. How could she enjoy this man's protection without telling him that the child so cosily cocooned at their feet was his son?

It will only be for a little longer, she told herself. She would tell him first thing in the morning. As soon as the cyclone passed she would come clean. She would risk Jack's wrath, and somehow she would find the necessary strength to let him take Harry away from her.

'Claire, are you OK?'

She took a deep breath and bravely blinked to banish her tears. 'I'm fine,' she said, perhaps a little too brightly. 'I guess I'm not feeling very brave.'

'I've actually remembered a game,' he said. 'It's one we played when I was sailing the Atlantic. We usually had two on watch at a time, and it helped to keep us awake.'

'What is it?'

'It's called Liars' Club. You have to make three statements about yourself, but only two of them are true. The other person has to guess the lie.'

The lie?

Claire went cold all over. Jack couldn't have chosen a worse game. 'That doesn't sound like fun.'

He laughed. 'Well, of course you can choose what you tell. There's no compulsion to reveal your darkest secrets.'

She forced a smile. 'That's a relief.'

'Do you *have* deep, dark secrets, Claire?'

She couldn't answer him. 'Why don't you go first, to show me how it's done?'

'Fair enough... Let me see... I'm six feet two inches tall, I'm allergic to shellfish, and I'm the youngest in my family.'

Claire answered quickly. 'I'd say...you're not allergic to shellfish.'

'You're right. How did you know I'm the youngest in the family?'

'Jack, everyone in Australia knows about your family.'

He pulled a strange face.

'Surely that doesn't surprise you?'

'I suppose I'm more surprised that you and I have spent a whole evening together and you haven't plagued me with questions about my family.'

'I—I didn't want to be a stickybeak. Your father's so famous. I thought you might be tired of being asked about him all the time.' Not to mention she'd been terrified she'd let something slip about Harry.

Jack smiled. 'That's very considerate. And you're right, actually. I do get tired of being quizzed. I guess that's why I'm surprised when it doesn't happen.'

'Is it a teensy bit daunting to be Theodore Dysart's son?' she asked now, keen to make amends.

Jack shook his head. 'I know my father has a reputation as a ruthless businessman, but he's actually very different when he's relaxed at home with his family. Soft as a pussycat. Dotes on his grandchildren.'

Claire gulped unhappily.

'My mother has an enormous influence on him,' Jack went on. 'He adores her, you see. And he actually listens to her—which is very sensible, because she's incredibly grounded, and a very calm and wise woman.'

'What a nice thing to say.' Claire knew she must have sounded surprised, but she couldn't help it. Flora had depicted Jack Dysart as some kind of self-centred black sheep, more or less hinting that his overseas adventures were his way of rebelling against his overbearing and difficult family.

'Now, that's enough about me,' Jack said decisively. 'It's your turn.'

'To tell a lie? Oh, gosh… OK… I wore braces on my teeth in my teens, I'm afraid of spiders, and I'm left-handed.'

Without a beat of hesitation he said smugly, 'You're not left-handed.'

'Very observant, sir. Now you get another turn.'

Jack responded quickly. 'I was blond until I was five years old. I love heavy metal music. I've always wanted to be an astronaut.'

Claire gasped. 'Were you really blond?'

'Claire, you're supposed to be guessing.'

'Oh, yes. Sorry. You—um—you don't like heavy metal music.'

He shook his head. 'Love it.'

'Oh. So you were lying about wanting to be an astronaut.'

'I win that round.'

She had to ask. 'But were you *really* blond when you were little?'

'As fair as a dandelion. As blond as your little Harry.'

She had to look away quickly, terrified that her face would betray her.

Fortunately Jack didn't appear to notice. 'Right,' he said. 'Come on—spill, Claire. Tell me another lie.'

There was no denying that the game deflected their attention from the terrifying sounds outside. Claire said the first things that came into her head. 'I love scrambled eggs with smoked salmon and toast. I don't like cheesecake. And…I'd like to stay on this island for ever.'

Jack's blue eyes gleamed warmly and he studied her face, watching her so intently and taking so long to come up with his answer that she felt bright heat creep up her neck and into her cheeks.

Eventually he said, 'So you don't want to stay here?'

'I—I'm not sure.'

'But that was the lie? The other two statements are true?'

She nodded. 'There've been times when I've felt very insular here. Insular in every sense of the word. The island's beautiful, and the people here are wonderful, but when you live on an island it's very easy to stop taking any interest in the rest of the world. I'm not sure that's what I want.'

'Interesting. I guess it's a bit like mountain-climbing. The mountain becomes your world, the summit your goal, and nothing else matters.' After a pause, he said, 'So *why* do you live here?'

Oh, help. Why did every question feel like a trap? 'It—it's complicated,' she said. 'But I feel closer to Flora here.'

Jack nodded slowly, and Claire realised that somehow they had moved towards each other. They were facing each other, bodies curved, knees fitting nicely, without quite touching. In the silence, their gazes locked.

Outside, the wind grew even stronger, but a delicious warmth spread through Claire.

'You want to try something different?' Jack spoke in a low, lazy voice that totally melted her bones.

Oh, yes. There was something *very* different Claire wanted to try, and she had a fair idea Jack was thinking about it, too. The very thought of it made her dizzy, sent her pulse pounding in her throat.

But no way would she make the first move.

Shyly, she said, 'At least this game keeps my mind off the wind. It's your turn again, isn't it?'

'I guess.'

She saw his knowing smile.

'Get on with it, then.' She spoke in her bossiest tone.

His eyes shimmered. 'OK… I've been to London to visit the Queen. I've climbed five of the world's famous seven summits. And—I do not want to kiss you.'

Claire's heart banged against her ribcage. 'I—I—' She swallowed. As soon as Jack had mentioned kissing her brain had fused and she couldn't remember anything else. What *had* he said? 'Could you—um—repeat those statements, please?'

He laughed softly. Dull colour shaded his cheekbones. 'I said: I've been to London to visit the Queen. I've climbed five of the seven summits. And I have no desire whatsoever to kiss Claire Eden.'

She was flooded with heat. 'I—I don't believe you've met the Queen.'

'I have the photo to prove it.'

'You've climbed more than five of the seven summits?'

''Fraid not.'

Now her heart was thumping so hard she was sure he could hear it above the roar of the wind. 'Then you've climbed less than five summits?'

Very slowly, Jack shook his head, and Claire felt small explosions inside her, spreading deep. Desire, stronger than anything she'd ever known, took hold.

He lifted his hand and his thumb gently traced a burning line beneath her lower lip. 'So what's the truth, Claire?'

You want to kiss me.

Which means I'm in deep water.

For all kinds of reasons she shouldn't let it happen. He'd once been her sister's lover. And she still hadn't told him about Harry. Finally, he was a Dysart—way out of her league.

But how could she find the will-power to stop something that felt so amazingly fabulous?

Fortunately Jack didn't wait until Claire had found a suitable answer. His hands framed her face and he dipped his head until his lips touched hers, and then he kissed her with slow and tantalising thoroughness.

Her skin began to burn from the inside out. She had

no choice but to close her eyes, to part her lips and to surrender to darkness and sensation.

Jack tasted just as a man should taste—clean and strong, and with an additional hint of coffee and chocolate. Lingering traces of her rose soap clung to his skin, and she caught a trace of something fresh and tangy, a whiff of the wildness outside. As for his lips…

Oh, man…

His lips…were…mesmerising. This man really knew how to kiss. For one daunting moment Claire thought of all the other women he must have kissed, including her sister. But almost immediately that thought was banished by Jack's flattering, shameless eagerness. He kissed her deeply, urgently—as if he could never have enough of her kisses, as if he never wanted to stop.

Happiness flowed through her and mingled with her desire. She felt as if she were flying and melting and drowning and dancing…drifting into a dark place where the world stopped.

Wait…

There's something wrong…

Claire couldn't believe she was distracted on the very brink of being consumed by bliss, but a diminishing part of her concentration was aware that the howling roar of the wind had morphed into a bewildering silence…

It was *silence* that had distracted her.

'Oh, my God,' she whispered. 'The wind's stopped.'

CHAPTER SIX

JACK didn't care what the wind was doing.

His limbs were happily entangled with Claire's, his fingers were threaded in her silky hair, and his lips were exploring the ivory smoothness of her throat. And as if that wasn't fabulous enough, her soft, needy little sighs were launching him into the stratosphere.

Why the hell should he care about the wind?

But Claire cared. She lifted her head and tilted it to one side, listening. Jack watched the way her straight hair fell in a shiny curtain. He traced the slender curve of her throat and thought how especially pretty she looked, all rosy and flushed. Not conventionally beautiful, perhaps—not groomed to within an inch of her life, like many of the women he'd dated.

Claire was something else—something more important. She was womanly and interesting and...*real*.

Kissing her just now, he'd been crazy with lust, but he'd also felt truly happy and unexpectedly *at home*. For the first time in years. First time ever?

'The wind's stopped,' she said again.

Jack listened. The roaring had indeed stopped. The only sounds from outside were water dripping from the eaves and, intermittently, the soft, whistling flurries of a much tamer wind.

'The eye of the cyclone must be moving over us,' he said. 'Once it passes the wind comes back—just as strong, but from the opposite direction.'

'How long will it be calm, do you think?'

'I'm not sure. Apparently it depends how big the eye is and how fast the cyclone is moving. Perhaps half an hour?'

Claire sat up and almost bumped her head on the tabletop. 'This is a good chance to check on Dorothy.'

Check on Dorothy? Now? 'You can't go chasing off down the street now, Claire. It's still too dangerous.'

'I have to see how she is. She's old and she's all alone. She must be terrified.'

Chivalry prevailed. Before Claire could leap out of their cosy nest, Jack caught her hand. 'I'll go.'

'But—'

'Don't even try to argue. I'm not letting you go out there in the dark, Claire. Besides, you need to stay here in case Harry wakes up.' Already he was scrambling to his feet.

Claire smiled shyly. 'Thank you, Jack.' The shining sparkle in her eyes made him feel as if he was saving the entire world rather than one old lady.

She said, 'You will be careful, won't you? There'll be fallen trees everywhere, and power lines down.'

While she checked Harry, still asleep in his basket,

Jack took the torch and turned up the wick on the lantern for Claire. 'Don't worry. I won't take any risks.'

She followed him to the front door, and he couldn't resist drawing her in.

'I plan to come back for more of this,' he murmured.

Demurely, she turned her face, offering him her cheek. But as Jack prepared to make the most of this disappointing option she suddenly turned back, and her sweet, warm lips were on his.

She kissed him hungrily and then laughed. 'You'd better go.'

'In a minute,' he murmured, stealing another kiss. One on her mouth and then, oh, another just below her ear. 'Would Harry's father object if he knew I was kissing you like this?'

Momentarily she stiffened, but then she said, 'No, of course he wouldn't mind.' Setting her hands against his chest, she gave him a gentle push. 'Now, off you go. We don't know how much time we have before the winds come back.'

He opened the door, flicked the switch on the torch—and felt a slam of shock as the beam of light lit up a scene from Armageddon. The front steps, the path, and the footpath were almost completely obscured by fallen branches and leaves.

'Oh, my God.' Claire, behind him, was staring in disbelief.

Jack flashed the light over the hillside at the back of the house. It looked as if a bomb had exploded there. All that was left were bare pale trunks, scoured of bark, branches and leaves.

Shocked, he flicked the light out to sea, where the bay thrashed and heaved, then down the street. 'Which house is Dorothy's?'

'The pink one, three houses down. Jack—' Claire gripped his arm. 'Please try to persuade her to come back here.'

'With or without her Labradors?' he asked dryly.

Her shoulders lifted in an uncertain shrug. 'Your call. I trust you to know the right thing to do. Just be very careful. And remember to stay away from the power lines.'

'Of course.' He sent her a grin in a vain attempt to banish the worry in her eyes. 'I can hear Harry crying. Go to him. I'll be fine.'

He had to fight his way just to reach the front gate. Even the patches of ground that were clear of fallen trees or pieces of roofing iron were ankle-deep in leaves. And already he could sense the wind picking up again.

Flashing the light up and down the path along the cliff top, he saw power poles leaning drunkenly, their wires dipping low to the muddy ground, but as far as he could tell unbroken.

Carefully, he made his way past the two houses next to Claire's. Holiday homes, according to Claire, their owners back on the mainland. Just as well, he thought, eyeing a partly missing roof.

As he turned in at Dorothy's gate, loud barking erupted.

'Who's there?' called a shrill female voice, and the yellow beam of a light waved at him in the blackness.

'It's Jack Dysart. I've come from Claire Eden's place to see how you're faring.'

'Oh, how nice.' The light bobbed towards him.

'Stay there,' Jack called. 'I'll come to you.'

He hadn't shone his torch directly at her, for fear of blinding her, so she didn't become visible until after he'd made his way through the obstacle course of debris that littered her front yard.

He found her on the front veranda, a stout, round-cheeked woman, with silver hair that stood out in spikes all over her head. She held her torch high, while in her other hand she clutched the leads of two Golden Labradors.

'Dorothy, I presume?' Jack said, smiling.

'Jack.' She set the torch down and held out her hand to him. The Labradors growled. 'Quiet, you pair. This is Jack, and he's a friend. Claire and Harry sent him.' Dorothy gave Jack's hand a vigorous shake. 'How kind of you to come down. It's been quite a blow, hasn't it?'

Gesturing to the tangled ruin that had once been her front garden, she drawled in a fair imitation of an American accent, '"I've a feeling we're not in Kansas any more."'

Jack laughed. In the midst of disaster, she was quoting Dorothy in *The Wizard of Oz*. He wasn't sure what he'd expected to find, but her sense of humour was a pleasant surprise.

'Claire's been very worried about you,' he said. 'How are you holding out?'

'Oh, we're fine. This place is as solid as a rock. I had the roof thoroughly checked last winter, you know. I told Claire not to worry.'

Picking up the lantern again, she held it high in front

of her so that its light fell onto his face. Her dark eyes were as beady and bright as a bird's, and she studied him for rather longer than necessary. Eventually a huge smile spread over her face, like dawn on a summer's morning.

'So you're looking after Claire?' She sounded as if she was highly amused by this. Her eyes twinkled wickedly. 'Lucky Claire.'

Jack cleared his throat, but he was absurdly pleased to have received approval from Claire's friend. 'I'm under strict instructions to persuade you to come back with me before this storm turns around,' he said.

Without hesitation Dorothy shook her head, and her hand strayed to rub the nearest Labrador's head. 'That is kind of Claire, but I'm fine here. Honestly.'

After a beat, he said, 'There'd be plenty of room for the dogs as well.'

'No, no, no. Pluto and Venus are big sooks. They hide under my bed in any kind of storm. If I took them to Claire's they'd howl the roof off without the wind's help. And they'd terrify poor little Harry.'

Jack wasn't about to argue. He couldn't pretend he didn't want Claire to himself for the rest of the night.

All about him the wind was gathering speed again, leaves swirling in menacing circles.

'You'd better get back,' Dorothy told him.

'Are you sure there isn't something I can do for you while I'm here?'

She shook her head. 'You get back to Claire and take good care of her. Is little Harry OK? He must be frightened by all the noise.'

'He's been great. Next to no trouble at all. So far he's slept through almost everything.'

'What a darling. I've been so impressed by how beautifully Claire's cared for that baby,' Dorothy said. 'It was very big-hearted of her to give up everything to look after her little nephew.'

'Her *nephew*?'

The word reverberated in Jack's head like the echo of a rifle-shot.

A sudden gust of wind sent a spray of dirt and leaves onto Dorothy's veranda and she ducked her head. 'This is about to get nasty again. I'm going into the house, Jack, and you should get back while you can.'

He took two hasty steps towards her. He had to ask. 'Did you say that Harry is Claire's nephew? Is he Flora's son?'

Something in his face must have alerted Dorothy. She frowned, and her dark eyes became shrewd and wary. Her mouth pulled in, tightening her farewell smile. 'Thanks so much for coming to check on me.' She spoke warmly. 'I'll look forward to seeing you later, Jack. Good luck!'

He wanted to insist that Dorothy repeat what she'd said, but in truth he didn't really need to. He'd heard her clearly enough.

It was very big-hearted of her to give up everything to look after her little nephew.

It would have been a damn sight more big-hearted if she'd shared that news with him. Why had Claire let him assume she was a single mother? She knew he thought Harry was her son.

Hell, he'd felt sorry for her, thinking she'd been abandoned by Harry's father. In reality, Harry *must* be Flora's child. Claire had no other brothers or sisters.

With a wave of her torch Dorothy disappeared inside, taking her dogs and pulling the door shut behind her. Jack, tussling with her unsettling revelation, worked his way back through the messy yard to the footpath.

Flora had had a baby.

Whose baby?

He came to a dead stop. Wind gusted and bellowed around him so savagely it almost lifted him off his feet. A tree branch flew past, missing him by inches, but he hardly noticed it.

The arithmetic was elementary—and yet he felt a desperate need to repeat the simple calculation several times over. Harry had been born nine months ago—and of course had been conceived nine months before that.

Eighteen months ago *he'd* been here on the island…with Flora.

And, unless she'd been incredibly promiscuous…

A chill wind swept through Jack, and this time the weather was not the culprit.

Surely not…?

He threw back his head and stared at the blinding black of the swirling sky, while anger and despair stormed through him.

Bloody hell. Had another woman—a woman he liked very much and had begun to trust—deceived him?

* * *

At last.

Claire sighed with relief when she saw the torch beam threading through the black night towards her cottage. She'd spent a nervous time waiting, wondering what Jack would find at Dorothy's place. She wished she'd thought to give him her mobile phone number so they could keep in touch.

Now she peered through the inky blackness, trying to see whether he was bringing Dorothy and her dogs, but with clouds blanketing the moon and stars and the streetlights out she couldn't see anything much.

Harry, who had woken, stirred restlessly in her arms, and she joggled him up and down and patted his back.

'Jack will be here soon,' she told him. *He's your daddy.*

Thud. Just thinking about the news she must share with Jack sent a burst of anxiety shooting like a gas flame in her throat.

In a few more hours she would have to tell Jack everything. She hoped it would be cathartic to come clean with her secret as she watched the return of daylight—almost as if the cyclone had arrived for a reason, to break down the lie, smash through the subterfuge.

Bring the truth to the surface.

But would it be a painful process? Honesty could be brutal.

Claire shivered and hugged Harry closer. Knots tightened in her stomach. Now that she'd kissed Jack—hungrily and with reckless abandon—she felt more nervous than ever about telling him he had a son.

Then again, she supposed she shouldn't read any particular significance into one steamy bout of kissing.

It was probably water off a duck's back for a man like Jack Dysart.

Admittedly, for Claire it had been the most perfect kiss in the entire history of the planet—but she'd only had a handful of boyfriends, so what would she know? It was a whole year since she'd been kissed by anyone who wasn't wearing a nappy.

Jack, on the other hand, kissed women all the time. For a playboy, women were mere wildflowers—to be plucked and enjoyed, then discarded without a backward glance before he moved on to greener pastures.

Claire heard the stamp of feet on the front steps and went to open the door. As Jack entered, a gust sent debris flying down the hall. The door slammed before Claire could close it.

Jack hadn't brought Dorothy with him, and he looked so grim her heart faltered. 'Is Dorothy all right?'

Dark fury smouldered in his eyes. 'Dorothy's absolutely fine.' He sounded weary, but there was a jerky tension in his movements as he shrugged out of the rain jacket and hung it on a hook beside the door. 'I couldn't convince her to come here.'

Outside, the wind renewed its strength, rushing like a jumbo jet overhead.

'You just got back in time.' Claire conjured an overbright smile. 'I'm sure you could do with a cuppa. I'm heating water in a saucepan on the gas ring. It's almost boiling.'

Halfway across the lounge room, Claire turned and frowned. Jack hadn't made any move to follow her. He was standing still, just inside the front door.

What was the matter? He'd said that Dorothy was fine, but something had happened. *He'd changed.* When he'd left her he'd been flirting, trying to steal last-minute kisses. Now he looked distanced and worried, like a man who'd had very bad news. Had he seen something terrible outside?

'What is it, Jack?' She began to walk back to him, jiggling a grumbling Harry on her hip. 'What's wrong?'

His eyes were as frigid as an Arctic shadow. 'You haven't been honest with me.'

'What do you mean? What are you talking about?'

'Harry.'

Whoosh.

'He's your nephew, isn't he?'

Claire gasped as if he'd thrown icy water in her face. *Dorothy must have said something.* She'd never dreamed that this might happen.

'Yes,' she said. How could she deny it? There was no point.

But this was too soon. All wrong. She'd wanted to tell Jack herself—gently, framing her story carefully, justifying her silence before he could object.

'So,' he said coldly, 'I assume Flora was Harry's mother?'

Claire nodded. Felt sick. Jack wouldn't be this upset if he hadn't already guessed the possible link to himself. 'Come—come and sit down, Jack.'

'No, thanks.'

Harry complained loudly, and rubbed his sleepy face into Claire's shoulder. It was still the middle of the night and he should have been asleep.

'When did Flora die?' Jack asked, lifting his voice to reach her above the strengthening wind and Harry's cries.

'A few days after Harry was born. Jack, please don't look at me like that.' She couldn't bear to see the agonised fury in his face.

Tears sprang in her eyes, and Harry's wails grew louder than ever. Outside, it sounded as if a giant was hurling heavy furniture about.

Squeezing her eyes tightly shut, to stem the flow of tears, Claire hugged Harry closer and pressed her lips to the silky top of his head. As she tried to rock and soothe him, she heard Jack's footsteps approaching across the timber floor. Any second now he would demand the truth, the whole truth and nothing but the truth.

He would claim this little boy and leave her with...*nothing*.

The footsteps stopped beside her. 'Why don't we play another round of Liars' Club, Claire?'

Claire didn't want to open her eyes. The iron-cold contempt in his voice was bad enough without seeing the expression in his eyes.

'My turn,' Jack continued, in a cruelly mocking tone. 'Which of these is the lie? I'm Santa Claus. We're trapped in the middle of a cyclone. I'm Harry's father.'

She had no choice. She couldn't stand there cringing like a guilty criminal. After all, she hadn't done anything terribly wrong except blindly follow her sister's wishes.

Chin high, and praying that he wouldn't have too bad an opinion of her, Claire faced her fear. 'He's your son, Jack.'

CHAPTER SEVEN

'I WAS going to tell you,' Claire quickly added, jolted by the bleak shock in Jack's eyes.

'Oh, really?' There was a haughty threat in his voice now. No doubt his Dysart genes were rearing their scornful heads.

'I was going to tell you in the morning,' Claire tried to explain. 'As soon as this cyclone had passed.'

He gave an icy little laugh. 'How convenient to have a cyclone to hide behind.'

Something inside Claire snapped. It had been a dreadful night and their lives were still at risk. She was too tired and tense to handle an arrogant Dysart. She stamped her foot, and Harry let out a roar of protest. Another crash sounded outside.

'Do you really think this is the right time to discuss this?' she cried. 'Shouldn't we get under the table?'

Jack's lips curled as he cast a contemptuous glance towards the kitchen. 'You can get under there if you want, but the rest of the storm won't be any worse than what we've already been through.' He lifted his voice above the ruckus. 'And, for what it's worth, the right time to discuss this was eighteen months ago, when Flora got herself pregnant.'

'Oh, so getting pregnant was her fault, too, was it?'

'As it happens, yes.' His jaw squared, and without meeting her gaze he said, 'Flora was very insistent that she had taken care of contraception.'

Claire stared at him, stunned. She'd never discussed this delicate matter with her sister. She'd assumed Harry's conception had been accidental. But, given Flora's unconventional and capricious approach to life, it was quite possible that she had decided she would like to have a baby and then used Jack as an unwitting donor.

Not that Claire would dream of suggesting this possibility to Jack in his present mood. 'A wise man might have asked a few pertinent questions,' she said. 'I'm afraid my sister often found shades of grey in matters that are clearly black and white for the rest of us.'

A low curse broke from Jack and he looked angry enough to commit a serious crime. Plunging his hands in his pockets, he paced to the other end of the room, but his long legs got him there too quickly and he was forced to turn back.

'What about when the baby was born?' he demanded. 'Couldn't she have notified me then?'

'She didn't know where you were.'

'I wasn't in hiding! I left forwarding addresses all over the place. My family always knew where I was.'

'Jack, this is a pointless discussion. You know Flora's not here to defend herself.'

'You could have found me if you'd bothered.'

Oh, so now he was going to drag her into it too! 'I had enough on my plate without looking for wayward playboy fathers!'

Damn. She'd lost her temper.

How had this fallen apart so quickly? Less than an hour ago she and Jack had been so happy, playing a game that had led to sensational kisses and to an amazing feeling of connection. She'd thought Jack was gorgeous and delicious—quite possibly the nicest man she'd ever met.

Now they were at war.

To put a finishing touch to Claire's despair, Harry stiffened, threw back his head, and bellowed at the top of his lungs. Claire glared at Jack. He glared back at her. Outside, a thumping great crash was followed by the sound of splintering wood.

'Couldn't you have left this till the morning? Go away, Jack! Let me try to calm Harry down.'

He did exactly as she demanded. After bestowing a final blistering glance on the two of them, Jack spun on his heel and strode out of the lounge room into the spare bedroom, where he closed the door sharply.

Good riddance.

Tears streamed down Claire's cheeks as she kissed Harry and tried to soothe him. She knew her tension was flowing into the baby and upsetting him further, but what could she do?

Flora, Flora, why did I listen to you? I knew keeping the baby a secret from his father was asking for trouble.

Jack's door remained stubbornly shut and Harry continued to cry. Claire went through to the kitchen and turned off the gas beneath the boiling water, wondering what on earth she could do to calm the baby down. She'd already given him another bottle. If she gave him any more he'd end up with a tummy ache.

'Hush,' she soothed. 'There, there.'

The wind outside was as savage and scary as it had been before, but Claire was too preoccupied to pay it much attention. She walked up and down the length of the lounge room, cuddling Harry, rocking him, patting his back.

She tried to sing lullabies—'Rock a Bye Baby', 'Hush Little Baby'. When they didn't work she tried nursery rhymes—'Little Boy Blue', 'Hey diddle, diddle'.

Harry didn't seem to like any of them.

Eventually, on the point of dropping from exhaustion, she sang a song from the top of the charts—a hip-hop number about a guy falling in love with a girl with green eyes.

Harry stopped crying and listened.

Claire had to sing the song over and over and over before he started to relax and grow heavy in her arms, his head lolling on her shoulder. She went into the hall, where there was a mirror, and in the dim lantern light checked her reflection from the back to see if Harry was indeed asleep.

His eyes were closed and his plump little cheeks were flushed and wet with grievous tears. Every so often he gave a little shuddering whimper in his sleep.

He looked so little and vulnerable, so sad and sweet. Poor little man.

She'd had such a struggle to settle him, and now she had to tackle the other sad and upset male fuming away in the next room. It would take more than a pop song to soothe Jack. He'd had a terrible shock tonight.

Feeling calmer now, she tried to imagine what it had been like for Jack to suddenly learn that this dear little fellow was his son—and to receive that news in the middle of a cyclone from a complete stranger. Hurt and angry didn't go halfway to describing how he must feel.

With tender care she put Harry back in the basket beneath the table, then tiptoed to the door of Jack's room and lifted her hand to knock. She'd been wrong to give in to Flora's demand for secrecy, and after Jack had turned up her silence had indeed become a deception. The least she could do was offer an apology.

But her hand froze in mid-air. Jack had been so very angry, and he might not be ready to listen. They might start fighting again. Perhaps her original idea was the best. She should wait till morning.

Miserably aware that she'd chosen the cowardly option, she went back to the kitchen and made herself a mug of hot chocolate. She took it through to the lounge room and drank it, curled in an armchair. She cast another anxious glance to Jack's closed door and wondered if he was asleep, then she yawned hugely. And she realised she was completely worn out.

The baby had stopped crying.

Jack sat on the edge of the single bed in the spare room with his head in his hands. The cyclone continued to rage outside, but he'd only been focused on the sounds that came from within the house. The cries of his son. And Claire's light soprano voice singing on and on.

How patient she'd been—while Jack was still fit to burst from the anger that roiled inside him. Frustration too. He was cut off. In a prison of his own making. He'd shut the door on his own son's crying.

And here was the irony—earlier this evening, when he'd thought Harry was another man's child, he'd calmed the kid down. He'd felt like a miracle-worker just because the little fellow had fallen asleep in his arms.

But now, when he knew the baby was his, he'd virtually abandoned him. Left him to cry his lungs out.

That was what anger did to a guy. Righteous anger. Valid, reasonable, justifiable anger.

Hell. What was it with women? Did they think their biology gave them a divine right to make every decision about parenthood?

First his fiancée had cheated him of his chance to be a father, and then Flora had excluded him from her entire pregnancy. Finally, Claire had carried on the tradition.

If Dorothy hadn't blurted out the truth…

Who knew? Based on his past experience, he thought Claire had probably planned to wave him off once the cyclone was past, without a whisper about his connection to his son.

That strong possibility disappointed Jack more than anything else.

He'd known Claire for less than a day, but in their

short encounter they'd prepared for a cyclone, they'd fussed together over a baby, they'd played stupid funny games under the table. And then they'd kissed. Under the table.

If he were to measure kisses from ordinary to exceptional, kissing Claire had been off the scale. Everything about this evening had felt more special than any evening he'd ever shared with any other woman.

That sounded crazy, but it was the honest truth. It was different from simple attraction. He'd been filled with admiration for Claire. Single motherhood was tough, and she'd done a fabulous job of caring for Harry. And then there was the way she cared about Dorothy. And the old woman thought the world of her.

It was so maddening that Claire could be compassionate and caring and also collusive and devious. He found it hard to accept she was a liar, but the evidence was inescapable, and it was asleep in a basket under the kitchen table.

Jack, on the other hand, would get no sleep tonight.

Claire woke in the armchair.

She'd been sleeping with her legs hooked over the upholstered arm, and her head had fallen at an awkward angle. Now her neck was stiff. Actually, she was stiff all over. She felt as old as Dorothy as she took a few seconds to get her bearings.

She listened to the silence outside—the cyclone must have passed. So they'd survived, which was something. Cautiously, she lowered her feet to the floor and used the arms of the chair for support as she stood and took stock.

The cottage was filled with pale, creamy light. Morning?

What was the time? How long had she slept?

The door to Jack's room was open. Her heart skidded sideways.

A few hasty steps, however, showed her that the bedroom was empty. In fact, the bed was as neat as when she'd made it. It looked as if it had never been slept in. And Jack's duffle bag was gone.

Claire sagged against the doorframe, intensely dismayed by the empty room. He hadn't even said goodbye, hadn't given her a chance to explain that she'd never intended to cut him off from his son for ever.

What did this mean? Was he coming back for Harry?

Oh, heavens—Harry!

She dashed to the kitchen and her heart plunged from a great height when she saw the laundry basket lying on its side. Empty.

Surely Jack hadn't taken him? Not like that.

No! Oh, help.

'Harry!' Her voice was shrill with horror.

No answer.

'Harry!' she almost screamed.

'Da!'

The sound came from the open doorway of the pantry. Claire flew across the room and discovered Harry sitting on the pantry floor, covered in honey and sugar crystals.

'Da!' he crowed, showing his three teeth as he grinned up at her, then gleefully plunged his hand back into the opened honey pot.

'Oh, thank God.' She almost cried with relief, but that was quickly followed by dismay when she registered all the mess. 'How did you get that open, you little monkey?'

Harry was coated in honey and sugar, like a Greek pastry, and he'd obviously crawled through the debris blown in from the storm on the kitchen floor, so bits of leaves clung to his clothing and his knees were streaked with mud.

Claire looked at the clock and was shocked to see that it was already half past eight. How could she have slept so late? How long had Harry been awake? And where was Jack?

She supposed she should be grateful he hadn't kidnapped Harry.

But she was sick that he'd left without a word. She wanted to apologise. She needed to explain—to make him understand.

Most of all she wanted to see him smile again.

Silly of her, but last night—before their fight had erupted—she'd had fantasies about Jack staying on for a bit and helping to clean up all the mess in her yard.

She'd been spoiled yesterday, having him here to help with the shutters and the roof. For a brief moment it had been like having a partner, a helpmate…a husband…

Dream on.

Claire bundled Harry into a towel, but she would have to heat water before she could clean him up. It was while she was waiting for the warm water that she realised something was wrong with the house. It shouldn't be filled with light, but it was. Light streamed in through every window, and when she looked more closely she saw that the storm shutters had been taken down.

How about that? Surely Jack must have done it? Was he still here, working outside?

With Harry in her arms, she hurried outside and stopped, shocked by a landscape virtually obscured by a horrible, stomach-churning mess. Almost nothing was left of the pretty garden that Flora had started and Claire had maintained. As for the hillside... The sight of hundreds of leafless, limbless tree trunks brought tears to her eyes.

But when she looked higher she saw sunshine and patches of blue. The sky had a washed-clean, post-storm freshness, and she couldn't help feeling happy because Jack had taken her shutters down.

'Where is he?' she asked Harry.

An abrupt mechanical snarl broke the morning stillness, rapidly followed by the jarring whine of a chainsaw. The baby jumped in Claire's arms, startled by the sound, which came from behind the garden shed.

Gingerly, Claire stepped over a pile of branches and saw Jack wielding a chainsaw. His dark hair gleamed in the sunlight and his back muscles strained his navy blue T-shirt as he cut through the tree that had smashed over the fence and onto the shed's roof.

Where had the chainsaw come from? Had he already been down to the hardware store?

How kind. And how little faith she'd had to doubt that Jack would stay to help. She wanted to call out to him, but he would never hear her above the noise of the saw. And she didn't like to wave and distract him when he was working with such a lethal weapon.

She went back inside to get on with the task of cleaning up Harry and then cleaning the house. They had survived the night, the cottage was still standing, and Jack was still here. Her heart was as light as the morning air.

CHAPTER EIGHT

JACK, halfway up the hillside behind Claire's cottage, looked out through a tangle of broken trees and dangling limbs to the sulking waters of the bay and punched his brother's number into his mobile phone.

'Nick, how are you?'

'Jack? Is that you?'

'No one else. How's the family?'

'The family's fine. Fighting fit. But where the hell are you? Which hemisphere?'

'I'm back in Australia. On Sapphire Island, actually.'

'You're joking. Sapphire Island was blown off the map last night.'

'Is that what you heard?'

'It's on TV and in all the papers. Cyclone Fred.'

'Yeah, well, for once the media aren't exaggerating. Fred was a savage blow, and it's a miracle no one was killed. Huge amount of property damage, and the island's vegetation is devastated.'

'Trust you to be there in the thick of it, Jack. Are you OK? Can you get off the island?'

'I'm fine. But no one can get off at the moment. The seas are still too rough, and the jetty was badly smashed, so it'll be close to a week before the ferry from the mainland can moor here.'

'We could send a boat and a tender to pick you up. Or a helicopter. Hey, why don't I do that? I've got my licence now. I could fly Dad's chopper up there—say tomorrow?'

'Nick, calm down. Thanks all the same, but I don't need to be rescued.'

After a beat of silence, Nick became the teasing big brother. 'I see—so there's a woman involved, is there?'

Jack gritted his teeth. 'No woman.' Somehow he held back his sigh. 'As a matter of fact I'm on a completely different mission. I'm going to hang around here to see what I can do to help the islanders. It's going be a long haul before they recover from this. I'm at a loose end, and the State Emergency Services need volunteers.'

'I can't argue with that, mate. Good for you. Let us know if there's anything we can do.'

'Yeah, thanks. Can you let Mum and Dad know where I am? I'll ring them later.'

'Sure. They'll be pleased to hear you're back on Australian soil. But Sapphire Island? Are you *sure* there isn't a woman involved?'

Jack looked down at the cottage: at the red iron roof he'd climbed all over yesterday, at the windows where he'd fitted shutters and then removed them again, at the neat pile of sawn timber piled beside the smashed garden shed, at the flattened plants, at the clothesline with washing—mostly Harry's baby clothes—blowing gently in the sunshine.

While he watched, Claire came out of the back door and lifted a hand to shade her eyes as she scanned the yard. She looked up at the hill, and Jack's heart gave a heavy, dull thud.

Stiffly, he said, 'I can assure you I'm not staying on here because of a woman, but there are complications that I have to work through.'

Nick chuckled. 'Why am I not surprised?'

'Yeah, well, this time you might be very surprised. But you'll have to cool your heels. I'm not going into details now.'

'Fair enough, little brother. But a word of warning. With all the media interest in the island at present, you'll have a hard time lying low.'

'I swear I won't stick my head above the parapet. Listen, I've got to go. Give my love to Alice and the girls.'

'Will do. Stay in touch, Jack.'

Jack was back.

Claire didn't know where he'd been, but she'd heard the chainsaw start up again. All morning she'd kept busy—she'd removed the bedding from beneath the kitchen table, swept and mopped the cottage floors, washed out Harry's clothes by hand and hung them in the sun, then set a huge pot of tomato soup on the burner for lunch. When it was ready, she went out into the yard to call to Jack.

The fallen tree was now sawn into three neat piles:

the thick trunk in one pile, branches in another, spindly twigs and leaves in yet another.

She hadn't been able to catch Jack's eye. It was pretty clear that he was avoiding her, so she supposed he was still angry. But she didn't know if he'd eaten breakfast. She felt nervous and jittery when she found him cutting the last of the branches behind the shed.

'Jack,' she called. 'Come and have some lunch. It's all ready.'

He yelled back over his shoulder. 'Don't worry about lunch for me. I'll eat at the pub.'

She hurried closer. 'You don't have to go all the way to the pub. You're welcome to eat here. There's hot soup and rolls, and left over casserole from last night.'

She almost told him the soup was homemade, not out of a tin, but when he set his heavy chainsaw on the ground and glared at her, hands on hips, she was glad she hadn't said anything so pathetic.

'I've moved to the hotel,' he said. 'I'll be staying there for the rest of my time on the island.'

She saw the resolute iciness in his eyes and knew instantly that it would be pointless and demeaning to protest. Miserably, she said, 'But I—I haven't even thanked you for your help.'

'All part of the service,' he said, with a frighteningly cool smile.

Her throat was so tight she struggled to get the words out. 'We—we haven't talked about Harry.'

'Oh, yes, we have.'

'But last night was all wrong. Won't you let me explain, Jack?'

His mouth took a bitter down-curved dive. 'No, thanks. I don't think I could stomach your list of excuses.' He turned to go, then halted, sent her a quick frowning glance. 'I'll give you plenty of warning before I leave the island.' After the briefest pause he added, 'And of course I'll be taking my boy with me.'

She felt the colour leave her face.

Perhaps Jack saw it, too, for he sent her one sharp, searching look, then, with a deepening frown, spun on his heel, grabbed the chainsaw and marched out of her yard.

OK, Jack thought as he took the steps down the cliff, so he'd been hard on Claire. But what had she expected him to say?

I have a son? How nice. But don't worry. I understand perfectly that nobody had time to tell me about him during the past eighteen months. And even though you kept it a secret all through yesterday and last night, I knew that one day you'd get around to telling me. That's fine. No worries. Don't give it another thought, sweetheart. I'll just leave Harry here with you and drop in again—say when he turns twenty-one.

Pigs might fly.

Unable to bear her own company, Claire took the soup to Dorothy's and found her old friend coping with the devastation of her beautiful island with stoicism. She'd already been down to the shops, and she was full of news about which island residents had lost their roofs, and who'd been unlucky enough to have trees fall on their homes.

'No lives were lost, thank God,' she reported, as she ladled their steaming soup into bright yellow bowls. 'But old Archie Bell's in hospital. He was badly cut by flying glass, poor chap. And the library lost a big section of its roof. Hundreds of books have been damaged.'

'I suppose the government will provide some kind of disaster relief?' Claire suggested, determined to prevent her thoughts from dwelling on her personal disaster. 'There's so much to be done—clearing all the mess, restoring electricity and water, re-roofing homes, mending damaged roads. Not to mention all the insurance assessment and compensation.'

Dorothy nodded. 'There's talk of a retired army general being sent up from Canberra to co-ordinate it all.'

'Really?' Claire felt the tiniest flare of excitement. 'I used to do that sort of work. Not actual disaster relief, but logistics and co-ordinating. I wonder if I'd be any help?'

After lunch, while Harry slept in the back bedroom, the two women cut away allamanda and wisteria vines from Dorothy's smashed pergola.

Dorothy wanted to talk about Jack. 'What a sight for sore eyes he is.' She chuckled, and her brown eyes were as bright and round as buttons. 'And he has such nice manners, too. It must have been so reassuring to have him with you and Harry last night.'

Claire winced inwardly. The only assurance she'd received today was a promise that Jack would take Harry away from her. It was news too awful to share. She tried to steer the conversation elsewhere, with little success.

* * *

Two days later, Dorothy arrived on Claire's doorstep on top of the world. 'Your Jack is going to rebuild my pergola,' she announced, waving a glossy magazine under Claire's nose.

'He's not my Jack,' Claire mumbled as she invited Dorothy inside. She'd been hearing Jack's praises sung by several of her island friends whose yards Jack had helped to clean up. Somehow everyone seemed to know he'd spent the night of the cyclone with Claire. She'd chosen not to tell them he hadn't spoken to her since then.

It was killing her. Everyone else saw Jack as a wonderful saviour, but she now knew him as a harsh and unforgiving Dysart—a man who planned to coldly and cruelly claim Harry and wreck her happiness without a care. The worst of it was, she felt so guilty about deceiving him that she almost believed she deserved his ill treatment.

As soon as Dorothy was comfortably settled, Claire steered the conversation away from Jack. 'I was wondering if I could ask an enormous favour, Dorothy?'

Her friend didn't blink. 'Certainly, dear. What is it?'

'I've volunteered to help with the disaster relief coordination, and I was hoping you could possibly mind Harry for a couple of mornings a week.'

Her friend's face broke into the most enormous grin. 'I'd be delighted. I was never blessed with children, but I've always fancied myself as the grandmotherly type.'

They discussed which mornings would be most suitable, and then Dorothy simply had to share more news about the pergola. 'Jack brought me this magazine so I could choose a design. Who would have thought? I built the old pergola myself twenty years ago, but I didn't care a hoot about any particular design. I just wanted something to grow a creeper over.'

Dorothy flipped pages merrily, showing Claire photographs of pergolas with lattice, with slats, with knotty undressed timber, with arches, with curlicues. She looked quite pink and girlish in her excitement… Jack suggested this and Jack said that… No doubt Dorothy had been batting her eyelashes at him too.

Foolishly, Claire let out a heavy sigh.

Dorothy pounced. 'Excuse me for being terribly nosy, Claire, but have you and Jack been fighting?'

'No…we haven't been fighting. We haven't been… *anything*…really. I haven't even spoken to him for days.' Claire's hands fluttered nervously and she curled them onto her lap. 'Honestly, I only met him on the day of the cyclone. We're not—not an item—or anything.'

Dorothy looked utterly unconvinced, and Claire knew there was nothing to be gained by hiding the truth. 'Jack was looking for Flora, actually. He'd been away overseas. He didn't even know Flora had died.'

Her friend's eyes grew thoughtful, and it was ages before she spoke. 'So Jack's Harry's father.' It was a statement, not a question.

Now it was Claire's turn to be surprised. 'How d-did you guess?'

'Flora told me her baby's father was away overseas.'

'I see.'

'But she gave me the impression he wasn't really her type. A high flyer. Very self-centred.'

'He is. More or less.'

'Oh, Claire, how could you say that about Jack?'

'Very easily.'

Dorothy's eyes narrowed. 'Don't talk rubbish. Did you know Jack had half a dozen generators flown in at his own expense for the people in Blue Bay because they won't have power for another six weeks?'

Of course Claire knew. People hadn't stopped talking about it. And another friend had found a magazine article that raved about Jack's contribution to disaster relief after a terrible snow storm in Nepal.

Dorothy said, 'He's hurt you, hasn't he?'

Claire's face threatened to crumple, but she struggled to hang on to her composure. Any minute now she would tell Dorothy that Jack was going to take Harry away, and the black cloud of nameless horror she'd been fighting ever since he gave his ultimatum would descend and consume her. 'I'm sorry, but I'd rather not talk about it.'

'Claire, darling, what's the matter? You look quite ill.'

'I'd like to take a closer look at those designs. Have you decided what kind of pergola you'd like?'

Jack walked to the end of the bay and climbed the rocks on the promontory. The boulders were smooth and huge and littered with the trunks of fallen hoop pines, but he continued on, keen to reach the top.

Climbing had always been a release for him. It helped to clear his head, and he'd made many of his best decisions while looking out at views from mountain peaks.

At the top he stood on a smooth flat-topped rock, looking to the west at the heartrending sight of the island's flattened vegetation. This evening he found it utterly depressing. He would get no answers there. He turned instead to the east.

He could see the next bay, and the one after that—aquamarine blue scallops, edged with sand that curved like slices of lemon peel. He looked further out to sea, to the horizon, where clouds floated like islands.

He thought, *I have a son.*

It actually felt amazingly good. He'd wandered the world aimlessly and come home to find he had a son—a fragile root, a tiny anchor, a line stretching into the future.

But the secrecy surrounding Harry was a bitter pill. Still. Always.

Claire might never have told him.

Do you really believe that?

Sure. She had plenty of opportunities. We talked non-stop.

She was focused on the cyclone. Terrified. And her fear was justified. Look at the devastation. Look at the number of homes you're helping to rebuild.

Yeah. Whatever.

He looked back to Claire's bay, saw the cliff behind it and the row of cottages, some of them unroofed, saw her cottage in the middle, with its secure red iron roof. He stared at it, remembering the afternoon he'd worked up there. He remembered the two of them in the rain, and the urgency of his need to kiss her.

He saw a flutter of blue in the front garden. Claire, wearing the same dress she'd worn that day, was looking his way.

Watching him? A sudden flare of hope came out of nowhere—an irresistible impulse to reach out to her. He lifted his hand to wave, but she quickly bent down and retrieved something from the ground—presumably Harry, crawling on the lawn. Her dark hair floated behind her like a ribbon in the wind as she turned swiftly, with the white bundle in her arms, and went back into the house.

Closed the door.

Cool, salty wind rose from the sea and smacked Jack in the face, and he stood there, looking across the chasm of the bay to her closed door.

Perhaps the door spoke more loudly than any words. Perhaps the salty wind had cleared the clouds in his thinking. As Jack watched, he felt beyond his own pain to Claire's pain.

Of course.

Of *course.*

He straightened his shoulders, took a deep breath and smiled. Something complicated was suddenly simple. He knew what he needed to do.

CHAPTER NINE

CLAIRE was feeding Harry in his highchair when she heard the commanding knock on her front door. Instantly she thought of Jack.

Was this the moment she'd dreaded? How many days, hours, minutes were left to her before he took Harry away?

Her hand trembled so violently she spilled mashed vegetables all over Harry's cheek. 'Sorry, darling.' Hastily she wiped his face and set the plastic bowl and spoon on the highchair's tray. 'Here—do your worst with this, while I see who's at the door.'

On her way down the hall she shot a frightened glance in the mirror. In the past stressful week she'd lost weight, and her face was all cheekbones. She tucked her hair behind her ears and wished she felt more prepared.

For days she'd been trying to gather the courage to go to Jack, to entreat him to listen to her side of this situation. She'd thought of little else.

In the middle of the night she found it easy to construct brilliant defences, stating her case reasonably and persuasively.

Harry was her family too…her *only* family. Flora had entrusted him into her care. For nine and a half months she'd been his mother. Jack's demands were excessive…he should be prepared to negotiate a fair way to share Harry…

She'd never had trouble standing up to domineering males when she was in business.

But this was different. This was Jack and, try as she might to deny it, her emotions were involved. Damn it.

She'd fallen in love.

After just one night. How feeble could a girl be? Ever since the night of the cyclone, whenever she'd caught a glimpse of Jack—in his hired ute, driving from one job to another, climbing cliffs, chatting with locals—she'd been afflicted by a terrible pang.

Whenever people spoke about him—and there was always someone who wanted to talk about Jack Dysart—her insides churned and she had to find an excuse to leave the room.

She knew if she tried to confront Jack she would remember the way he'd kissed her, and how much she'd loved it, and she would break down and make a complete fool of herself. And, honestly, what could she tell him that he didn't already know?

Another sharp knock sounded and her hand shook as she opened the door. *How silly I am. It might not be Jack.*

Of course it was.

Jack stood there, dressed in a white open-necked shirt and carefully laundered jeans, holding a bottle of red wine in one hand and a white pizza box in the other.

His tan had deepened and he'd shaved away his habitual layer of stubble. He offered her a shy, almost boyish smile. 'I owe you one dinner.'

Claire's throat tightened so painfully she couldn't speak. Helpless, she shook her head.

'I need to talk to you Claire.'

'About Harry?'

He was no longer smiling. 'Among other things.'

From the kitchen came the splat of Harry's bowl hitting the floor, and then his wails of protest.

'He was in the middle of his dinner,' she said.

'My apologies. A young man should be allowed to eat in peace.'

'I guess you'd better come in.' It felt like a repeat of the day they'd met, when she'd found Jack on her doorstep.

As they entered the kitchen Harry was bellowing with rage, but when he saw Jack he stopped in mid-howl. His little mouth, rimmed by mashed pumpkin, remained open as he stared at Jack—and then he grinned.

Jack grinned back at him, and Claire bent quickly to retrieve the bowl from the floor and wipe up the spilled food.

Jack set the wine and pizza box on the kitchen table. 'So, what are you having for your dinner, Harry?'

'Mostly mashed pumpkin with a dash of Vegemite,' Claire supplied, as she found a fresh bowl and scooped more vegetables from a pot on the stove.

'Vegemite?' Jack grinned again, watched Harry open his mouth for another spoonful. 'So you're a fair dinkum Aussie?'

'Of course,' Claire snapped, hating that Jack could suddenly turn up here and be so relaxed—like an executioner, making a joke before the axe fell.

Jack said, 'Shall I pop the pizza in the oven to keep it warm?'

'If you like.' She was sure she wouldn't be able to eat a mouthful.

'It's tandoori chicken.'

She didn't reply, and for the next few moments silence smouldered while she spooned food into Harry's mouth and Jack fiddled with oven knobs. When Harry was finished she lifted him out of his high chair.

'He normally has his bath now.'

Jack's eyebrows rose.

Sighing, Claire reached for a face-washer and cleaned Harry's face and hands. She removed his bib, put him on the floor and gave him his favourite toy—a hammering set. 'His bath can wait. Perhaps you'd better tell me why you're here?'

'All right.' Jack's air of relaxation vanished. His throat worked and he swallowed. 'Would you like to sit down?'

She pulled out a kitchen chair and sat stiffly, hands clenched in her lap. Jack sat opposite her. His eyes drifted to the bottle of wine. 'Would you like a drink?'

She shook her head. On the floor, Harry smashed his hammer onto wooden pegs.

Hooking an elbow over the back of his chair, Jack said, 'Are you enjoying your disaster relief work?'

'Yes. Are you enjoying yours?'

'Very much. I've listened to a host of people singing your praises.'

'Ditto.' If only he would stop beating about the bush.

He smiled awkwardly, and she saw a flash of vulnerability in his blue-green eyes. 'Claire, I'm sorry.'

Her heart thudded. This wasn't quite what she'd expected.

'I've handled the business about Harry very badly,' he said, and he began to rotate the wine bottle round and round and round and round…

'So have I,' she admitted, watching his nervous movements and feeling unexpectedly generous. 'Flora and I shouldn't have kept him a secret.'

Jack shrugged.

'I'm sorry, Jack. You've no idea how sorry I am.' She leaned forward, eager to cast off the burden of her guilty secret, needing him to understand. 'I kept quiet because I knew it was what Flora wanted, but deep down I've always felt it was wrong. And then you turned up at the wrong moment—just when the cyclone was coming.'

Hastily, she corrected this. 'Actually, it was the right moment—because Harry and I really needed your help. But in every other way it was such bad timing. I'm afraid I couldn't deal with two crises at once.'

Jack nodded. 'And, to be fair, you thought you were dealing with a no-good adventurer who'd abandoned your sister.'

'At first, yes.'

He twisted the wine bottle again. 'I'm afraid I took it hard because this isn't the first time I've learned too late about an unexpected offspring.' His mouth twisted into a bitter smile. 'That makes me sound very careless, doesn't it?'

'You have another child?'

'No.' He looked at her and released a small sigh. 'Before I met your sister I was engaged.'

Yes, Claire had read about it. He'd dumped the poor girl.

'My fiancée was expecting my baby, but she chose not to tell me.'

'Oh.'

'And she had the pregnancy terminated, hoping I would never find out.'

'I…see.'

Terrible shadows dimmed Jack's normally bright eyes and his mouth tightened into a thin line. Claire was shocked to realise how deeply upset he was about being cheated out of fatherhood. Twice.

Jack cared about Harry—*really* cared—in the same way she did.

He turned the bottle again.

This was *terrible*. Far worse than she'd ever imagined.

'I'm so sorry,' she said again, but it sounded inadequate.

She couldn't look at Jack and she had to bite her lip, fighting tears. She loved Harry so much—had almost tricked herself into believing he was *her* baby. But really she'd been no better than a thief. Harry belonged to Jack. And she couldn't deny that Jack was perfect father material.

'Claire, don't look so worried.'

'Can you ever forgive me?'

'Of course.' He smiled gently. 'It was a tricky situation for you. A very sad situation. You loved your sister. I should be asking *you* for forgiveness.'

She frowned. 'Why?'

'I've spent too long licking my wounds.' He sent her a sheepish smile. 'Wallowing in self-pity, I guess. But I was so caught up in my own problems I didn't give much thought to yours. I know you only wanted what was best for Harry. And you've done a wonderful job. I'm really grateful, Claire. You've been a fabulous mum for him.'

But now I have to give him up.

She held herself super still, hardly daring to breathe for fear she would burst into tears.

'Something else might surprise you,' Jack said, as he twisted the bottle yet again.

He paused and threw Claire a cautious, almost hopeful look, as if he was asking permission to continue. But she was steeling herself for the last act in this tragedy. Any minute now he would ask her to surrender Harry, and she was so tense she couldn't speak, couldn't move, could barely breathe.

'Claire, the night I spent with you here was one of the happiest nights of my life.'

Clunk.

That was her heart.

Claire looked up, and her eyes met his, and the temperature in the kitchen rose ten degrees. Her ribcage ached from the sudden storm of emotions inside her. Fear. Uncertainty. And now a tingling, bubbling sensation that didn't dare give way to hope.

Earnestly, Jack continued. 'When I was here with

you the simple things—like fixing your roof, eating here at your kitchen table, helping to get little Harry to sleep, playing crazy games—they were—it was—'

He stopped turning the bottle and looked at her. His eyes were suspiciously bright. 'It was so much like my idea of—of how I want to live my life.'

His sad smile made her ache all over, as if her very bones might shatter at the slightest touch.

What about the kiss? He hasn't mentioned the kiss.

'Da!' shouted Harry, and they both jumped. They'd almost forgotten the baby, but there he was, grinning at them as he stood in the kitchen doorway beneath the fringe of Flora's beads.

He was standing all alone—not holding onto anything.

'He's never done that before,' Claire cried. 'You clever little man.'

'Do you think he's going to walk?'

'I don't know.'

As she spoke, Harry took a step—just one wobbly step—then fell flat on his bottom. He looked surprised and disappointed, and his bottom lip trembled.

Jack laughed, and in an instant he was out of his chair and scooping him into his arms. 'What a champ!'

'Wow!' Claire smiled at them. 'You saw him take his first step.'

'I want to see him take more. I want to be there for all his important milestones.'

Her smile faded. Jack had every right to take Harry away, but she could feel the black cloud descending, threatening to suffocate her.

'What about it, Claire?'

She blinked. 'What about what?'

Switching Harry onto his hip, Jack held out his hand to her. 'Come here,' he said, pulling her gently but confidently out of her chair.

Her legs were shaky, but Jack's arm tightened around her shoulders, and before she knew quite what was happening he leaned in and kissed her.

He smiled happily, and kissed her again. 'Your kisses were the best thing about our night together. You have the sexiest lips in all history.'

It was just as well his arm was supporting her. 'B-but what about Harry? Weren't we talking about him?'

'Of course.' Jack pulled her closer. 'Harry needs you, Claire. You're his mum.'

'We both know I'm not.'

'We both know you've been a wonderful mother to him. And you're the only mother he has.'

'Th-that's true.'

'And I'm his father.'

'Ye-e-es.'

'What say we give it a go?' Jack pressed his warm lips to her forehead.

'Pardon?' He'd lost her.

'Why don't we try bringing Harry up together?'

'Together?'

'Yes.'

'As in *live* together?'

Jack was grinning as he nodded. Was he laughing? Was this some kind of joke?

'Do you mean all three of us?' Claire asked. 'In the same house?'

'Why not?'

'But what about—what about your family?'

'They won't be living with us.'

'But what will they think?'

He grinned some more and kissed her cheek. 'They'll be delighted.'

'I don't see why.'

'Trust me, Claire. They'll be very happy. So, what do you say?'

She wanted to tell him it was all too good to be true. She wanted to shout and jump up and down. Dance a jig. Scream. She restrained herself and said instead, 'I'd like to give it a try.'

They began by bathing Harry together, laughing at his antics in the water. After he was dried and dressed and had drunk his bottle Claire put him to bed while Jack rescued the pizza—it hadn't dried out too much—and opened the wine.

And over the kitchen table they shared their simple meal while they talked and talked. Later, on the sofa, they didn't talk very much at all. But much later they sat in the dark and talked long into the night, making plans…

They would stay on the island until the cyclone repairs were finished, and then Jack would take Claire and Harry to meet his family.

'Don't worry. You'll like them and they'll love you, Claire.'

With that sorted, the world would be their oyster. They might go into business—with Jack's money and interest in construction and Claire's organisational skills, who knew what they might achieve? Or they might travel while Harry was still small. Or they might stay here on the island and build another storey onto this cottage.

Claire very bravely suggested that if things didn't work out for them Jack should feel free to go his own way—and Jack kissed her again to put an end to such negative thinking…

Harry ran ahead along the deserted beach, close to the water's edge where lazy waves lapped. At two, he was a happy, robust child, with eyes as blue as his striped T-shirt and a fringe of blond hair that flopped when he ran.

He'd spent his second birthday in Paris, with his doting grandparents, while Jack and Claire attended a conference on eco-friendly housing for remote area communities. They'd come away from it bursting with exciting plans. But first they'd wanted to visit the island.

'Hang on a minute,' Jack called to Harry now. 'I think you just ran past a magic rock.'

Harry spun around, eyes popping.

'Over here.' Jack pointed to a small rock further up the beach, shaped like a turtle shell and encrusted with barnacles. 'I'm sure that rock is magic.'

A year ago Claire might have reproached Jack for raising the little boy's expectations. These days she knew better. Jack was always coming up with happy surprises, and life with him was a continual adventure. A romantic adventure.

Today, as he walked with her on the beach in a baggy old T-shirt and even baggier shorts, with his hair windblown and his tanned face creased with laughter lines, she was sure he'd never looked more handsome.

Harry ran up to the rock and crouched beside it, hands cautiously resting on his chubby knees, not sure whether he should touch it. 'Where's the magic?' he demanded.

Jack lifted the rock and, lying in a little hollow in the sand lay a toy plastic fish—bright red with white stripes.

Harry squealed. 'Can he swim?'

'Of course.'

Amused, they watched as the little boy ran with the fish to the edge of the shallows and threw it into the water, then danced with excitement as it floated back and forth in the small frothy waves.

With casual nonchalance Jack threw an arm around Claire's shoulders, and she sighed with deep contentment and let her head rest against him, wondering how she'd ever earned the right to be so happy.

'I'm so glad I've kept Flora's cottage,' she said, looking up at the hills behind the beach, timbered once more with healthy regrowth. 'It's good to come back to the island.'

'I think we should come back every year.'

Her heart missed a beat. For some time they'd tiptoed around the edge of a serious discussion about their feelings for each other. Was this the moment to take it a step further?

No. Jack was already calling to Harry. 'Hey, little mate, I think there's another magic rock over here.'

'Where?' Harry cried, grabbing his fish before it could float out to sea.

Jack pointed. 'Just a bit further—up here. The round one. See?'

This time Claire did reproach him. 'You're spoiling him. One surprise is enough.'

Harry was already ahead of them and, confident now, he rolled the rock away. 'A little box!' he exclaimed, and held it high.

'Bring it here,' said Jack. 'That looks like a Mummy-sized surprise.'

Claire's heart began to thump. She looked at Jack, and he was watching her with a glowing, heartbreaking smile.

He took the box from Harry and lifted the lid. Claire saw the sparkle of diamonds and goosebumps broke over her skin.

'What is it, Mummy?'

A ring. An impossibly beautiful ring. Set with diamonds and—and rubies. Claire's vision blurred and she was forced to swipe at tears so she could see properly.

'I hope you like this, Claire.'

'It's beautiful!'

'I know it's a bit old-fashioned, but it means a lot to me. Seventy years ago my grandfather had it specially made for my grandmother.'

'Oh!'

Jack reached for her left hand, slipped the ring on her third finger.

'You gorgeous, crazy man.' She was laughing and

crying and trying to kiss him. 'I can't believe you risked hiding an heirloom ring under a rock!'

'I've been standing guard over it all afternoon, waiting for you and Dorothy to stop gossiping.'

'Oh, Jack.' She threw her arms about his neck.

He wrapped his arms around her waist and drew her in. 'I think we've made a pretty good fist of this past year or so, don't you?'

'Yes—yes, I do.' She kissed his jaw, then closed her eyes, so deeply happy she thought she might explode.

'Each day I've fallen more deeply in love with you, Claire.'

'I adore you, Jack. You know I do.'

'Please say you'll marry me?'

'I'd love to.'

'Me, too!' piped a small voice, and an eager hand tugged at the hem of Claire's beach shirt.

Laughing, they lifted their son and cuddled him between them.

Claire kissed Harry's cheek. 'Of course you, too, Harry. We owe everything to you.' She looked up at Jack and said quietly, 'And to Flora.'

'Yes, to Flora.'

Behind them the island's hills were rimmed with the pink and gold glow of the setting sun. Claire, looking over Jack's shoulder, was sure the sun winked and smiled.

* * * * *

Expecting His Child

MEREDITH WEBBER

Meredith Webber says of herself, 'Some ten years ago, I read an article which suggested that Mills & Boon were looking for new medical authors. I had one of those "I can do that" moments, and gave it a try. What began as a challenge has become an obsession, though I do temper the "butt on seat" career of writing with dirty but healthy outdoor pursuits, fossicking through the Australian outback in search of gold or opals. Having had some success in all of these endeavours, I now consider I've found the perfect lifestyle.'

Dear Reader,

Six months before I wrote this book we had an unexpected family drama with my son and daughter-in-law's first baby arriving ten weeks early. It was my first experience of the world of premature babies, of the equipment that is in place to keep them alive and the wonderful men and women who care for them. I've since found that this care is on-going, for when wee Grace Victoria eventually came out of hospital – seven weeks later – she had home visits from a premmie nurse for another couple of months, appointments at the hospital with therapists, and plenty of support provided for the parents. She now goes to weekly 'playgroup' with her 'friends' - the other babies who were in the hospital with her – as the mothers, not unexpectedly, have the common bond of the experience.

Grace is now eight months old and thriving as I'm sure young Sam in my story is. As for his parents, well, where better to meet than a tropical island paradise, and who better to care for him than a couple of doctors and a loving big sister?

This story was a special story for me to write because, although it brought back so much angst, it also reminded me of the joy a baby brings into the lives of all around him or her. Babies are definitely special.

Meredith Webber

CHAPTER ONE

GEN took one look at the swimming pool, which apparently, for all its size, was standing room only, and walked on towards the jetty and marina where the boat had docked the previous evening. She was on an island—there had to be water all around it in which she and others could swim. So why were all those people packed into the pool?

But when she checked the water that lapped the island near the jetty a dozen answers suggested themselves. Sharks, stingrays, electric eels and atomic submarines were only a few of them, for the blue-green depths into which she peered could hide an assortment of vicious predators, just waiting to snap up her—almost literally—lily-white body.

She was hovering near the edge of the water, hot and uncomfortable in her borrowed bikini and matching sarong, longing to plunge into the cool water—*any* cool water—when a voice hailed her. A man was walking from the direction of the marina.

'That water's filthy,' he warned, coming close

enough for her to see battered denim shorts, faded to grey and ripped not by fashion but by age. A T-shirt, also well-aged, hung limply over his solid torso, while his face, as he drew closer, seemed as battered as the shorts.

A lived-in face, deeply tanned, with white lines showing in the wrinkles near his eyes—too far away to see the colour—and why was she wondering?

'The big boats all come in there, and bits of oil and fuel float out from their exhausts. If you want to swim in unpolluted water I'll run you round to the other side of the island. There's a great beach there.'

'Is that your job?' Gen asked. 'To run guests around the place?'

'Hardly a job,' the man said, then he smiled, and for the oddest moment Gen's mind flashed back to her sister Marielle, to seeing her off at the airport, hugging her goodbye and whispering in her ear—urging her!

'Be irresponsible for a change—have fun, have an affair!'

'But—' Gen began, in response to the man, although she'd probably said it to Marielle as well. Too late. The man had turned away, obviously expecting her to follow.

Her hesitation was so brief it hardly counted before she was following him along the rock wall, onto the jetty, and down a ramp onto a floating walkway between parked boats.

He leapt onto a long white boat, with the name *Carlotta* painted on its side, and leant over to unhitch a small black rubber dinghy from behind the boat beside it.

'Come on,' he urged, and Gen, feeling irresponsibility positively surging through her veins, went on, stepping cautiously onto the polished decking of the *Carlotta*, then edging along the side to where the stranger held the little craft.

'I'm sure white slave traders would have bigger boats than this,' she said, aware of a certain rashness in her actions.

He didn't respond immediately, holding her hand to steady her descent while the little rubber boat rocked alarmingly.

'Much bigger boats,' he assured her, and though she heard a smile lurking in the words it certainly wasn't visible on his face.

Was she taking irresponsibility too far?

No, people were about—on other boats, some hailing the man who'd now joined her in the unstable little craft and was casting off the rope that held it tethered to the bigger boat. And she was at a resort, booked for a massage this afternoon, she'd be missed...

'Hold on to the rope,' the stranger told her, then he revved the engine and they were off, the front end of the black rubber craft lifting out of the water, slapping against the mild swell, the wind rushing past her face, tearing her hair out of the hairband she'd used to tame it so it streamed behind her.

Clinging to the rope that looped around the side of the boat, she stared ahead, breathing in the salt-laden air, such exhilaration filling her soul she had to turn her head and smile at the man.

Not that he noticed. With one hand on the tiller—she

knew some boat words, even though she'd little experience of sea-going vehicles—he stared ahead, although there wasn't another boat anywhere near them, nor other islands for them to bump into.

He's paid to run the tourists around the place, Gen reminded herself, not to enjoy their delight.

But she was a little disappointed anyway—although when they rounded a heavily wooded point and pulled into a small, secreted bay, she forgave him everything. On the eastern side of the island, it was bathed in sunlight. The sand that curved in an arc along the shore was dazzlingly white, while the water, shallow near the shore, was the palest blue. Or was it green?

The boat engine died suddenly, and in the absolute silence that followed they drifted towards the beach, the water so clear Gen could see small fish darting around beneath them. Then suddenly there was noise again, bird calls, and the soft shushing sound of the wake of the boat washing up onto the sand.

'It's beautiful,' Gen breathed. 'Thank you so much.'

The little boat was now beached and steady, so she stepped out and then turned to repeat her thanks. But the man had also stepped out, and was pulling the little dinghy further up the beach.

'Oh, there's no need for you to stay,' Gen said, as a new trepidation quite unconnected to the white slave trade juddered through her body.

'I was coming here anyway,' he said. 'It's the best place to swim on the whole island, but as it's not accessible by land few people come here. Not that most of the resort guests would think of swimming anywhere but the pool.'

He gave her an assessing look—a why-not-you kind of look—but she had no intention of explaining to this boat person why she hadn't wanted to swim in a pool so full of people that movement would be minimal and body contact far too close.

She dropped her beach bag on the sand, took out her towel and spread it carefully, aware of the man's presence, although he was fiddling with the boat engine and seemed unaware of her existence. Settling on the towel, she delved again into the bag and found a hat and sunscreen. It might be winter, but here in the tropics the sun would still burn fiercely.

And as she rubbed the lotion into her shoulders she sighed, feeling the warmth of the sun seep into her bones, feeling tense muscles relax, and all the worries in her head blur into such a tangled mess she knew she'd never sort them out.

Which was good, considering that the whole idea of this trip away—provided so generously by her siblings—was to *not* think—*not* worry—for two whole weeks. Although worry had become so much a part of her life she'd doubted it would be possible to leave it behind.

Until now, when her mind floated free of her jumbled thoughts and she looked out at the cool, inviting water, and revelled in the sun heating her shoulders.

'You're very fair; you should time your exposure to the sun—move into the shade at the far side of the cove in half an hour.'

She turned to find the boat man had left off fiddling with his engine and was walking past her, stripping off his tatty T-shirt as he headed for the water.

'I tan easily—I just haven't been in the sun for a while,' she said, feeling hot again and deciding she had to swim soon—although if he was going in…

'You could still burn,' he pointed out—totally unnecessarily. He didn't know he was talking to a doctor, but most adults these days—in fact most children—were only too aware of the damage sun exposure could do.

He dropped his T-shirt—little more than a rag—on the beach, and strode forward a few more paces before diving cleanly and easily into the sea.

Gen waited until he'd swum, with strong, full strokes, almost to the headland, before standing up, untying her sarong, then walking across the rather gritty sand to test the water. Warm, but not too warm.

She walked in, letting her body revel in the increasing sensation of weightlessness, until she was almost shoulder deep, then she lifted her feet and floated on her back, arms outspread, hands moving slightly to steer her in no particular direction.

Bliss!

The sun kissed her face, the slight tidal movement of the water shifted her hair around her head, and she wondered if she'd stay afloat if she fell asleep for just a short time.

She'd drown—of course she'd drown—and she could feel her nose getting sunburnt.

Turning over, she breaststroked towards the shady area of the cove, moving her arms slowly and lazily, letting the power of her legs push her along.

Bliss!

But once in the shade she realised the exercise had

felt good—she'd had as little of that as she'd had of free time recently—so now she swam, head down, freestyle, across the bay and back, then, in the shade once more, dived beneath the water, revelling in the freedom, the water, the sheer bliss—there was no other word—of being alone.

'I'm going back in ten minutes.'

She wasn't alone.

Surprised by the strength of her disappointment, she faced the man who'd swum to about three body lengths away. Close, but not close enough for her to see his face clearly—though why that would matter she didn't know.

'Oh, can't we stay longer? I can pay you extra,' she said, and saw his quick frown, followed by the definite shake of his head.

'I have to meet the morning boat,' he said. 'I've a motor part coming over from the mainland, and if I'm not there it will go in with the general mail and it might take me a week to find it again.'

Gen nodded—the explanation was entirely reasonable. The man had a job to do, she could hardly hold him up. She swam back to the shore, then felt a rush of embarrassment. She'd have to stand and walk up the beach in front of this man—in Eloise's itsy-bitsy, teeny-weeny bikini.

He was a boat man on a resort island—he'd seen worse sights in a bikini than her pale size twelve body squeezed into her sister's size eight bikini.

Could she run? Kind of casually—as if it was a bit of fun exercise?

No, running would make her boobs bob about and draw attention to them. There was nothing for it but to rise up out of the water, walk casually to her towel and get her sarong wrapped around her as quickly as possible.

Except that the towel and sarong had got tangled up together, and she dropped her sunglasses in the sand, and her hair was caught in the bikini tie at the back of her neck, so by the time she joined a very bored-looking boat man in his rubber boat, now afloat in the shallows—he'd been launching it, not looking at her at all—she was hot and flustered and desperately needed another swim.

'Here for long?' he asked, using a small oar to push the boat into deeper water before lowering the engine.

Staff members were probably given lessons in being polite to the tourists!

'Two weeks,' she said, too abruptly, as her embarrassment lingered.

'Come far?'

His voice was deep, but laced with boredom. He obviously hadn't taken the lessons very seriously.

'Perth!' she said.

'Far enough,' he responded, and he revved the engine so the noise put paid to any further scintillating conversation.

He dropped her back onto a low pontoon at the end of the jetty, the engine idling now, quieter, so she could thank him.

'Think nothing of it,' he said, and for the first time she saw his eyes—grey—and in them she read the pain that made his voice so lacking in emotion. The man wasn't only battered, he was bruised and hurting, holding onto some inner pain too bad to escape.

'My name's Genevieve Lucas,' Gen said, holding out her hand. 'And that thank-you wasn't just a token politeness. I meant it.'

He seemed surprised, but took her hand and shook it.

'Zeke Wilson,' he said, and for a moment Gen thought he might say more—offer to take her to the secluded bay again, or maybe meet her later—but his fingers gave hers the minimum of polite squeezes then dropped away. And as the loud blast of a horn told them both the morning boat was arriving from the mainland, Gen climbed out of the dinghy, which puttered away immediately.

Zeke Wilson. What kind of a name was Zeke? Short for Ezekiel? Who would name a son Ezekiel?

Gen smiled to herself. The same kind of people who gave all their children French names? Hers wasn't too bad—especially as most people called her Gen—and Eloise was acceptable, but Marielle hated having to spell her name all the time, while Jean-Paul had changed his to plain John the moment he was old enough.

Thinking of her siblings, Gen sighed. It had been so kind of them to send her on this trip, but could two weeks free from responsibility give her the strength she'd need to get through the years that lay ahead—the final years, the doctors said, of her mother's life?

She had lunch at the resort, chatting amiably about

nothing with a couple at the same table, and followed it with a wonderful massage in the resort's day spa, then a long afternoon sleep.

Maybe the fortnight away *would* do her good, if only so she could replenish her energy supplies by catching up on lost sleep. But by six she'd had enough of her deluxe room—beautifully fitted out, but still an anonymous hotel room—and was tired of the antics of the characters in the book she was reading. She needed to get out—to have a proper look around the resort and perhaps find out what happened on an island in the evenings.

According to a notice in the foyer, some group she'd never heard of was playing in the Coral Lounge at eight p.m., while the Seasprite Bar remained open until two a.m., and the Pool Bar's hours extended long enough to provide dawn cocktails at six. She didn't find any of the information particularly useful, so drifted outside, not wanting to eat dinner too early, because once she'd eaten she'd have to go back to the less-than-gripping book.

Her feet led her towards the marina, but on reaching the jetty she turned left instead of right, so she could walk past the mass of watercraft—some worth serious money, by the look of them, others little sailing boats, all jammed in together in their berths.

The man, Zeke, had the look of a man who had spent his life on a boat. She knew some people did, and for a moment she envied them—and him—the freedom it must provide.

But to have *no* ties? *No* responsibilities?

That would be taking things too far.

She was past the boats now, but the track, no longer paved, seemed to lead to the headland around which Zeke had taken her in the boat. Would she be able to see the bay from there?

Curiosity drove her on, but as she rounded a bend she found the track ended—not on the headland, as she'd expected, but at a small shack roofed with palm fronds, tucked back against the thick tropical forest so it was barely visible.

Light showed through the cracks in the wall—bamboo?—and a soft hum of voices suggested the little hut was occupied.

Should she walk on? Or leave whoever lived there to their privacy?

'Coming for a drink?'

The voice was familiar, deep and scratchy, as if it wasn't used all that often.

'I thought the track would lead to the headland,' Gen said, feeling incredibly embarrassed—as if she'd been caught snooping.

'No, just to the bar,' Zeke told her. 'The boaties use it, and some of the staff. People who can't be bothered putting on the kind of respectable clothing the resort bars require.'

'Respectable?' Gen queried, thinking of some of the barely clothed women she'd seen in the resort bars as she'd walked by.

He almost smiled—she was sure of it.

'Well,' he drawled, 'while a designer bikini covered by a diaphanous sarong might be acceptable, faded shorts and torn T-shirts definitely aren't.'

He studied her for a moment.

'Come and have a drink?'

Simple, harmless invitation. But Gen knew it was far more than that. It might have been some years since she'd had a relationship with a man, but that didn't mean she'd forgotten the silent signals of exploratory attraction. Her body had been aware from her first sighting of the man that this was someone in whom it could be interested. Its reaction to his handshake had confirmed it, and now the eyes that looked into hers were certainly suggesting *his* body, too, might be feeling the glimmers of attraction towards hers. Mind you, his body might feel glimmers of attraction to any female form—this was a tropical resort island, after all—there were all-night bars!

'I'd like that,' she answered, and now he did smile.

The smile lit up in his face in a totally unexpected way, taking away the bruised look, bringing it to life so that what she saw was an attractive man, maybe early forties, with rough, salt-thickened and grey-streaked black hair, a straight nose, and quite exceptional lips—for a man!—sculptured, almost…

She shouldn't be thinking about a stranger's lips!

He took her elbow and they walked together the twenty yards to the little hut, but before they entered his hand dropped away, and though he remained close behind her as he ushered her through the door he wasn't touching her.

Girlfriend in the bar? Needed to check first? And surely that wasn't disappointment she was feeling?

Then his hand, warm and somehow possessive,

rested on the small of her back as he steered her towards a table by a window that looked out over the sea.

'They don't do cocktails here, but they can rise to a gin and tonic or a whisky and soda. What would you like?'

'I'd like a really cold beer, if that's okay—mid-strength. But you don't need to buy me a drink. Let me shout as thanks for the boat trip this morning.'

'Impossible—this is a members only place; it will go on my tab. One mid-strength beer coming up.'

He walked away, and Gen glanced around, expecting to see curious glances from the other people in the small room, but no one seemed the least bit interested in her which meant—what?

Either Zeke was in here every night with a different woman, or these people really didn't care what others did or didn't do.

Was that likely?

She shook her head. This far out of her familiar environment, she had no idea, couldn't even guess, although a slight twinge in her belly suggested she'd rather it wasn't the first option.

She watched him as he spoke to the man behind the bar, then exchanged a few words with the two men sitting on bar stools beside where he stood. No eyes turned towards her, nor did heads swivel—these people couldn't care less that Zeke Wilson had walked in with a woman.

'Are they so used to seeing you come in with a woman they don't check her out?'

She'd *had* to ask!

Zeke looked puzzled.

'Did you want to be checked out?' He put down the two glasses of beer. 'You should have stayed in the resort bars if that's what you want. A good-looking woman like you would have got plenty of checking out.'

Sorry she'd started this conversation, Gen picked up her beer and took a sip.

'Of course I didn't want to be checked out, but these people seem so incurious.'

Zeke smiled again.

'Boaties,' he said, as if that explained everything. 'Most of the people in here—men, and a couple of women—live on their boats. At the moment they're here in the north of Queensland, but next month they could be in Jamaica. Well, maybe not Jamaica—most of them are sailors, and they wouldn't make Jamaica in a month—but somewhere else. Their boats are their homes, other boaties are their neighbours. They are more interested in new rigging systems or how to get the best out of the latest boating gizmos than they are in strangers they'll never meet again.'

'Boating gizmos?' Gen queried. The rest of his explanation made sense, even if she did feel a sense of wonder that people could live such lives. 'You mean they don't just hoist sail and blow where the wind takes them?'

His lips gave an infinitesimal twitch—the only sign that he'd accepted her teasing—but he answered the first part anyway.

'Wherever there's a market someone, somewhere, will be making something to fill it.'

Gen nodded her agreement, relaxing back into her chair and sipping again at her beer, looking across the table at the man who was a stranger, yet so easy to talk to she felt she knew him well. 'And you? Are you heading for Jamaica?'

'Regretfully, no,' he said, shaking his head to reinforce the reply, that look of sadness back in his eyes.

Of course he couldn't go sailing off to Jamaica, Gen told herself. He probably didn't even own a boat. He just worked on them, and no doubt loved them. Wouldn't you have to, to work with them?

'What about you?' he asked. 'Seachange Island is a long way from Perth—what brought you here?'

'Escape!' Gen answered, and then, looking at the man, at the grey eyes that studied her intently, she knew she had to explain. 'No, it's more than that. It *is* an escape from responsibilities, certainly, but it's a breathing space—a chance for a regeneration of energy and inner resources.'

His dark eyebrows rose.

'Sounds serious. Have your responsibilities been so onerous?'

Gen shook her head.

'Constant, but in no way onerous,' she told him. 'My mother developed multiple sclerosis when I was twelve. By the time I was fourteen she was in a wheelchair and my father had left us. My little brother was only three, and my two sisters fitted in between him and me, but last month John graduated with honours in Biochemistry, and my siblings, at his graduation, presented me with the tickets for this trip. *They* felt I needed a break from responsibility, although I'd never seen what I did as burdensome in any way.'

What on earth was she doing, pouring out her family history to this stranger?

She finished her beer and stood up.

'I'm sure they'll let me buy you one,' she said.

He shook his head.

'One's enough for me—besides, it's time to eat back at your hotel. Unless you fancy fresh caught fish? I hooked a nice coral trout this afternoon, and intend barbecuing it for dinner. Bit of a salad to go with it? A glass of white? Interested?'

She studied the man. She hadn't been so long out of the dating game that she didn't know where dinner with him might lead. Marielle's parting words were ringing in her ears.

'Yes, I am,' she said—because she was. Far more interested in eating barbecued fish with this man than in talking to strangers at a table in the resort dining room—even interested in where the invitation might lead, interested in whether she'd be interested if more was offered.

He carried their empty glasses back over to the bar while she made her way to the door, and although it was obvious they were leaving together, again no one took much notice.

'So, what do you do when you're not being totally responsible for your siblings?' he asked as they walked back towards the marina.

Gen hesitated. Tell people she was a doctor and they'd be peeling off their sandals to show her their ingrown toenails.

'I work,' she said, then she sighed. 'Actually, it's my work more than my siblings that I'm escaping at the moment—the responsibility attached to it can be overwhelming. That's what this holiday is really about. My next in age sister, as I was leaving, urged me to be irresponsible for a change, but I don't think that's the right word. Irresponsible means behaving stupidly, without thought for consequences, which is different to not being responsible, surely?'

She turned to her companion, who was watching her, his grey eyes assessing now.

'Irresponsible is certainly the wrong word—although if silliness comes under that description maybe it's not totally wrong. Is it so bad to be a little silly sometimes? Weren't you a little silly getting into a boat with a total stranger this morning?'

Gen smiled at him and nodded.

'Irresponsible too,' she said. 'But let's get off silliness and irresponsibility. You know my life story—what about yours? Why have you escaped to a desert island?'

He grinned at her, and shivery awareness prickled her skin.

'Hardly a desert island,' he said, but already his smile had disappeared, so when he added, 'My personal responsibility is singular—my daughter—and I'm not escaping her, just spending time I would have been spending with her on the boat instead.'

The pain in his voice was impossible to hide.

'Custody trouble?' Gen guessed.

'You could say that—although to label my ex-wife

"trouble" is like calling a cyclone a bit of wind. But now I'd just as soon go back to talking about silliness, if it's all the same to you.' His face was bleak again.

So much for sharing life stories!

Although maybe things were better this way, Gen decided, as he held her hand to steady her as she stepped onto the small boat's polished timber decking. He obviously had a lot of baggage, but she had enough of her own troubles right now…

She felt the rocking motion as her weight disturbed the boat's equilibrium, and clung more tightly to his hand.

'You'll be right—you'll get your sea-legs shortly,' he said, and although that might be true, she wasn't sure what kind of legs she needed to combat the sensations Zeke Wilson's touch was generating in her body.

He led her to the back of the small boat, where padded seats formed a half-circle on the lower deck. A table had been set up in front of them, and although she could see a small gas stove in the little cabin beyond the deck, she guessed Zeke ate most of his meals out here. And why not, when the setting sun had spread a soft pink wash across the water, and the only sounds were the cries of birds returning home from their sea flights and the clatter of boat riggings around them in the marina?

'Sauv Blanc all right with you?'

Zeke had ducked into the cabin.

'Sounds lovely,' Gen returned, still absorbing the peace and beauty of the setting. She didn't offer to help—partly because it looked a very small cabin and she would only get in the way, but mostly because she was content just to be.

Well, to be and to see where just being led her…

She was intrigued by that thought, and not wary at all, certain she was a good enough judge of character to know she was safe with this man.

The feeling of security grew as she watched him cook the slabs of fish on a small gas-fired barbecue attached to the back of the deck.

'Yacht,' he corrected, when she mentioned how compact everything was on the boat.

'There's a difference?' she asked, teasing him, because she knew boat people were usually passionate about their boats, or yachts, or whatever.

He frowned severely at her, then realised she was teasing and almost smiled again. But he did go on to explain what constituted a yacht—although, he conceded, he supposed they were, as watercraft, still boats.

It was a silly conversation, just easy talk, and so incredibly relaxing Gen could feel the holiday already doing her good—although she was certain eating in the resort dining room wouldn't have provided the same degree of relaxation.

He carried a plate full of thick fish fillets across to the table, then ducked into the cabin and returned with a tray bearing two plates, a bowl of salad, cutlery, a cut lemon, salt and pepper and the bottle of wine.

'Help yourself,' he ordered, offering her a plate, and Gen did, the smell of the fresh cooked fish so tantalising she was salivating.

Zeke watched her as she filled her plate, then did the

same for himself, but as she bit into the fish she knew he was watching again.

'Okay?' he asked.

She nodded, her mouth too full to speak, but when she'd swallowed she had to tell him it was far more than okay—it was delicious.

So they ate, and sipped wine, and Gen's feeling of relaxation morphed into something more, something dangerously like desire. Yet this man, apart from buying her a beer and feeding her dinner, had made no move to suggest he might be interested in her, and nothing in his words or his expression suggested more than politeness to a stranger.

'That was utterly wonderful,' Gen declared, finally pushing her plate away, her second piece of fish unfinished. 'Eyes bigger than my stomach, unfortunately.'

'That's all right; the cat will eat it.'

'Cat? You've got a cat? Surely it should have been twining itself around our legs from the moment it smelt the fish?'

Zeke smiled again, and Gen's feeling of desire deepened.

'He's a marina cat. Most of the inhabitants of the boats will be eating fish for dinner—he'll work his way round.'

'A marina cat—what a perfect job description,' Gen said.

'Isn't it just?' Zeke agreed, then he reached across and touched her lightly on the knee. 'Just how irresponsible do you want to get this fortnight?' he asked, his deep voice even deeper so the words scraped along Gen's skin.

CHAPTER TWO

GEN shifted in her seat so her swollen belly—or the bump, as she affectionately called it—was more comfortable. Not that she'd be sitting for long. The keynote speaker was finishing up, there'd be questions, then the MC would nod and smile towards Gen, and she'd rise and walk up on to the podium, ready to deliver her riveting paper on the weight-development ratio in preterm babies.

She was acutely uncomfortable, the bump having moved somehow during the long night flight from Perth to Brisbane. Brisbane—Zeke's daughter lived in Brisbane. She'd discovered that much about him in the idyllic fortnight they'd spent together.

And now she was carrying Zeke's son—although he didn't know that small fact, unless he'd got one of the letters she'd mailed off to 'Zeke Wilson, yacht next to *Carlotta*, Seachange Island'.

She shook her head at her own stupidity.

And irresponsibility.

Although she hadn't been totally irresponsible. Zeke

had produced an unopened packet of condoms from some corner of his yacht, and though he'd admitted not remembering when he'd bought them, he'd been sure they wouldn't have worn out.

'How could they when they've never been used?' he'd teased, and she'd been so eager and excited she'd probably have taken the risk without his dodgy condoms.

She patted the bump reassuringly, hoping it wouldn't read any regret in her thoughts. There was nothing in the world she wanted more than this baby, and knowing she had only two months to wait before she met him filled her with joyous delight.

'So, do you think we should be giving steroid injections to all women who might be at risk to go pre-term when they reach thirty weeks?' someone asked, and Gen returned her attention to the speaker, anxious now—she was thirty weeks, but there was no reason why her baby would be premature. Everything had gone beautifully.

So beautifully, in fact, she hadn't realised she was pregnant until she was more than twenty weeks, having put down all her symptoms to the stress of her mother's sudden final illness and subsequent death.

The speaker was assuring the questioner that, given the immune-suppressing qualities of steroids, wholesale injections to pregnant women were inadvisable, but for women at risk—women who'd previously had a pre-term baby—they should be considered.

The MC made a winding-up signal and Gen shifted in her chair again, this time preparing to stand—a less simple exercise than it used to be, given the shift in her centre of gravity. As the MC thanked the speaker, and polite applause echoed around the room, Gen made it from her chair to the stage, where she hovered, awaiting her introduction. Her laptop and the printed version of her speech were clutched in one hand. The laptop was essential, but she was fairly sure she'd be able to deliver her address without resorting to reading from the printed pages.

'And now it gives me great pleasure to introduce Dr Genevieve Lucas. Dr Lucas is one of the leading members of a Western Australian team following up pre-term babies, testing the children at two-year intervals until they reach the age of eighteen. Dr Lucas's special area of interest is social maturity, and it is on that subject that she will speak to us today.'

As polite applause once again sounded through the auditorium, Gen stepped forward, thanked the MC for the introduction, and launched into her speech, knowing the screen behind her would already have the first page of her presentation lit up. She moved the cursor on her laptop to indicate certain peaks on the first graph, turning slightly to make sure it was working properly.

Which was when she felt the twinge.

Braxton-Hicks contractions? Surely it was too early?

She plunged on, the twinge gone, and moved through her presentation—proud of the work her team was doing, pleased she'd had her work to keep her focussed after her mother's death.

The sensation of wetness meant little too—until she

heard a splashing sound. Her waters hadn't just broken, they were gushing out.

Calm! she told herself, and she turned to the MC, who was looking at her with horror.

'Would you mind reading the rest of it? You can use the laptop too, so you can put up the pertinent graphs—it's not hard.'

As the man stepped forward, looking relieved—perhaps because the guest speaker hadn't gone into strong hysterics *or* delivered her baby on the podium floor—Gen turned back to the audience.

'You'll have to excuse me,' she said. 'It seems I'm about to have a baby.'

And with total aplomb she walked off the podium, collected her handbag from the chair in the front row and headed for the door—by which time a woman in the audience had recovered enough to come scampering after her, sliding an arm around Gen's shoulders.

'Oh, poor you. But at least you're close to a hospital,' she babbled. 'Just up the hill. Do you want an ambulance or will you let me run you there? My car's here in the car park. If you wait just inside this door—' she was steering Gen along a corridor '—there's a chair. I won't be long.'

She squeezed Gen's hands and rushed off before Gen had time to agree or disagree with anything, or even thank the woman for her help.

But sitting seemed a ridiculous thing to do! Just sitting, when her baby was inside her with no nice amniotic fluid to swim around in. He'd get distressed. He could get tangled up with the umbilical cord. Infection—there was a definite danger of infection.

She stood up again, realised how stupid she was being, so sat down, her skirt wet and clammy, her heart racing, her hands pressing against the bump, trying desperately to feel a foetal heartbeat—trying desperately not to panic!

'You're how many weeks?' her good Samaritan asked as she reappeared through the door and helped Gen stand up.

'Thirty,' Gen told her, allowing herself to be led to the car, although her anguish was mental not physical.

'Thirty's good—but then you know that,' the woman said as she drove. 'Right, here we are. This is the private hospital emergency entrance. I'll get an obstetrician to you asap, but in the meantime let the ER staff do their stuff. They're good.'

'Did you phone ahead?' Gen asked, as she climbed out of the car to be met by two women, while a young man held a gurney just a pace away.

'One quick call as I was paying my parking ticket,' the woman said. 'Now, I can't park here, but I'll call in and see you later. Good luck!'

She was driving away before Gen realised she didn't know her name. But then a pain came, low and hard, and she stopped thinking about helpful strangers and allowed herself to be helped onto the gurney.

'Cubicle six is free,' someone said as she was wheeled into a bright ER department, filled with the bustle of staff and the chatter and moans of patients, their friends and family.

Cubicle six was roomy enough, but two of her three attendants disappeared, leaving the third, who introduced herself as Petra, to wrap a blood pressure cuff around Gen's arm and begin the process of admitting her patient to hospital.

Gen felt a strange detachment at being on the other side of the medical machine that had swung into action. Halfway through taking her personal details Petra poked her head out of the door and called to someone to check that an obstetrician was on the way.

Thank heavens they had foetal heart monitors, she thought as Petra, having single-handedly stripped off Gen's clothes and got her into a gown, strapped one on. But Petra wasn't thankful—she poked her head outside the door again and spoke sharply to someone, the only bit Gen heard being 'well, get a doctor in here, then'.

Not entirely comforting, but her pains were getting worse, and she was feeling fuzzy in the head and nauseous as well. She managed to mention this to Petra, who produced a basin before Gen threw up.

It was into this debacle—Gen being sick and feeling increasingly light-headed—that the boatie walked.

Obviously she was hallucinating. But just in case she wasn't, she wiped the back of her hand across her mouth, fixed him with a glare, and said, 'I don't want you here.'

'Gen?'

Even sounding incredulous, it was definitely recognisable as Zeke's voice saying her name.

'You two know each other?' the nurse asked—she sounded incredulous too. No doubt because she'd heard the story of Gen's waters breaking at the conference.

'He's a boatie—I won't have a boatie delivering my

baby,' Gen muttered. Although maybe no one heard, because Zeke was now acting like a doctor, asking questions, touching her belly, checking her chart and the read-outs from the monitors.

She wanted to protest further, but, ashamed though she was to feel it—and she'd definitely not admit it—it was kind of comforting to have Zeke there.

That was if it *was* Zeke and not a hallucination.

Voices, more people coming into cubicle six, too many people, talk of foetal distress, talk of blood pressure dropping, an injection… Hadn't she been talking about injections at the conference, or had that been someone else? Then the hallucination that was Zeke was holding her hand, explaining things to her—the injection was to help the baby's lungs, another one would try to halt or slow down her labour, although they doubted they could stop it, and as long as she was far enough into her pregnancy the baby would be viable…

'I don't want viable. I want a full-term baby!' she snapped, snatching her hand away from his—although holding hands with Zeke, even if it wasn't Zeke, had been nice.

'That might not be possible. But, speaking of full-term, just when would that be?'

His voice was so familiar—*too* familiar, considering he was a stranger with whom she'd spent some time seven months ago. She'd loved his voice—deep and slightly uneven, somehow, as if it didn't get a lot of use.

'We're both old enough to know the attraction's there,' he'd said that first night they'd had dinner on his boat. 'But being older and more in control of our bodies we don't have to act on it.'

But they had! Again and again. Turning a two-week holiday into a blissful memory of sea, sun and sex as far as Gen had been concerned. Irresponsible? Possibly! But she'd returned home totally relaxed and rejuvenated, ready to face whatever lay ahead.

Which, as it had turned out, had been a nightmare of stress and pain and grief and loss…

'I'm thirty weeks,' she mumbled at the man who might or might not be Zeke.

'I did wonder,' he said. Then more people came into the room and she was wheeled somewhere else, and the pains blurred the activity around her as her labour turned into delivery—although someone still held tightly to her hand.

Eventually someone handed her a baby—so small Gen immediately burst into tears, and sobbed against the chest of the man who held her in his arms.

'He'll be fine,' Zeke's voice said. 'You know that. I've been told it's what you do—ensuring little chaps like him not only survive but thrive.'

But because it *was* what she did Gen knew the danger—knew just how hard it would be for the little scrap of humanity that was her son to breathe and feed and grow and flourish.

'His Apgar—what's his Apgar?' she demanded, and a placid-looking nurse reassured her.

'It was low—three at birth, because he took a while to breathe spontaneously—but he was up to eight at five minutes, which is terrific.'

It didn't feel terrific. Gen cradled the tiny mite against her chest and cried even harder—she who rarely cried, carrying on like a big wuss, not even sure what she was crying for. Except when someone gently removed her son from her arms, explaining he needed special care, it was loss she felt, and separation—a feeling of total disconnection not only from her baby but from the world.

'My mother died,' she whispered at one stage, pressing her head hard against Zeke's chest. She'd accepted it was Zeke by this time. And if later it turned out he was some kind of drug-induced dream, well, she'd cope with that then.

'That was much sooner than you'd expected, wasn't it?'

She nodded against his solid bulk.

'She deteriorated suddenly two weeks after I returned home, and died six weeks after that. It was a bad time, but in the end definitely a release for her—she welcomed death with a peaceful acceptance that was as frightening as it was comforting.'

'I can understand that.' Zeke's arms tightened around her shoulders, and he shook his head at a nurse who had come in, wanting to help Gen shower.

'She didn't know about the baby—hell, *I* didn't know about the baby. My mind was so preoccupied with Mum it never occurred to me. It wasn't irresponsibility, Zeke. We used condoms, didn't we? We even bought another packet at the island pharmacy.'

'Yes, but it was probably the first lot that didn't do the job,' he said. 'But it's not a problem, Gen. Not as far as I'm concerned. I've always liked the idea of having a son.'

And Gen cried even harder, because it was ridiculous even *thinking* Zeke could be a father to this baby. The Zeke in her head was still a boatie—a wanderer—a man of no fixed address.

'I didn't even know the name of your boat. I know it must have been written on the back of it, but somehow I never looked—or if I did, I couldn't remember.'

'*Louise*. It's called *Louise*.'

Which was when Gen pulled away and actually looked at the man who'd come back into her life so unexpectedly.

It *was* Zeke, and he was real. He was also looking desperately tired.

'She's not still with her mother?' she demanded, and he stood up from the side of the bed and turned away from her.

'Shall I help you shower?' he asked, fiddling with something on a table by the wall.

She wanted to cry again, but knew that was just to do with her hormones being in such disarray after the birth.

The birth!

She had to forget about Zeke and his problems and find out where they'd taken her baby.

She had to—

Another nurse came in.

'Okay, so let's get you showered and dressed in something a bit better than that gown, then pop you into a proper bed. If you want to see your little man before you sleep I can wheel you down to the nursery, but first a shower. Are you leaving or staying, Dr Wilson?'

'Leaving,' Zeke said, but he came across to Gen again, with a smile she didn't for an instant believe on his face. 'But I'll be back. Lauren Cardwell tells me you were here for the conference at the convention centre—were you booked into the hotel down there?'

Gen nodded, suddenly so tired that even that much movement was an effort, and to ask who Lauren Cardwell was—impossible!

'Good. I'll phone them to pack your things and send someone down to get them, but in the meantime there's a shop downstairs. I'll ask them to send you up a nightgown.'

He was being brisk and efficient, and she should appreciate his efforts on her behalf. But she didn't want a brisk, efficient doctor. She wanted Zeke the boatie, who had held her in his arms on the back deck of *Louise* and named the stars he'd pointed out to her….

She was sleeping when Zeke found her room, sleeping in the soft, silky nightdress he'd had sent up, her shoulder-length fair hair rumpled and still damp from the shower. But that was how he remembered it—damp from dawn or midnight swims, smelling of the ocean. The tall, loose-limbed woman with sea-green eyes who'd wandered into his life when he was at his lowest ebb—

Was he *nuts* to be thinking like this? Okay, so having Gen's company had brought him great release from the tensions he'd been feeling when he'd flown north to the sanctuary of his boat. Having Gen around had meant he hadn't had to think—not about work, nor about his daughter, the bright, bubbly little girl who had somehow got lost in the tug-of-war between her parents.

Louise was living with him now, a quiet, well-behaved child—but Zeke's heart ached whenever he held her in his arms, ached with regret for the pain her parents had caused her—and ached with concern for her future.

Surely she was *too* quiet? *Too* good?

And now he had another child—a little boy whose face, when he'd called into the PICU on his way upstairs, was mostly hidden by a CPAP mask. Continuous positive air pressure—that was what his son needed right now to stay alive. That the child was his he had no doubt—it was what it meant that had him stumped.

Well, not entirely stumped. Somewhere deep inside was a welling of joy and delight—these were the things that had made tears prick his eyes in the PICU earlier, as he'd looked at the tiny mortal. And pride—that had been there too. The little chap looked like a fighter.

But how to even *think* about the future? Where to start? With geography? He lived on one side of a vast continent and Gen on the other. No. Geography could be solved, it was family that was important.

And family for him was Louise!

He sighed, aware as always of the frustration he felt when he thought of his daughter. She was beautiful, healthy, polite, did well at school—he could go on and on. Yet in his heart he knew she wasn't happy—knew that *something* was missing from her life…

But was that something a tiny, very dependent little baby?

Thinking what Louise needed most was the security of a settled home with a loving parent, he'd spent the last seven months providing it, desperate to regain his daughter's love and trust—to provide her with certainty and stability.

So how would she react to change?

He had no idea…

He was staring at the woman in the bed, not really seeing her as he thought about Louise, but now, as if his gaze had touched her, Gen stirred, then slowly opened her eyes. Her hands went to her no-longer-swollen belly as awareness of where she was struck her. Then the beautiful eyes focussed on his face.

'Zeke? I thought I'd dreamt you.'

She'd seemed pleased to recognise him at first, but as he watched a frown gathered her dark eyebrows and she sat up—the better, he realised as she spoke, to berate him.

'Why didn't you tell me you were a doctor? Why let me believe you were a boatie?'

'We neither of us talked much about our real lives,' he reminded her. 'It was that kind of "time out of the real world" affair. Not that it makes the slightest difference—I am a boatie. I love being on the boat, messing around in boats—that's a big part of my life. And does it matter? Am I not the same man, whether boatie or doctor?'

'It might have been easier to trace you if I'd known

you were a doctor,' Gen snapped, swinging her legs over the side of the bed. 'Not that I have time to argue about your profession. I need to see my baby.'

But as she stood up she turned towards him. Fear had replaced the anger in her eyes—fear so deep he could feel it chilling the air in the room.

'You've seen him? He's all right?'

'He's fine—and a good weight, considering his prematurity: one point six kilos. That's three and a half pounds in the language most parents understand, not bad at all.'

She was standing up and looking helplessly around.

'I've got no clothes,' she muttered, the despair he'd heard in the delivery suite creeping back into her voice.

'Here. Your things are all here.' Zeke opened the wardrobe to reveal her own clothes hanging there. 'But that nightgown came with a wrap.'

He unhooked it off the hanger and brought it over to her, holding it while she pushed her arms into it.

'Thank you,' she said, turning to face him. 'And now I need you to show me where my baby is.' Her eyes met his with the frank expression he knew so well. 'I know we have to talk, Zeke, but I can't right now. My mind's full of the baby.'

'Of course it is,' he told her, pleased that it should be that way.

Until she added, 'And guilt—there's plenty of that in my head as well. Is it my fault he came so early? Was it the flight? Should I have known something was wrong?'

He wrapped his arms around her and rocked her gently.

'I know telling you those kind of thoughts are all nonsense won't help, because you'll think them anyway—but it *is* nonsense, and when you're a little more rested and a little less shocked you'll realise that. These things happen—you know that as well as I do. The baby came early—now move on, so his needs and yours can be met and the best possible outcome achieved for both of you.'

She pushed away from the hug and looked directly at him again.

'His needs and mine—that's it? You don't come into the equation at all?'

Zeke shrugged.

'I've no idea where I come into things at the moment,' he said, speaking the truth because Gen deserved his honesty. 'Even with not knowing you were pregnant for quite a while, you've still had time to assimilate the knowledge and think about the future. I'm way back at the shock of discovering I'm going to be a father again—I've got to get over that before I can think about the future.'

Gen nodded her acceptance of his words but he sensed her disappointment. He caught up with her as she walked out the door.

'I'm your guide, remember,' he told her, but when he put his hand on her shoulder she moved, so it slipped away.

They went down a floor, and stopped in a small foyer to wash their hands at a basin near the door. The nursery—Gen refused to think of it as an ICU, even though all the babies in it were in special Isolettes, the air purified, the temperature monitored, their fragile heartbeats recorded—was new and shiny somehow, and soft classical music played in the background.

Zeke led her to a crib on the far side of the room, with a card reading 'Baby Lucas' attached to the side of it.

'All the other babies have names,' she said, her voice perilously close to a wail. Which was when she realised just how detached from reality she'd become. As if it mattered! Here she was, with a fragile little human to worry about, and she was being emotional about his not having a name.

'Had you thought of names?' Zeke asked, and she realised his arm was once again around her shoulders.

This time she didn't shrug it off, because it felt right, and warm, and kind of heavy but very comforting.

She nodded, but didn't tell him she'd been going to call the baby Zeke. Not, of course, because she'd fallen in love with Zeke—that couldn't happen in a fortnight—but because Zeke had given her so much in those two weeks. He'd reminded her how it was to be totally without care, how to relax and let the world pass her by, how to enjoy the physical pleasures of her body in every way—because swimming and diving and walking and sailing had also been part of their time together.

He'd given her joy!

And he'd also, if unknowingly, given her this baby.

She peered at the little scrawny scrap lying in front of her, legs and arms ridiculously long for such a tiny mite, and tried to think. This was what she did—her specialty—she should know exactly what came next.

But this was *her* baby, and all she felt was worry!

'He's breathing in concert with the machine, so they think they'll only need him to stay on the CPAP overnight,' Zeke told her. 'And over here is waterless hand-washing gel, so you can wash your hands and then touch him through the ports.'

He handed the dispenser to her, but though she took it she didn't use it, fearing if she touched her tiny baby she might break down again—and surely she'd cried enough for one day?

Yet he needed touch—her touch—although he probably wouldn't know it was her touching him. She washed her hands very carefully, then slowly pushed her fingers through the porthole and curled her hand around the tiny black-haired head.

And she did cry, but somehow that didn't matter any more as with firm but gentle fingers she explored the limbs, the hands, the perfect feet. Tiny monitor pads rested on his pigeon chest, and a tube ran into his belly button, but here he was—her baby.

Hers and Zeke's!

No, she couldn't think about Zeke's rights to this child right now. Although, with her mind refusing to move past Zeke as a name, the man might as well make himself useful.

'You name him,' she said, looking at Zeke across the Plexiglas crib.

He looked startled, then shook his head.

'And forever get the blame for choosing wrong?' he said.

'I'd veto wrong,' Gen assured him, insensibly warmed by the 'forever'. 'But have a go.'

He frowned, but not at her, she realised, as his face cleared and he said tentatively, 'I don't think I should have sole naming rights, but my father's name was Samuel—and although that's an old-fashioned name these days, I think Sam is quite acceptable.'

'Your father's name *was* Samuel? Your father is dead?'

'Both my parents died young.' He must have realised it was too bald a statement, for he smiled at Gen as he added, 'You don't have to worry about a genetic predisposition for the baby—they died in a light aircraft accident the year I started school.'

'Oh, Zeke, that must have been terrible for you!' Gen removed her hand from the crib so she could reach out and touch Zeke's shoulder. Hearing this—and picturing the orphaned little boy—she could understand how he'd become something of a loner.

In fact, the picture was so clear in her mind her voice cracked as she asked, 'Who brought you up?'

He hesitated, and for a moment she thought he wouldn't answer, but he did. Although the reply, a laconic, 'Various people,' told her nothing at all.

'And your father's name was Samuel,' she said, trying not to think of the little orphan child. 'I think that's lovely, wanting to call the baby after him, and Sam's a good name for a boy.'

Damn! Her voice was going shaky again.

'Sam Lucas,' she tried quietly, speaking to the baby, hoping for a sign, but his eyes didn't open nor a limb twitch, though she hadn't really expected a reaction.

'Sam Wilson,' Zeke said, equally quietly, and Gen's stomach clenched.

She stared across the crib at Zeke and saw his grey eyes fixed on her face—watchful, wary, but also determined.

Or so it seemed—although who was she to be trying to read looks in this man's eyes?

Not that the look in his eye was the issue—what should be bothering her was his obvious determination to be involved in bringing up her son.

She looked at him again, aware it was ridiculous to be trying to guess at his thoughts or intentions—she barely knew the man!

Yet even as the thoughts flitted through her head she knew she was wrong. She knew so much about this man—knew he was kind and caring, considerate, well-read, intelligent, fit and healthy. They'd walked and swum and sailed until she'd been exhausted, but he'd barely warmed up most times. And most of all she knew he loved his daughter, and that his sole focus on returning to his home in Brisbane after their time together had been to stabilise her life.

'Louise?' she said, following her thoughts to that daughter. She'd been mentioned earlier, but Gen couldn't remember the conversation. 'Has she settled in with you?'

'Physically, yes. She's as settled as she could be. But emotionally—hell, I don't know, Gen. I look at this little fellow and I think it should all be easy—well, easy once we get him out of hospital—but bringing up children is a minefield, and sometimes I wonder if love and security—which are the only extras I can offer on top of board and keep—is enough.' He paused, then added, 'And when I think maybe I've failed her, I can't help but wonder if I shouldn't just walk away from this little fellow right now.'

'Because love and security are the only extras you can offer?' Gen demanded, her voice rising with her incredulity. 'Isn't being an example of a kind, generous, compassionate, understanding, intelligent and thoughtful adult equally important? We tell sports stars they should behave themselves because they're role models for our kids, but the first role model and the most important one in any child's life is a parent.'

Was she right? Was being there—being an example—enough?

But how could he be there for this baby too, if introducing Sam into his family upset the delicate relationship he was building with Louise?

But he couldn't walk away. How could he, when Gen undoubtedly needed someone by her side?

How could he, when seeing her again—in the flesh, not in his dreams—had reminded him of just how good things had been for those two weeks? She'd come into his life when he'd been drowning in despair and not a little self-pity, and her frank enjoyment of his company, her delight in all they did together, had chased away the shadows and sent him back to work with new vigour—back to Brisbane with a renewed determination to overcome the mistrust his ex-wife had planted in his daughter's head.

Although a holiday romance was very different from a long-term relationship, and his only experience of the latter had been a failure…

Gen walked around the crib to stand beside Zeke.

'Is there anywhere we can eat in this place? I'm starving.'

He laughed, and she relaxed. For a moment she'd been sure he *would* walk away, and she'd have hated that—and not entirely because it would have left her all alone in a strange city. When they'd parted on the island there'd been no question of their taking their relationship further. She'd been committed to caring for her mother during the last years of her life, and she'd understood his commitment to stabilising his daughter's life. Family, for both of them, had had to come first, and their families had been on opposite sides of a huge continent.

'There's probably a hospital meal sitting by your bed right now,' he was saying, as she studied him and wondered why one person became special while others didn't. 'But when they built the new hospital they put in some good eating places—from coffee shops to restaurants—all of them accessible to patients in their night attire.'

'Then let's go,' she said, and then realised she probably looked a mess. 'No, let's go back to my room first. Night attire might be acceptable, but I'd prefer to change and brush my hair and do stuff like that.'

He smiled at her.

'By all means—but I like your hair all tousled like that—reminds me of the island.'

Gen felt a catch in the region of her heart.

'Do you think about it often—the time we spent there?' she asked, super-casual though her muscles had tensed and her nerves were tingling.

'Only all the time,' he said, and put his arm around her shoulders to give her a hug.

Gen's muscles relaxed and her nerves settled down. So it had been special to him too—that gave her confidence. Though confidence for what, she couldn't have said.

CHAPTER THREE

BUT as she left the PICU, her feet faltered.

'I don't think I can leave him,' she said to Zeke. 'I'm sorry—I'm behaving irrationally, I know—but—'

'You need to eat—you need to be strong. Think of what he's going to have to go through—the tests and scans—that's when you'll want to be there. Right now he's recovering from being born—that's enough for him at the moment. Doubtless they've done the heel prick for his PKU test, but tomorrow, if he's off the CPAP, a battery of tests will really start.'

Gen stared at him.

'I know all this, so why can't I think of it? Why do I feel as if it's all a dream?'

'Because he's yours, not someone else's baby,' Zeke told her, guiding her out of the secure unit and along a passage to the elevators. 'And that's also why you need to look after yourself, so we'll go up to your room, and you can change if you want, or you can go back to bed and we'll get food sent up.'

Gen allowed herself to be guided—but only because

she was so confused she couldn't have made a decision for herself if her life had depended on it. Was it hormonal, this detachment she was feeling, or was it the result of shock, a double shock at that? Her baby's birth and, the ultimate coincidence, the reappearance of Zeke.

Although that was something she *could* question!

'If you're a doctor here why aren't you at work? How can you stay with me all this time?'

He smiled, and ripples of excitement she hadn't thought she'd ever feel again spread through her body.

'Down in the ER I'm the boss, so I can take time off whenever I like,' he replied, nodding to the people who greeted them while they waited for the elevator. 'Actually, I can't—but officially I'm not supposed to be doing a great deal of hands-on medicine, so there are always other people on duty to cope with whatever comes in. I get involved because being involved is what I like. What's the point of being an ER doctor if you don't get the rush that comes when the place is flooded with emergencies and you get to use all the skills you've learned over the years?'

The elevator arrived and they stepped in. Gen studied him, seeing a different man from the one she'd known—different and yet the same.

'I can see that ER medicine would appeal to you, but isn't it the worst job in the world for—?'

She stopped, aware that what she was about to say would be hurtful. Fortunately they'd reached the maternity floor, so getting out of the elevator and to her room should cover her unfinished sentence.

'For someone with a family?' Zeke finished for her

when they were back in her room. 'You're right—it's probably what happened to my marriage. Too many cancelled arrangements, too many interrupted holidays—that's my ex-wife's line, anyway.'

The bitterness in his voice pressed against Gen's chest, causing physical pain.

'Oh, Zeke,' she whispered helplessly, blinking back the stupid tears that seemed to be a permanent part of her postpartum state.

'Don't pity me,' he growled. 'I'm not stupid enough to believe my work was the sole cause of the breakdown of my marriage, and as far as the present is concerned—well, being the head of the department does mean more regular hours so, providing there's no mass disaster, I no longer miss Louise's ballet recitals or school sports days.'

'Then surely it's all good?' Gen said. 'Louise must be settling in really well?'

'One would think,' he said. The bleakness in the words hurt her again, and though she longed to offer comfort to him she had no idea how, nor even what he would accept from her. For all they'd spent two weeks together, they were still strangers…

'Let's eat,' he said, solving Gen's problem by changing the subject. 'Do you want to change? You don't have to.'

Gen considered the contents of her conference suitcase. One skirt—maternity—one pair of jeans—maternity—but she'd packed some leggings and a T-shirt, thinking they'd be comfortable to explore the park around the hotel if she had time.

'I'll change. I won't take a minute.'

She opened the wardrobe, grabbed the clothes she'd need, and headed for the small bathroom, turning back in the doorway to look at Zeke. He'd crossed to the window and was staring out, although whether or not he was seeing the view over the river, she didn't know. Miraculously he had been there for her today, when she'd so desperately needed someone to hold and comfort her, yet she couldn't comfort him…

'I won't be long,' she repeated helplessly, and shut the door.

Was he mad? Staying here, seeing more of Gen, getting his life into an even more complicated tangle than it was currently in?

But he could no more walk away from Gen than he could forget that the baby downstairs in the PICU was his. Gen was alone here in a strange city, with all her family on the far side of the continent, no one to support her *except* him. As for the baby—well, Sam—he also needed his support—not only now but for all of his life.

How to do it?

How to find a solution that would work for both his children?

And Gen? How would she feel about his determination to be involved?

And, thinking of Gen, the logistics of it seemed impossible. He shook his head, shoving the future away into a far corner of his brain. He had enough to deal with in the present.

'You look gorgeous!'

Gorgeous? Gorgeous wasn't a word he'd ever heard

his lips utter—but she did. She looked ravishing—especially now, as a faint flush of pleasure—well, he hoped it was pleasure—coloured her pale cheeks.

'Thank you, but I don't need compliments.'

'Rubbish,' he responded, recovering well enough to let the conversation slip into harmless banter. 'Everyone needs compliments. We all need reassuring that we'll do—though in your case it's more than just doing, you definitely look great.'

Okay, so he wasn't quite recovered, he was still babbling a bit, but what had really shocked him was the hot flash of desire he'd felt when Gen had emerged from the bathroom. She was wearing black things on her legs that seemed to emphasise the length of them, and a dark green T-shirt—unremarkable, really, but it had seemed like the sexiest attire he'd seen in a long time.

Probably since the first time he saw her on the island, wrapped in a sarong, with the sun shining right through it so her curvaceous body had been delightfully revealed. He'd seen her naked after that—often—but it was that first sighting that had stayed in his mind, stirring his libido so he'd ached with regret that their lives had been on such diverse paths.

'Shall we go?' She sounded uncertain, and he realised he must be staring at her. Hopefully she couldn't read his thoughts.

'Yes,' he managed, although what he really wanted to do was run his hands through her hair to see if it felt as silky as it looked. He had liked her hair looking damp and ropy earlier, but he hadn't wanted to touch it the way he did now.

He kept his hands to himself and ushered her out through the door, stopped at the desk to tell the sister on duty where they were going, letting her know he had his pager on him if Gen were needed.

Though wouldn't he be needed as well?

'Hard for a baby to have parents on opposite sides of Australia,' he muttered as they waited, again, for an elevator.

'Is that what you're thinking? That you do want to be involved as a parent?'

Green eyes scanned his face, as if something of his thoughts might be written there.

Heaven forbid, given his earlier thoughts!

'Of course,' he said, and Gen frowned.

'I don't see that it's "of course",' she told him. 'You didn't even know about the baby until today! You said that yourself—*and* said you'd need time to assimilate the idea.'

'The length of time I've known about it doesn't make any difference to the fact that he's my son!' Zeke told her—unfortunately just as the elevator doors opened, and the visitors heading for the maternity ward all heard the last bit—the 'he's my son' bit, which, out of context and in the harsh voice he'd probably used, didn't sound too good.

'Oops!' Gen said, but she was smiling as she said it—though at his embarrassment, not, he guessed, at his assertion of parental rights.

But because she was smiling he smiled too, and some of the tension that had built up in his body dissipated. Right now he had to concentrate on being supportive to

Gen—and on hiding the attraction he still felt towards her. Talk about inappropriate…

Gen wasn't sure whether to be pleased or affronted by Zeke's assertion that he wanted to be a father to her baby. What she mostly felt was disconcerted, but that was mainly because the attraction she'd felt towards Zeke from the day they met had re-awoken in her body, and although she was reasonably certain immediately postpartum women shouldn't be feeling attraction towards anyone, it was there—as strong as it had been back on the island.

He guided her into a small restaurant, and he'd been right—there were women in their night-attire, suitably covered with robes, sitting at the tables, usually with just one man, though some were in family groups as well.

'Very civilised,' she said to Zeke, as a waitress showed them to a table.

'It's all part of making hospitals more user-friendly. If patients feel at home, they don't fear asking questions. You get much better patient-staff communication, and from that much better outcomes. Or that's the thinking, anyway.'

Gen nodded, knowing from her own work how daunting it sometimes was for patients and their families to ask questions of the staff. But her mind was still on attraction, and she studied him as he went on to explain that the hospital had only recently opened this new wing.

Was his hair showing more grey? Or did the shorter haircut, no doubt necessary for work, reveal more of the unwelcome streaks age brought?

And his tan had faded, but nicely. Some tans went yellow, but his had faded to a very pleasant—okay attractive—olive colour.

'Are you listening?'

She smiled her apology.

'Not really. I was looking at you.'

She'd spoken honestly, but as soon as the words were out she realised they sounded dreadful—like some soppy teenager with a crush!

'Wondering if Sam will have grey eyes.'

Zeke reached out and took her hand.

'It's okay to look at me,' he said, squeezing her fingers. 'I've been looking at you that way since we met again—looking at you and wondering how I let such a beautiful woman slip out of my life.'

The words made her heart flutter—which was stupid. And they made her just a little angry.

'Did you charm your wife with words like that?' she asked, and, because she was still studying him, she saw him flinch.

'Probably not,' he admitted, and the grey eyes met hers with a degree of defiance, as if to say *you asked for this*. 'We were both young, with hormones, testosterone—who knows what to blame?—raging through our bodies. All we wanted was to spend our lives in bed together. We didn't think much past that.'

And though Gen knew it couldn't possibly be jealousy eating into her, she also knew that talking about the past might help Zeke work out where things had gone wrong with his daughter.

'Until Louise came along?'

He shook his head.

'No, I'd got out of bed and got serious before Louise came along. I realised I had to grow up and be responsible. I'd always found it relatively easy to study and passed exams well, but that first year of marriage I actually failed and had to re-sit an exam—that was my wake-up call.'

'And your wife? Did she get on with her life?'

Zeke stared at her, thinking back—although he didn't need to think too hard. When Sharon had felt she'd lost his interest she'd stopped taking the contraceptive pill.

'She got on with having a baby. But the weird thing about babies is that while for most people a baby becomes the focal point in their life, with Sharon it was different. Babies don't give much back.'

'Of course they do!' Gen argued. 'My heart turns over every time my little niece smiles at me—right at me, because I'm me and not some stranger!'

Zeke smiled at her certainty.

'You're right. They smile, and gurgle eventually, and we tell ourselves it's because they know us. But they're not that much into other people. They don't constantly tell you how beautiful you are, how adorable, how funny. They are far too involved in learning all about themselves—you must have seen babies discover their hand for the first time—they way they stare at it, and turn it this way and that, working out that it's attached to them and also able to be manoeuvred. Anyway, they don't worry too much about giving positive feedback to their mothers.'

'But surely *having* a baby was enough positive feedback for your wife? The achievement of it, the satisfaction, the sheer joy?'

'For most people that's true,' Zeke said, sorry he'd started this conversation. He'd never talked about Sharon with anyone—not to any great extent—now suddenly he was pouring out this acid from the past onto Gen, who least deserved it.

Fortunately a waitress appeared to take their order, but as she departed he realised he wasn't going to be spared.

'Not for your wife?' Gen pursued determinedly, but she grinned at him. 'I know you don't want to talk about it, but think of it as therapy for me—it stops me worrying about Sam. And I refuse to go on calling her "your wife"—or "ex-wife", which is even worse—what's her name?'

'Sharon—and, no, it didn't work for her. She found Louise—well it could have been any baby—incredibly boring. There was good and bad in that. We employed a nanny. She isn't Mary Poppins, but she must be the next best thing—Elsie is the one constant in Louise's life, so that's the good.'

'And you're not going to tell me about the bad?' Gen guessed softly, recognising the expression on his face—one he wore to hide any emotion he might be feeling.

Zeke nodded, *really* not wanting to talk about this any more. His experience of marriage had left him scarred, and he had no intention of picking open any of those barely healed wounds. He lifted his knife and began to score lines in the tablecloth, marking the squares for noughts and crosses—as futile a game, if you knew the play, as marriage.

'But you have custody now?' Gen confirmed, reaching out and taking Zeke's hand, stopping the restless doodling.

'For what it's worth! Have you ever been to court to witness a custody hearing? It's not pretty, Gen, and in the middle of it all is a gorgeous little girl with long dark hair and serious grey eyes. And for all she might be living a stable life with her daddy, I doubt there's a little girl in the world who doesn't fall for her mother's tears—her mother's cries—her mother's "but darling I love you so much; I want you home with me".'

Gen shook her head, her stomach twisted into knots at the thought of the little girl torn between two parents. Could this happen to Sam?

No way! There was no way she would allow that. Better he never knew his father than have to make choices no child should ever have to make.

Or was it?

'It puts the child through terrible emotional trauma,' she said softly.

Grey eyes dark with pain looked into hers.

'Which is why I worry about her now, for all that she seems settled.'

Gen felt his fingers grip hers more tightly, but she had no words to help him—nothing to offer except the warmth of her hand.

Their meals arrived, and though Gen knew she had to withdraw her hand from Zeke's she didn't want to. But it would be impossible to eat the steak she'd foolishly ordered with one hand!

Zeke solved the dilemma, squeezing her fingers before releasing them.

'Enough talk of problems and misery. Let's think about Sam. My neonatal knowledge isn't anywhere near as good as yours. What next for the little fellow?'

Sam! Gen had to put down her knife and fork and breathe deeply for a minute, until the pang—part emptiness, part worry, part joy and excitement—passed.

Think medically, she told herself, and returned to cutting up her steak.

'Blood tests—zillions of them. Checking for infection, checking all is as it should be in his blood. And tomorrow, I'd say, or within five days of birth anyway, a Hep B vaccination. Jaundice—they'll check for jaundice all the time. A head scan—but not till he's off CPAP—to make sure there's been no brain haemorrhage. They might do that twice.'

'Hearing? Sight tests?'

'He's really too immature for those at this stage—they'll check his eyes, but probably not until four weeks.'

Then the full realisation of what lay ahead, with all its implications, struck her, and she put down her knife and fork and stared at Zeke across the table.

'They won't let him out until his due date—or close to it! He'll be here for weeks—*I'll* be here for weeks.'

'Eat your dinner,' Zeke ordered, and because her brain had gone all fuzzy again, and she couldn't dredge up one single logical thought, she picked up her cutlery and ate, trying desperately to get enough clear space in her head to think things through.

'I imagine you made some arrangements for maternity leave from your job?' he continued, so calmly Gen couldn't help but feel comforted. 'It will just have to start early.'

She nodded, a small bit of brain matter now producing a sequence of thoughts.

'Because Mum had deteriorated so much I arranged a year off from clinical work. I've been supervising the study we're doing and working on my doctoral thesis. It won't be hard for my 2-I-C to take over the study, but—'

'But you're here and your home's over there. Is that it?'

Zeke spoke so gently Gen felt tears prickle at her eyelids again, even threaten to leak out and run down her cheeks, but she refused to give in to them, blinking them away.

'I suppose,' she muttered, disconcerted that she, who prided herself on her composure, could be behaving so pathetically. 'Not that home's really home without Mum. I'm the one who stayed, you see. But the others were always in and out—now it's empty, and in fact it's up for sale. It's far too big for me, and it was left to all of us—and the others could all do with the money.'

'And just when, in between pregnancy and selling a house and supervising a study and writing a thesis, were you going to look for a new home?' Zeke asked, sounding so incredulous Gen had to smile.

'I *had* realised it was impossible,' she admitted. 'I'd decided to rent. In fact, on the flight over I checked out some possible rental units I'd downloaded from the net.'

'Well, it's a good thing you didn't settle on anything,

because it would be a waste to be paying rent on an apartment in Perth when you're stuck in Brisbane—'

He stopped rather abruptly, as if he'd been about to say more.

Gen waited. She'd learnt to do that with this man.

'The best solution would be for you to stay with me—at my place. It's just up the hill from the hospital, so you can ferry breast milk back and forth for Sam, and it has plenty of bedrooms, so you can be completely private.'

Gen studied his face, trying to read it, wondering…

She'd certainly not been able to read anything into his tone of voice—not even a smidgen of welcome…

'You don't *have* to do that for me,' she said. 'I know most hospitals with PICUs have arrangements with places nearby for parents in just this situation.'

'Soulless motel units! You didn't even feel at home in a luxury hotel room at the resort,' Zeke reminded her. 'You'd die in a motel room.'

He paused, then sighed.

'And, no, I didn't *have* to offer you accommodation—although as Sam's father I should have some obligation to seeing you well-housed. I offered because I wanted to, Gen. I offered because I'd like to have you in my house. I'd like to know you're safe and looking after yourself—even, time permitting, do a little looking after you personally.'

He must have realised the ambiguity of the statement, for he quickly added, 'With no strings attached. No, that's making it worse. What I mean is that—well, I guess you know what I mean.'

Gen stared at the tongue-tied, embarrassed man

across the table. Was this really Zeke, stumbling over words, digging himself deeper and deeper into a conversational minefield? Zeke, who was always so controlled—so in charge!

It was, and with a sudden clarity of insight Gen realised why. Her staying with him might imply a relationship, which they didn't have—not really—and, judging by his embarrassment it was something he didn't want.

Was that a twinge of disappointment?

Surely not.

But, just in case, she decided to treat his disjointed ramblings lightly, shrugging them off with a teasing, 'No sex? Is that what you're saying? Not possible for a few weeks anyway.'

Zeke glowered at her.

'That is *not* what I was saying,' he muttered. 'And well you know it!'

Gen shrugged. Maybe she shouldn't have teased him.

Maybe she should have been more forthright. Suddenly it seemed important to find out exactly where they stood.

'Yes, but it's not as if we have some kind of ongoing relationship, now, is it?'

His frown deepened.

Did he think they *did* have a relationship?

Gen's poor heart wasn't certain how it felt.

'We have our son,' he reminded her, the frown fading to be replaced by the faint glimmer of a smile.

And although that didn't help sort things out one bit,

Gen experienced—not for the first time since they'd met again—a totally inappropriate charge of sexual desire.

She hadn't said yes to his invitation.

Given the charge, should she?

Wouldn't moving in with him complicate matters between them? Yes, they shared a child, but they were still strangers for all the physical attraction they felt towards each other.

And was it two-way attraction?

She thought so. It hadn't been good manners prompting Zeke to tell her she looked gorgeous. But attraction was only part of any relationship, and moving in with him—into the same house, not into his bedroom—could give a false sense of belonging.

She sighed—shouldn't she be thinking of the baby—of Sam, not attraction—right now?

'It's very kind of you—' she began, but his pager was bleeping and she'd lost his attention.

He checked the number and pulled out his mobile, glancing across the table at Gen as he thumbed in a number, then apologising as he stood up and walked out to the doorway to talk.

Gen studied him from this safer distance, seeing immediately the tension that had gathered in his face, imagining she could see it in his shoulders—in his stance.

Work or Louise?

It couldn't be a summons about Sam—he'd have told her immediately. But now she'd thought about the tiny baby boy again her worries returned, together with an almost physical need to get up and go to him.

She looked at their plates, half-eaten steaks congealing on them, and stood up, crossing to the desk and handing over a credit card to cover their meals, knowing she *had* to go, and suspecting Zeke would insist on accompanying her.

The bill paid, she moved towards the door. He was pacing as he talked, back and forth across the foyer by the elevator, one hand holding the phone to his ear, the other one waving in the air, as if he needed to emphasise whatever point he was making.

'Tell Elsie I'll be home in ten minutes. If you haven't had dinner we'll get some takeout. See you soon, darling.'

There was a slight pause while he listened to the other side of the conversation, then a quiet, 'Love you too,' and he slid the phone back into his pocket.

'That was Louise,' he said to Gen—quite unnecessarily, given what she'd heard. 'She was supposed to be spending the night with her mother, but apparently Sharon had other ideas.'

He pressed the button to summon the elevator.

'And Louise, naturally, is upset?' Gen murmured, thinking how hard it must be for children to juggle divided loyalties between two parents.

'It's the way it happens that upsets me,' he said. 'Sharon gets a new man and suddenly there's no room in her life for Louise. Can't she see the damage it does to her daughter? Doesn't she understand that Louise will see it as a rejection of her? Is it any wonder the poor kid is so—so cowed, almost?'

'But she's getting plenty of positive input from you,' Gen reminded him, certain this man would be providing the stability and love the little girl needed. He was a man with enormous empathy for others, and his daughter was the main focus of his life.

'Sometimes I think it's not enough,' he said, his voice so low Gen barely heard the words.

The elevator arrived and they stepped in, their conversation halted by the number of passengers already inside. They squashed into the limited space still available, and rode down to the PICU floor in the strained kind of silence only found in elevators in big hospitals, where the stark realities of human frailty were all too frequently present.

Gen was close enough to feel the tension in Zeke's body, which was strong enough to be puzzling. Louise had been with him for seven months now—surely the bond between him and his daughter was strong enough to withstand disappointments like this one?

She turned to look at him and saw the frown, a distracted look—he was thinking, and his thoughts were far from happy.

Why?

As they left the elevator on the PICU floor light dawned. His relationship with his daughter was obviously still delicate—but with a strange woman in the house? To say nothing of introducing a new half-brother into the mix!

'I don't *have* to stay with you. You've got to do what's best for your daughter,' she told him. 'I'll be perfectly all right in whatever accommodation the hospital finds for me. Not that that's an issue right now anyway. I saw the obstetrician who delivered Sam this afternoon. She wants me to stay in hospital a few days at least.'

Zeke stared at her in silence for a few moments, then he shook his head.

'That is so wrong!' he muttered. 'Yes, I'm worried about the effect your presence would have on Louise, but, Gen, isn't this what went wrong in the first place between myself and my daughter? I put other things—work—first. I can't start life with my son the same way…'

'It's *not* the same,' Gen told him, then she leaned forward and kissed him lightly on the lips. 'Right now Louise needs you—she needs to know at least one of her parents wants her—really wants her. And you need to give whatever time you have available to making sure she knows it.'

She smiled and touched him on the cheek.

'I'm a mature woman—even though I haven't been behaving like one at times today. I can look after myself *and* Sam—although the nurses won't let me do much of that. So you go home and be with your daughter. As for you and I—well, let's take things one day at a time.'

He didn't reply, simply looked at her for a moment, then put his arms around her and drew her close, so her body pressed against his. It was comfortable, and comforting, and so familiar it surprised Gen to think her body remembered his so well.

Surprised her even more to find herself wishing she could stay in Zeke's arms for ever…

Hormonal weakness—it *had* to be…

CHAPTER FOUR

SAM was still a tiny, scrawny scrap in the Isolette. Gen stood and looked at him, then pressed her hands against the Plexiglas cover that protected him and fought back stupid tears.

Definitely hormonal.

'Hi—you won't remember me, but I did want to know how things worked out.'

She turned her head to find the woman who'd rescued her at the conference—had it been only this morning?—standing beside her.

'I'm Lauren Cardwell. I'm actually a paediatrician right here at this hospital, and I'm not toting for business, but if you'd like me to look after your son I'd be only too happy. I realise another paediatrician checked him out when he was born, but you *can* appoint someone yourself.'

She paused, and Gen looked at the woman standing beside her, an older woman, motherly…

'Damn these tears!' Gen whispered, swiping the back of her hands across her cheeks to get rid of the cascading water. 'Yes, I think I'd like that.'

She put out her hand. 'Genevieve Lucas,' she said as she offered it.

Lauren took it and squeezed her fingers, then she put her arm around Gen's shoulders. 'You look as if you need a hug more than you need a handshake. I know from the conference info that you're from Perth. I imagine all your family's over there, so as well as the shock of a premmie birth you're feeling isolated?'

'And how,' Gen told her. 'Although—'

She stopped. She'd never talked to anyone about Zeke—refusing, even after her pregnancy had become obvious, to admit to anything more than a holiday fling—wanting, without knowing why, to keep her memories of Zeke and the magical fortnight they'd enjoyed to herself.

'Although everyone's been so kind,' she finished, and Lauren smiled at her.

'Including our esteemed ER boss Zeke Wilson, I hear?' She grimaced. 'Hospital gossip—at least *you'll* understand how quickly word gets around in a hospital. Zeke's a good guy, but he's had it tough and had to grow a hide like a rhinoceros to cope with some of the stuff he's had to deal with.'

She said no more, and nor did she question Gen about her relationship—if any—with Zeke. This was good. If Lauren was looking after Sam they'd be seeing a lot of each other, so trust and confidentiality between them was essential.

'The nurses tell me you've called him Sam. I've got a Sam—fifteen, and still a great kid. So far so good, I keep telling myself. What you'll want to know is that your Sam's now breathing well enough to come off the CPAP, so we'll take him off that shortly and watch him overnight. If he's breathing well on his own we'll let him graduate to the big kids' room in the morning. I know this is like teaching your grandmother to suck eggs, but I have to tell you everything we do as if you're just a normal mother—because it's different when it's *your* baby lying there.'

'And how!' Gen said. 'I don't know how mothers without training feel, but I'm freaking out inside—it's really scary, a detached feeling, as if something's been ripped away from me.'

Lauren looked at her with interest.

'You know,' she said, fairly hesitant for someone who'd come across as full of confidence, 'it would be really good if you could keep a diary of the next ten weeks, noting down all your feelings and reactions. Think how useful a tool it would be for us neonatal people to have first hand info on what the mothers of our charges are going through—physically and emotionally.'

'Mainly emotionally,' Gen said, interested in spite of herself. 'Zeke had my things sent across from the hotel. I've some small notebooks in my case. I'll start tonight.'

They talked a little longer about the treatment and tests Sam would have to endure over the next few days, then Lauren excused herself, leaving Gen with Sam, although she turned back before she reached the door of the unit.

'Do you need anything? Clothes? Nightgowns?'

Gen shook her head as the friendliness of this

stranger made her feel weepy again and she found it hard to speak.

Telling herself she had to handle this better, she did eventually manage a thank-you, adding, 'I packed for a four-day conference, and although most things will be a little large for me now it doesn't really matter. After all, who'll be seeing me?'

But although Lauren apparently found her response quite reasonable, it started a few niggling doubts in Gen's head—because her answer hadn't been completely honest. For reasons she didn't want to delve too deeply into, she didn't really want Zeke seeing her in over-large pregnancy clothes.

Ridiculous thought! There was no guarantee she'd be seeing Zeke at all. Not now she'd decided that moving in with him might upset the delicate balance between him and his daughter.

'Oh, Sam,' she whispered, and she washed her hands so she could reach in to cup his head, to feel his tender skin and the throb of his valiant little heart beneath the bony chest. As emotion threatened to overwhelm her again, she remembered Lauren's suggestion and, with a whispered goodbye to her son, she slipped back to her room to get a notebook and pen. She *would* keep notes on how she felt—but whether those notes would be a useful tool for the future or just a record of a personal journey of some kind, she didn't know.

She was asleep again, her head resting on her hand as she lay, uncomfortably folded into a reclining chair, beside Sam's Isolette. A red notebook lay in her lap, and a pen had fallen to the floor beside the chair. Zeke picked up both items and put them on a shelf behind the crib, then he sat the soft grey rat he'd found in the toyshop downstairs beside them.

Sam's first toy. And while a rat was hardly a normal children's toy, the animal's wise face and cute outfit of shirt and shorts had appealed to Zeke more than any of the profusion of rabbits and bears.

He washed his hands and stretched one through to touch his son.

His son!

Pride swelled in his chest—well, he hoped it was pride, and not some other stupid emotion. Although he'd been overwhelmed by emotion when Louise was born, unable to hold back tears as he'd held his daughter for the first time.

Poor Louise! Tonight he'd held her in his arms again, assuring and reassuring her—not of *his* love but of her mother's as well. But this time he believed Sharon's rejection of her daughter had bitten deep—at ten, Louise knew when her mother was making up an excuse to not see her.

'How do I undo that kind of harm?' he asked the small mortal asleep in front of him. 'How?'

He'd whispered the words, but they must have penetrated Gen's sleep for she was moving, stretching—and looking so incredibly sexy he was again thinking things he shouldn't.

'Zeke?'

Her voice was husky with sleep, and full of wonder,

then her hands went to her flat belly and she sat up to peer into the Isolette.

'I thought I'd dreamed it—you and Sam and everything that's happened—but I didn't, did I?'

He took her hand and held it firmly.

'No, you didn't. But Sam's okay, and you're okay, and we'll work things out eventually.'

He mustn't have sounded as positive as he'd have liked to, for she frowned at him.

'Louise?'

Zeke sighed.

'She's asleep at home—it took a while to calm her down, but she'll be okay.'

'I'm sure she will be, with you as her dad,' she said, but there was enough false bravado in the words for him to guess she was thinking that little girls needed a mother as well. Hell, he knew that! It was why—again and again—he made arrangements for Louise to spend time with Sharon. Although the more often Sharon let Louise down, the less Zeke felt like doing it.

'I can only hope so,' he said grimly, wondering just what it would feel like to be ten and let down by your mother…

'I was thinking, before I fell asleep, about you and her,' Gen said, dragging him out of his depressing thoughts. 'She's still settling in with you—I know it's been seven months, but that's not all that long. And now we've got Sam. I imagine it's going to be hard enough for you to introduce him into her life, without introducing me as well. Can she handle all these changes at the moment?'

Zeke smiled at her.

'You stole my thoughts! Although as a female you can probably get closer to imagining than I can. But I'm here for you, too, Gen, and I still want you to come and stay when you're discharged from hospital. Who knows? Your presence might be a welcome diversion!'

Was he saying this to be polite? Or because he felt he had to, given he was the father of her child? Gen studied him, but if she'd happened to guess his thoughts earlier she couldn't even come close now.

'We'll wait and see,' she told him. 'By the way, Sam's got himself a paediatrician—Lauren Cardwell. She's the woman who rescued me at the conference when my waters broke and brought me to the hospital. Oh!'

She put her hand to her mouth and tried to take back all she'd said.

'I should have asked you—you'd have known best—you know these people—it's your city.'

He touched her lightly on the cheek.

'Lauren's one of the best—certainly of those who work at this hospital. Sam will be in good hands with her.'

Gen grasped the hand that had lingered by her face and held it tightly.

'Oh, Zeke, I know I should be able to do this on my own, but I am so utterly and entirely grateful to have you here, I can't put it into words.'

'Hey,' he said, retrieving his hand so Gen felt embarrassed that she'd grabbed it. 'He's my baby too!'

Then he turned into Dr Wilson, and began to chide her for not looking after herself.

'You should be asleep up in your room. You know Sam's being well looked after, and there's not one single solitary thing you can do, so how about I take you back up there and tuck you into bed?'

'I'd like that,' Gen said. But when they reached the maternity ward and walked down the corridor to her room, although all the doors were closed, she heard the murmur of voices and knew couples lay together in the double beds this hospital provided for new mothers and fathers.

She'd be lying in the big bed on her own, and though she'd thought about the ramifications of single parenthood from the time she'd known she was pregnant, tonight it would have been nice to sleep in some man's arms—in Zeke's arms…

Had he sensed her need? Because once inside the room he put his arms around her and held her close, then bent his head and kissed her, at first gently—a caring kind of kiss—but as she responded, his kiss deepened, until it told of need and hunger.

Dangerous stuff, as it fired the same desires in Gen. She pressed against him, her hands exploring, remembering, her breath coming in little gasps, catching air from Zeke, who finally gave a low moan and eased away from her.

'Drugs! Flames! Wildfires! All the words they use about sexual attraction seem to apply to whatever it is between us,' he said, his voice hoarse and grating.

Gen held on to his shoulders—as much to steady herself as to stay in touch with him—so she felt the deep breath he took to steady himself before he added,

'Whatever it is, it's totally inappropriate for me to be feeling this right here and now. Probably inappropriate at any time and in any place, but my mind's not working too well right now.'

He leaned forward and gave Gen a very chaste kiss on the lips.

'Go to bed,' he ordered. 'And I know I said I'd tuck you in, but if I see you in that nightgown again I won't be answerable for the consequences, so I'm removing myself from danger. Okay?'

He touched her lips with his forefinger as he said the last word, and she kissed his skin and nodded, totally bemused herself. The problem was that as well as being so incredibly attracted to this man, she liked him. Liked him a lot! Probably more than she'd ever liked any man…

'Oh, Zeke,' she whispered helplessly, leaning against the closed door after he'd departed. 'What *are* we going to do?'

Exhaustion provided the immediate answer—she had to sleep. A warm shower first, a liberal application of the apple and aloe body lotion Eloise had given her for her birthday, then into bed. She'd think about all that lay ahead tomorrow. Surely by tomorrow all the fuzziness would have left her head and she'd be a normal functioning adult once again?

But it wasn't a normal functioning adult who awoke the next morning, when a kindly woman in pink, speaking softly, left a cup of tea beside her bed. It was a desperate, frightened mother—leaping from the bed, throwing on her gown and demanding to know how to get to the PICU.

The kindly woman, apparently used to new mothers, calmed her. 'Sit down and drink your tea first. If your little one's in the PICU he or she is fine—there are more nurses per patient down there than in any other part of the hospital, and at the slightest hitch they'll contact you.'

Gen knew this was probably true, but that didn't stop the clenching of her stomach, nor the panicky hammering of her heart.

'I have to go to him,' she said, and left the room, trying hard not to break into a run as she skirted the tea trolley and the nurses on changeover, intent only on getting to the nursery to see her baby.

To see Sam!

The CPAP mask was off his face and she could see him properly. Oh, he still had tapes and tubes and wires around his tiny body, but his face was fully visible.

'He's done well—breathing on his own,' the nurse who was watching Sam informed her. 'One small incident of apnoea, but although it rang the alarm he was breathing again by the time someone touched him.'

The young woman looked at Gen.

'Apnoea's when they stop breathing for a few seconds,' she explained, speaking slowly and carefully. 'Some premmies have up to eighteen episodes of apnoea a day, so it's nothing for you to worry about. You might find this is the only one Sam will have. It happened soon after we took him off the CPAP, so he probably forgot he had to do all his breathing for himself.'

Gen knew all this—well, not about Sam's incident

of aponea, but about apnoea in general and more specifically in premmies—but she found the nurse's explanation very soothing. Something else to write down—it didn't matter how much you knew, when it was your baby you wanted the experts who were working with him or her telling you things.

The nurse was still talking, and though Gen had missed most of what she was saying, she did hear the end bit—'brothers and sisters?'

'Brother and sisters! I haven't told them—haven't phoned them. Good grief, what is wrong with my head? And now it's too early!'

She sounded waily again—feeble and inadequate—and the nurse was looking at her strangely.

'It's after six,' she told Gen. 'Most kids are up and about by now.'

'They're not kids, and it's only four back home,' Gen said, puzzling the nurse even more. 'I have to go back to my room—no, I need to touch him first. And I need to know things—what you're doing next—I want to be here.'

The nurse was back on more solid ground.

'We won't do anything until Dr Cardwell has seen him and checked his chart, and she won't be in until eight. Why don't you go back to your room, do whatever you have to do, then come back and see her as well as Sam?'

Gen was so relieved someone had taken control of her life that she obeyed, stopping only to touch her little boy once again and peer more closely at his face, trying to see shape in his features—an impossibility at this stage.

But once in the lift, returning to her bedroom, a different kind of guilt struck her. She'd turned off her mobile before she'd entered the conference room yesterday morning and hadn't turned it back on since. Would one of her siblings, not able to get her, have phoned her at the hotel?

And, not getting her there, be worrying?

She doubted it. They'd known she was going to be very busy for the few days she'd intended being away, so they were more likely to have left text messages if anything had happened she needed to know about.

Or text messages of love and support—they did that to each other all the time. Her phone would be loaded. And they'd begin to worry if she didn't at least text them back…

Had baby? No. Squashed into text-talk, the message wouldn't be enough. She'd have to phone Marielle and get her to let the others know.

Someone would want to come flying over, and she began to wonder how she'd feel about that. The thought struck her as forcibly as a blow—that she, who'd held her family close for all these years, should suddenly have to think about whether she wanted them close now.

Yes, it would be a support, but—

But wouldn't it also come between her and Zeke?

What was she thinking? That there might actually be something between her and Zeke—something for one of her siblings to come between?

Get a grip. He was being kind—and the physical attraction was still there—and he *was* Sam's father—but apart from that…

She made her way back to her room, from where the cup of tea had disappeared. A breakfast plate, covered by a slightly battered silver lid—obviously the new hospital was using old equipment—was on her table.

Zeke was waiting by the bed, somehow emphasising the doubts she'd been having about her family.

'Louise is not an early riser,' he said quietly. 'I checked on Sam, called into my office, then came on up. You can tell me to go if you'd rather not have me here.'

Gen shook her head. How could she tell him to go when her heart had given a little excited skip on seeing him, and a warmth she didn't understand was spreading through her body just looking at him?

'Are they bringing you some breakfast?' she asked, and he smiled.

'Thank you—I'd like to stay, but I'll have cereal with Louise later,' he said, and, although she wasn't entirely sure why he was thanking her, she knew he was pleased to be there.

Which was a puzzle.

She could understand his wanting to be involved with Sam—but to do something so mundane as sitting with her while she ate her breakfast?

And be happy doing it?

Was that hope making her feel kind of empty inside?

Maybe eating would help. Toast to fill the emptiness, eggs and bacon—protein—brain food to help her think.

'Here you are, Dr Wilson.'

One of the women in pink bustled in, carrying a cup of coffee on a tray. 'Real coffee—not that hospital stuff.

Dr Cardwell keeps a machine in her office and lets us use it for special people.'

'Special, huh?' Gen said to Zeke, when the woman had left.

He smiled at her, and she knew for certain why she didn't want her loving, helpful sisters fussing around the place—nor her protective although much younger brother checking out this man. Not yet! Not until she'd worked out just what was happening with her and Zeke—or her side of it, at least.

Zeke sipped the coffee—strong and black. What sleep he'd had last night had been intermittent and tortured by weird dreams—although the one where he, Gen, Louise and Sam had sailed off around the world had been quite pleasant.

And very definitely a dream!

She looked a little better this morning—Gen, not Louise. He'd only looked in on his sleeping daughter, who even in sleep had still looked a little wan, but there'd been no sign of tears on her cheeks, and he hoped the resilience of youth would get her through this latest disappointment in her life.

Setting aside some murderous thoughts about his ex-wife, he turned his attention back to Gen, now attacking her breakfast with gusto.

'How did your siblings react to the news?' he asked, thinking it a reasonable question, given how close they all were.

But the green eyes that met his held a mix of guilt and defiance.

'You haven't told them?'

She shook her head, realised that was wrong, and nodded, then finished the mouthful she'd been chewing and began a rather halting explanation.

'At first I simply didn't think about it—I mean, I was having a baby, I was in pain—then the realisation that Sam was ten weeks premature and all that meant tumbled down on my head. To say nothing of you, appearing like a genie from a bottle—'

'I hope you wished on me,' he teased, unable to resist the interruption, because she was getting more and more tied up in her explanation.

She gave him a scorching look and tried again.

'What I'm trying to say is that it wasn't until this morning I realised I hadn't been in touch. I came back up here, intending to check my mobile for messages and get in touch with one of them at least—but then you were here, and breakfast.'

She paused, then added, 'I *will* tell them.' And Zeke had the strangest notion that she was trying to convince not him but herself.

'Well, I have to go. So you can get on with your phone calls,' he said. Then he wound back through her conversation and added, 'Unless you'd like me to stay? Or you'd like me to phone someone for you?'

'Call my sisters? They'd be on the next plane—they'd charter a plane—certain there was something desperately wrong because I didn't phone myself. No, it's a kind thought, but I'll ring them. Thank you, Zeke.'

He accepted her reply, although she still sounded very unlike the usual positive Gen he'd come to know, and the fact that she was worrying about contacting her family worried him. Not that he didn't have enough of his own family problems to be worrying about!

He leant down to kiss her goodbye, as naturally as if he was a husband leaving his wife in the maternity ward, promising to come back when he could get away—so casually domestic he felt a shiver running down his spine.

As if it could be, given the situation he was in at the moment. He wasn't even sure he could have Gen stay at his place without upsetting the delicate balance that was his life with Louise.

Surely life wasn't meant to be this complicated? Hadn't he settled into a good routine where he went to work and came home, helped Louise with her homework and generally minded his own business?

Okay, so he worried about Louise—about whether she was *too* good, *too* quiet, *too* composed—but apart from that she seemed fine.

The complication had begun seven months ago—he was honest enough to admit that. And for the last seven months he'd known that the life he'd forged for himself—the routine of work and home he'd developed—would never again be enough. He hadn't dreamt that Gen would come back into his life. In fact, given the circumstances of her life and her mother's illness, he'd known she wouldn't. But he'd known, for sure, that he needed more to make his life complete, and if he couldn't have Gen then maybe some other woman…

Although in seven months he'd done little to find that other woman—any other woman. He'd gone to a couple of hospital events with female staff who'd asked him to accompany them, finding their company pleasant enough but no more than that.

He turned in through his gate and looked at the big old wooden house he called home. It was a family house. There should be kids' toys on the wide verandas and music and laughter echoing through the high-ceilinged rooms. There should be a woman in the kitchen—well, there probably was. But Elsie was sixty-seven, and didn't have green eyes…

Gen could still smell the rich aroma of good coffee in the air, and was feeble enough to feel peeved that Zeke had been so honoured and she hadn't. She really had to pull herself together! She'd get her phone, check her messages, phone Marielle—it was after five now. Not all *that* early to be waking her…

But how to say *don't come* without offending the sensibilities of her siblings?

She checked her messages while she considered this—nothing urgent, all of them accepting she was probably busy either conferring or having fun. With a thudding heart she pressed the button that would connect her with Marielle, determined not to cry, not to worry her sister in any way.

An hour later, thoroughly cried out, she disconnected. She had at least convinced her sister she didn't want any member of the family flying over. She was fine, she'd insisted, and being very well looked after, having made a friend of Lauren Cardwell and having Zeke there as well.

The name had slipped out, but once she'd heard it

Marielle had demanded explanations—and expressed incredulity! The *boatie* Gen had refused to name was really a doctor? He was a doctor right there, where she'd been admitted? He was being supportive? He was happy to have a son?

Gen was in the shower when Eloise phoned, and just about to leave her room to return to the PICU when John got on to her.

'I'll keep the girls at home,' he promised. 'Unless you phone me and tell me you need someone—then we'll all come over. But in the meantime you can get to know your baby's father all over again. And remember that now Mum's dead there's nothing holding you in Western Australia. We're all grown up, and though we'd miss you, with e-mails and texts and phones we can stay in touch—and with cheap airfares we can all get together often. So think about yourself for once, Genevieve Lucas. You and that nephew of mine!'

Gen cried again. But John's call had been more comforting than either of her sisters'. John had reminded her that it was time to get on with her own life, which had been on hold for far too long.

Not that she regretted one instant of the time she'd spent with her mother, or the efforts she'd put into her siblings, but now she had a son to consider…

CHAPTER FIVE

'THIS little boy is in for a busy day.' Lauren Cardwell was in the PICU when Gen entered. 'We'll give him a Hep B shot today, and if he handles that all right we might move him into the special care room—do a head scan to check for any bleeding in his brain on the way.'

She eased away from the crib so Gen could touch her little boy, but Lauren wasn't finished.

'What about you? Have the nurses up on the ward been talking to you about your milk supply? Has it come in? Are you happy to express? If you do it down here, the nurses will refrigerate or freeze it. Do you have a breast milk bank at your hospital back home? Are you willing to donate milk if young Sam doesn't want it?'

'What is wrong with me?' Gen muttered, running her hands through her hair as if a scalp massage might help her brain. 'Why aren't I thinking about things like that? I know it all!'

Lauren patted her arm.

'I've had three children, and I went into the same

kind of fugue state with the births of all three of them. The doctor turns off—heavens, the brain turns off—and you work on some kind of instinctive level for a few days. Worse, of course, with premmie babies—you're just not ready, mentally or physically. But think about it, will you? We always need milk for the bank.'

'I don't need to think about it at all—of course I'll donate milk to the milk bank. I had a patient recently—the young mother had breast cancer and they wanted to get on with chemo and radiation immediately after the birth—and we used milk-bank milk. We've actually started a programme at the hospital where I work to send it to women in country areas whose infants can't tolerate anything else.'

Lauren smiled at her.

'We do that too. I sometimes wonder whether the parcel delivery people have any idea they're delivering breast milk when they drop off the foam boxes packed with dry ice. But, like all programmes, it's expensive, and it's hard to get funding from the government when there are so many other demands on what money is available. But to get back to Sam…'

'Blood test to check for any infection?' Gen asked. 'You'll do that today?'

'Blood and urine,' Lauren agreed. 'And, though you're welcome to be here and to be involved, he's your son, not your patient. Are you ready for that level of detachment?'

Gen remembered how certain she'd been she could talk to Marielle without tears—and how many tears she'd shed.

'I hope so,' she said. 'Although I'm less sure than I thought I'd be.'

Lauren nodded.

'In that case, I'm going to get one of the nurses to show you the expressing machine and talk to you about it. We'll be feeding little Sam intravenously for another day, then we'll slip a feeding tube into his nose and try him on breast milk day three.'

Gen felt a lurch of concern. Would Sam's immature gut be able to tolerate breast milk? Tolerate anything?

If it would take breast milk, then the immunoglobulins in it would be enormously beneficial to him. But as she started to think about the studies done on the benefits in PICUs—which were mostly inconclusive—she realised she was thinking like a doctor again.

She touched her son, talking quietly to him for a few seconds, then went off with a nurse, leaving the professionals to do their job.

'The detachment is the worst part of it,' she told Zeke a little later. He'd appeared as she was about to break down the door of the treatment room where Sam was being injected—or scanned, or something. 'I feel as if they've stolen him, yet I take babies away from their parents in this situation all the time.'

Zeke pulled her out of the recliner beside the empty space where Sam's crib had been, sat down in it, then pulled her back onto his knee. He rested his head against her back and held her in a loose clasp, relishing just being with Gen—he'd think about that later—and hoping his presence was some comfort to her.

'Sharon had a Caesar—refused to be involved in

what she considered the very messy business of natural childbirth. She stayed in hospital for four days after it, but refused to have Louise in with her. While as for breastfeeding… With her perfect breasts? No way!'

'Poor Louise!' Gen murmured, relaxing back against his body. 'How was she this morning?'

'Happy enough. I walked her to school. It's just down the road from the house—one of the best things that's happened, enrolling her there. She's had continuity in her school-life at least.'

'And friends? Are there schoolfriends who live close by? Does Elsie mind them coming to play after school?'

Zeke thought about this, puzzling over it.

'Her best friend from the beginning was Rowena, who does live close by, but now you mention it Louise's afternoons and weekends seem to be taken up with dancing lessons, or piano practice. I haven't seen anything of Rowena since Louise came to live with me.'

'Kids change friends all the time,' Gen told him, although Zeke was fairly certain *she* probably still had friends from her first year at school. She was that kind of woman—loyal and true.

He tightened his arms around her, so pleased to have her back in his life—though for how long he dared not think. There were so many obstacles in the way of the two of them getting together—the biggest being that she might not want to…

A nurse appeared, pushing Sam's crib. Lauren Cardwell walked behind her.

'Well, look at you two!' she teased, then touched Zeke on the head. 'Congratulations, Dad,' she added.

'You've got a beaut little fellow here. Scans fine, took the needle like a champ, gave up some of his precious blood and treated the whole performance with disdain.'

Gen leapt off Zeke's knee, embarrassed to be caught in such a position—though couples all around them were sharing the comfortable recliners.

'He's okay? You're sure he's okay?' she said to Lauren, who grinned at her.

'I've always thought he was more than okay. But I'm a happily married woman, so I can't do more than look!'

Gen felt her cheeks heat in a way they hadn't since her teenage years.

Definitely hormonal!

And, although Lauren knew full well Gen had been asking about Sam, she had to admit that Zeke *was* a more than okay guy, and having him with Gen was helping her through this traumatic time.

Not that he wasn't going through a traumatic time himself. As well as having a fragile new son, Gen had a feeling—from things he'd said and his reaction to the phone call the previous evening—that his daughter might be emotionally fragile too.

And she, Gen, was doing nothing to support him…

Could she?

Was there anything she could do?

Only make life even more complicated for him, she realised, studying the man who was now reading the latest notes on Sam's chart and talking quietly to Lauren about her findings.

He wasn't particularly tall, but he had a solidity about him that made him seem taller, and though now she'd decided that his grey eyes were even more memorable than his lips as his best feature, her own eyes were still drawn to his lips.

Lips that had slid all over her body, that had worshipped her with words and kisses so she'd felt beautiful and special and any number of things she'd never felt before.

Now the warmth that had coloured her cheeks seeped through her body. Was it purely physical—this attraction to Zeke?

As if her thoughts had tapped him on the shoulder, he glanced up at that moment, and winked at her.

No, it was more than physical—the man was special.

He was also, if she was honest with herself, totally off-limits. Oh, he was happy enough to have Gen stay with him—man-like, he thought it was that simple: she needed somewhere to stay; he had space. But the more she saw of him the more she—fell in love with him?

Surely not!

But if it wasn't love, what was it?

And if it *was* love, then she, who'd watched her own father walk out of her mother's life, knew love had to be two-sided…

'I'm going back to my room,' Gen said, anxious to get away. She was feeling weepy again—but this time it was self-pity, and she'd never cry for that! 'The obstetrician is coming to see me.'

Zeke handed the chart to Lauren, and reached out to give Gen a hug.

'I have to show my face in the ER department, but I'll be up to see you later. I'm taking leave from the end of the week, and things will be easier then.'

He kissed her lightly on the cheek, a gesture so natural and loving Gen felt her heart grow heavy in her chest.

If she couldn't have his love, should she be seeing him at all?

And wouldn't having him around more during the day make the nights longer and lonelier?

She left the PICU, checking on her way out what time she should return to express more milk. The routine in the premmie units was geared to allow parents to spend as much time as possible with their babies, but with so many babies, and so many parents, they had to have some structure.

The obstetrician had departed, satisfied that Gen was recovering well from the birth, and Gen was sitting on the bed, clad in the leggings and big shirt that were the only things she felt comfortable in, when there was a brisk knock on the door.

'Come in,' she called, and was surprised when one of the pink ladies came in, bearing two floral arrangements. She was followed by an aide with even more flowers, and an older woman carrying a large box.

The pink lady and the aide departed, but although the older woman put the box down on the end of the bed, she didn't leave.

'I'm Elsie Moore,' she told Gen. 'Zeke might have mentioned me?'

'Mary Poppins,' Gen said, remembering Zeke's words. She put out her hand and introduced herself. 'Did you bring the box?'

Elsie shook her head.

'It was out at the desk when I asked for your room, and as the others were busy carrying all the flowers that had arrived while you were with the doctor I offered to carry it.'

Gen studied it. The distinctive black and white squares on the wrapping paper told her it was from a large department store.

'Go on—open it,' Elsie said, settling comfortably into a chair and looking as if she intended staying quite some time.

Gen opened it and gave a cry of delight. Inside, neatly folded and packed, was a mass of clothes. Gen lifted things out one by one: a linen shirt in dark green—her favourite colour, a filmy white cotton shirt, and a patterned shirt in green and black and purple—brilliant, riotous colours. Beneath them were three pairs of stretchy capri pants—one white, one black, one green—and below that again a gorgeous pair of black trousers, slim-looking, but with an elasticised waist to make them easier to wear.

Underwear—soft, beautiful camisoles in black and white, maternity bras in two different sizes in case one didn't fit—and finally two beautiful nightgowns, each with a matching wrap. Gen couldn't believe it, shaking her head and staring at the largesse, tears running down her cheeks.

'My siblings,' she whispered to Elsie, when she'd read the card enclosed with the gift. 'Eloise would have thought of it—she's the practical one, and she has children, so she'd know how I feel about the awful pregnancy clothes I have with me.'

'You've a very loving family,' Elsie said, studying Gen with interest. 'But from what I've heard you deserve their support.'

Gen shrugged, using a tissue from beside the bed to wipe away her tears.

'Would you like a cup of coffee?' she asked Elsie, uncertain why the woman was there. 'Would you like to see the baby?'

'No, I'm going now. Louise has outgrown her ballet slippers, and I want to buy new ones before her lesson this afternoon.'

She stopped, as if that was enough explanation, yet there was a pause hanging in the air, broken when Elsie continued, 'And I certainly don't think I should see Louise's brother before she does.'

She'd lifted herself out of the chair as she was speaking, and now headed for the door.

'I hope we meet again,' she said, by way of farewell, and then she was gone.

Gen plopped down on the bed, wondering why Elsie had come. To check Gen out? Or to let Gen know she believed Louise should be told about her sibling? As Elsie probably knew Louise better than either of her parents, Elsie's opinions should be considered. And of course Louise should be told about her brother. It was just a matter of when—or of Zeke finding the right way to do it without upsetting the little girl.

Zeke again—somehow he was the one supporting everyone: Sam, Louise, Gen.

But who supported Zeke?

Gen thought about him, considering the man who'd always seemed in such complete control of his life. Yet while she'd burbled on about her family he'd never mentioned one—the 'various people' who had raised him not even worth naming.

And if he didn't have a family she was back to the question—who supported him?

Gen knew in her heart she could slot into that role, but he hadn't in any way suggested he wanted her permanently in his life.

He wanted involvement with Sam—he'd made that clear.

But with her? Gen didn't know.

She stood up again, shaking her head to shift her thoughts. She'd have a shower, dress in some of her new finery and visit her baby.

The thought—not of dressing up, but of seeing Sam—made her smile, and so it seemed only natural to smile even more widely when Zeke appeared as her next visitor.

But although she smiled she felt a little cheated.

'You couldn't go away and come back in a few minutes?' she suggested, then, seeing his puzzled face, she waved her hand at the largesse on the bed and explained, 'Look—clothes from my sisters. Well, from my brother too, if you count who paid for them. I was just about to have a shower and change into something other than these leggings.'

'You look just fine to me, though I've been wondering what you call them,' Zeke said. 'Have your shower. I want to check your chart anyway.'

Gen's smiles vanished as if they'd never been.

'You want to check my chart?' she demanded, not sure just how she was supposed to feel at this idea but affronted, somehow—as if her chart was something personal, not a series of pieces of paper everyone who walked in could read at will.

'To see what the doctor said,' Zeke told her, looking puzzled again. 'Is that okay?'

Gen shrugged.

'I really don't know. I hadn't thought about it. I don't see why you'd be interested…'

He looked at her then—really looked at her, his eyes scanning her face.

'Can you really not see why? Not see I might be as anxious about you as I am about Sam—more, in fact. I've known you longer.'

It still didn't make sense, but telling him he couldn't read it didn't make sense either.

'Do what you like—I'm having a shower,' Gen told him, but as she stood under the running water she puzzled over it.

Did his being anxious about her mean he cared?

He'd kissed her as if he cared—but that was sexual attraction, about which, right now, the two of them could do little. What if he cared in that other way—the way she was beginning to care about him?

No, it was impossible. The problems in the permutations and combinations of him and her, Sam and Louise, were too innumerable to pursue. They couldn't go caring for each other that way.

Except that Louise and Sam were siblings—half-siblings. They shared the bond of blood. They *should* know each other.

Was that what Elsie had been saying?

Reading Gen's chart only confirmed Zeke's thoughts—that she could be discharged any time now. Knowing she didn't live in the city, the ward staff would do what they could to keep her in, but if the room was needed…

What he wanted to do was take her home. Being so close, it was the perfect solution. But there were two problems—the least of which, he admitted honestly, was Louise. The major one was exactly where it would lead—having Gen living with them. His relationship with Gen had begun with a strong physical attraction, and the experience of his first marriage suggested this was not the ideal base on which to build a lifelong commitment.

In fact, in his and Sharon's case, it had been the worst possible base.

He was staring at the chart, not reading anything now, when the door behind him opened, and he turned to see Gen come out of the bathroom. She took his breath away.

She was wearing black three-quarter-length pants, and a black singlet thing that clung to her body and was low enough to show the deep cleft between her breasts. Over these clothes she wore a dark green shirt that made her eyes even greener. She'd put on a little make-up. More than he'd ever seen her wear. But with pink lipstick on her lips and her dark blonde hair gleaming she was stunning.

And he said so, shaking his head in wonder, the words, 'You look stunning!' barely more than a whisper.

'I thought you liked the leggings?' she teased, but a little extra colour in her cheeks told him she'd appreciated the compliment.

'I did—you always look good—and if I don't stop right now I'm going to get myself into all kinds of conversational trouble.'

'You are,' she said gravely, then she came across the room and kissed him lightly on the lips. 'But thank you for the compliments. You've no idea how insecure a woman gets after childbirth—heavens, *I* had no idea. Fortunately Eloise has had kids and *does* understand—hence the clothes.'

'You've a pretty special family,' Zeke said, which pleased Gen to the extent that she kissed him again. But that re-awoke all his own concerns, so he didn't respond as his body would have wanted. In fact he moved slightly away, hung the chart back on the end of Gen's bed and slumped down into the chair.

'You could be discharged,' he said, then regretted his bluntness as the glow of happiness faded from her eyes.

'I know that, Zeke, and I've thought about it. I think it's too complicated in too many ways for me to shift in with you. I've talked to a social worker here. She says there are good serviced rooms in a boutique hotel just across the road. They're a bit more expensive than the motel option, but more comfortable. I'll be perfectly all right there.'

He might have believed her had her voice not cracked on the last word. Not a big crack, just a little hesitation—more a hitch than anything—but it speared pain right into his heart, and he stood up and wrapped his arms around her, holding her tight against his body, wishing he could offer her the certainty she needed right now, but not knowing what that certainty was.

His mouth found hers and he kissed her deeply, drinking strength from her lips.

'That's not how it should be,' he managed, when they rather shakily drew apart a little later. 'This is something we should be sharing—a time for us to be together. Don't make any arrangements yet. Let me think some more.'

Gen slipped out of his arms, heartened by his words. He certainly sounded as if he wanted them to be together—but why? That was her worry!

'Elsie came,' she told him, and saw from his quick frown that the nanny hadn't divulged her intentions.

'Why?'

'It was either to check me out or possibly to tell me Louise has a right to be introduced to her brother. Do you think it could be that? Do you think it would be the right thing to do? For Louise? When you think what poor Sam looks like—more like a skinned rabbit than a lovely baby brother—it could put her off for life! That's even considering you want her to know she's got a brother…'

Gen stared at Zeke, embarrassed that all her muddled thoughts had come tumbling out in such a stream of confusion.

'Don't look at me,' he said. 'I'm just as confused as you are. Or more.'

His frown grew fiercer.

'Although surely I *should* have more answers? She's my daughter, after all.'

'Kids don't come with manuals,' Gen reminded him. 'So being her father probably doesn't qualify you any more than anyone else—except perhaps a child psychologist—to make the right decisions. I guess it comes down to gut feelings about what's right and wrong, and if what you decide is right turns out to be wrong, then you have to fix things up afterwards.'

'If I can!' Zeke said bleakly, then he checked his watch, kissed Gen lightly on the lips and departed.

Sam had been moved to the special care unit where, instead of having big machines around him, there were smaller machines. Women sat and read or slept beside most of the Isolettes, and although Gen exchanged nods and smiles with those who looked up at her, she didn't feel up to pursuing conversations with any of them. Her mind was choked with problems of the future.

Zeke spoke as if the only obstacle to Gen's moving in was his daughter's reaction to such a move, while Gen knew, in her heart, that moving in with Zeke meant more to her than temporary accommodation.

And if it didn't mean more to Zeke, what was the point?

She read through the latest information on Sam's chart, spoke quietly to him while she cupped her hand around his head, then realised she needed to get outside, into fresh air for a while. Maybe a brisk walk would clear her head, or at least make her feel more human?

But once she'd found her way out of the hospital she

realised that walking anywhere in this part of Brisbane would present the challenge of hills. And what hills! Steep and daunting, and the hospital exit she'd used was halfway up one of them.

If she started by going downhill, then turned left and left again, so she walked parallel to the road where she was now, she'd eventually reach a cross street and could end her walk downhill to the hospital. She strode out, drinking in the crisp fresh air, so glad to be out of the air-conditioned closeness of the hospital she felt nothing but pleasure.

The feeling diminished slightly as she pushed uphill again, but as she was passing big old wooden houses, some beautifully restored, she was glad she was going more slowly. It meant she could look at her surroundings—at the neighbourhood in which Zeke lived.

Was one of these houses his?

One of the done-up ones? Or one of the sad old ones that needed a coat of paint? Perhaps that one there, where restoration was in progress? She stopped to catch her breath and turned to see the view. She could see glimpses of a park and the river, but from the veranda of the house the view would be superb, straight across the river to the cluster of high-rise buildings of the central business district—a very pleasant outlook by day, and a magical one, she imagined, by night.

She pushed on to the top of the hill, where a road did lead back towards the hospital, and though she was pleased she'd had the exercise to get her heart-rate up, she was even more pleased that it was all downhill from here.

All downhill—if only her relationship with Zeke could be that way. Although didn't downhill with relationships usually mean they'd gone bad?

Theirs had never been strong enough to go bad—not really. It had been a holiday romance, nothing more, and that was how it should have stayed.

Love didn't come into holiday relationships.

Not that love had got a mention in the current situation.

And probably never would…

Walking downhill, while physically easier, was obviously not good for positive thoughts…

Gen was wondering if she should do a quick uphill walk again, before going back into the hospital, when she overheard a bit of the conversation of two young girls sitting on the wall outside the hospital, scuffing their good school shoes by kicking them back against the wall.

CHAPTER SIX

'HE'S my brother. Of course they'll let me in,' said the one who sat with shoulders squared, back very straight—a kid who definitely took ballet classes.

'They won't let you in without a grown-up,' her friend said, looking a little slumped in posture compared to the dancer.

'They will if I say Dad sent me. Only I won't say Dad; I'll say Dr Wilson. He's the boss here—not the big boss, but a big enough boss.'

'They still won't let you,' the friend persisted. 'And someone will phone your dad or the school and we'll be in awful trouble.'

This brought Louise—for it was undoubtedly her—off the wall. Elsie would be pleased, because it saved further scuffing of her shoes, but the friend wasn't. She shrank back as if she feared Louise might hit her, which Louise did—but just with hurtful, hateful words.

'All you care about is trouble, Rowena Ward. You're not my friend any more.'

Gen moved forward, knowing she had to intervene, but with uneasiness curdling in her stomach at the situation. Somehow Louise had overheard a conversation about Sam and learned what Zeke—and Gen, to a lesser extent—had been worrying about telling her.

'I think Rowena has been a good friend to you,' she said quietly, standing in front of the two girls so they had little room, with the wall behind them, to escape. 'Ducking off school with you, coming here with you. Wasn't that very brave of her?'

'You shouldn't talk to us. You're a stranger, and how do you know we've ducked off school?'

Louise spoke very politely, but it was obvious she wasn't going down without a fight.

'I know because you've both got your school blouses on over your jeans, and I bet your school tunics or skirts and your ties are in your backpacks. My sisters tried this trick when they were young. I hope you folded your tunics carefully—do you wear tunics or skirts?—because otherwise they get terribly creased and that's a dead giveaway.'

'I folded mine carefully,' Louise said disdainfully, then when Rowena giggled she realised what she'd said and sat back down on the wall with a bump.

'We're not really dodging school. It's senior school sports day and we just didn't stay and watch,' Rowena said, her voice quavering as if the full magnitude of what she'd done had suddenly struck her.

Fortunately at that moment, with thoughts of stranger-danger flitting through Gen's mind, and possibly the minds of the girls, Lauren Cardwell walked out of the hospital. The mother in her took in the situation with a glance.

'Oh, hello, Louise, Rowena. Have you come up to see Louise's dad while the sports are on? Do you know Dr Lucas? She's from Western Australia. Genevieve, this is Louise Wilson and Rowena Ward. They're both at school with my daughter, Jenna.'

The two girls stared at Lauren, who remained unperturbed, though she did give Gen a warm smile.

'Shall I leave you with them?' she asked quietly.

Gen nodded.

She had no idea what to do next, but she knew she had to do something.

Lauren said goodbye and walked on towards the car park, while Gen turned back to the girls.

'Well, now we've been introduced and you know I'm not a stranger—actually, I am, but not a dangerous one—what if you both come up to my room in the hospital? You can change into your uniforms, then duck back into school and watch the sports.'

Rowena looked relieved by this solution, though still somewhat anxious. Louise looked plain rebellious, her bottom lip jutting mutinously.

'Louise,' Gen added carefully, 'I couldn't help overhearing some of your conversation, and Rowena is right. You won't be allowed in to see babies without an adult. Why don't you ask your father to bring you up after work?'

Gen thought she was doing rather well, but when Louise burst into tears she knew she'd failed. She put her arms around the little girl—because ten *was* still little—

and hugged and patted her while mumbled words about Daddy not telling her and him not loving her and her mother not loving her all tumbled out in a confused mess.

Gen found tears trickling down her own cheeks.

'Don't worry about me,' she said to Rowena, who also looked about to cry. Probably because the person she was relying on—the sensible adult—had broken down. 'I've just had a baby and it makes me weepy. Come on. We'll go up to my room and sort this mess out.'

She hurried the two girls through the hospital, glad she knew the way to her room fairly well by now. But once in there she didn't have a clue what to do. There was no way Louise could be sent back to school, but Rowena should be returned there—and with an adult to explain, so she didn't get into trouble…

'Look, pop into the bathroom and wash your faces and hands, and get back into your school clothes. We'll take it from there,' she said, ushering the girls into the bathroom. Then, remembering there'd been chocolates with some of the flowers, she passed those through the door as well.

She shut the door and picked up the phone by her bed—surely a hospital phone would be able to connect her to Zeke? She studied the information on it—'For exchange dial ten'. The woman on the exchange didn't think she should connect a maternity room to the head of ER, but after Gen put on her hospital voice she eventually complied.

'I need you up here now. Louise and her friend are

here,' she said to him. 'But don't come in. Wait at the desk and I'll bring Rowena out to you. You'll have to take her back to school. I thought of Elsie, but I don't know her number, and anyway you'll have more authority. You can let them know Louise won't be back today as well—it's sports day, so it doesn't matter, and, no, I can't explain more now. Ask Rowena as you walk her back to school.'

She hung up before he could ask the questions he must be burning to ask.

Would he come?

Gen was fairly certain he would—if he could—if he wasn't tied up with some ghastly accident.

The two girls emerged from the bathroom, looking like schoolgirls again.

'Right,' Gen said. 'Now, here's what's going to happen. Rowena, you've been a really true friend to Louise, but now it's time for you to go back to school. I've got someone you know coming to take you back and explain to the teachers what happened so you won't get into trouble. I would take you down to see Louise's baby brother, but he came far too early and he's in special care. They only let in siblings—that's sisters or brothers—but she'll tell you all about it tomorrow at school. Won't you Louise?'

Louise, having recovered her composure, was looking mutinous again.

'You can't make me stay here!' she said. 'And I won't tell *her* anything!'

She sent an angry glare at poor Rowena, clearly still put out by what she saw as her friend's betrayal.

'No, I can't make you stay,' Gen said. 'But if you do, I can and will take you down to see your brother. Just sit down for a moment while I get Rowena sorted. There are more chocolates somewhere—in a box, I think. Maybe you can find them?'

The chocolates won, although Gen knew it was a very minor victory. She hurried Rowena out through the door, and nearly cried with relief when she saw Zeke approaching along the corridor at a hospital jog, a worried frown creasing his brow.

'Thanks—here's Rowena. Rowena—you know Dr Wilson. He'll make everything all right for you at school, and explain to them that Louise won't be back today. And *I* think you're the very best friend any girl could have.'

Rowena smiled and tucked her hand into Zeke's. He was obviously bemused, and no doubt had a thousand questions to ask, but when Gen said, 'Go!' in a very firm voice, he went.

Back in Gen's room, Louise had found the chocolates—but she wasn't eating any of them. She was checking out the flowers, reading the cards. Gen took a deep breath and held out her hands, hoping Louise might take them. But the little girl, straight shoulders bending now under the weight of all she didn't understand, turned away from her.

'Your little brother is called Sam,' Gen said gently. 'I'm his mother. But before we go to see him you need to understand that he came very early. He wasn't meant to be born for another two months, so he's not properly grown yet.'

Louise turned back, interest in her eyes, although her pale face worried Gen—the child had been through too much this morning. Been through too much all her life, poor kid!

'So when you see him he won't look like pictures you see of new babies. He's very small, and because he was so early he needs a lot of help from machines. These are called monitors, and they make sure his heart is beating, and that there's plenty of oxygen in his blood, and that his blood pressure is okay. So he's got wires and tubes all over him, and he's in a special crib that keeps the air warm and purifies it, because he could easily pick up an infection if he was out in the open air.'

Gen had been sitting on the bed as she explained, and now Louise came and sat beside her—close enough for Gen to put an arm around her.

Keep it about Sam, her head warned, although her heart ached to give this little girl the love she needed.

'I'm telling you this so you won't be shocked or worried. Babies as little as him survive, and they do well. Back home in Perth I've studied babies like him as they grow up, and by the time they're two most of them have caught up with other kids their age.'

Louise appeared to be thinking about this, then she stirred and stood up.

'Can we see him now?'

Gen stood up as well. Might as well get it over and done with. Thank heavens Sam had been shifted into Special Care. The staff there would probably be more lenient about siblings visiting than they would have been in the PICU.

Down in the ante-room, she showed Louise how to wash her hands and forearms, then led her in. The little girl's hand crept into Gen's, and she held the slim fingers in a firm clasp.

'This is Sam. Sam—meet your sister, Louise.'

Louise pressed her face against the Plexiglas top and looked and looked.

'Can I touch him?' she asked.

Gen hesitated—but only for an instant.

'Use this first, to wash your hands again, then when you touch him, touch him firmly. He has physiotherapy to help him develop, so he's used to being touched, but a really, really light touch might startle him.'

Gen guided Louise's hand through the port, and watched as the little girl touched her brother for the first time, picking up his hand and studying his fingers, then lifting one foot and looking at it, wonder and amazement in her eyes.

They stayed for fifteen minutes, then Gen led Louise back out. The child was obviously thinking—but about what Gen didn't have a clue.

'Do you want me to walk you home?' she said. 'I can explain to Elsie that you came to see Sam and now it's too late to go back to school.'

Louise regarded her with Zeke's grey eyes.

'I think that would be best,' she said, very formal and grown-up now. 'Then you can explain to Elsie how to look after him when he comes home. If he needs special stuff done for him and all that.'

They were walking towards the exit on the ground floor, and although Gen wanted to stop and demand to know exactly what Louise had meant by that remark, she really didn't need to. Louise's next words made it perfectly plain.

'You needn't worry that Elsie won't know what to do with babies. She looked after me.'

And while Gen longed to ask this small manipulator just where *she*, the baby's mother, fitted in, she didn't want to upset the child—nor talk about a future even she and Zeke hadn't fully discussed.

They walked up the hill in silence, and found the house—renovated some time ago, from the look of it—empty. Elsie was no doubt out buying ballet slippers.

'You can come in if you like,' Louise said, and Gen hesitated.

Go into Zeke's house?

Wouldn't that be the thin edge of the wedge?

But she could hardly leave Louise on her own…

'Perhaps we could sit on the veranda,' Gen suggested. 'And you can tell me about your school. It's close enough for you to walk? Do you like it?'

Louise studied her for a moment, no doubt—childlike—seeking an ulterior motive in the questions, though to Gen they were simply easy subjects to discuss.

'It's okay.'

Typical kid answer, but it left Gen with the responsibility of starting another conversational thread.

'And your ballet? Do you have your lessons at school or somewhere else?'

Once again Louise's eyes scanned Gen's face, before the child replied with the single, conversation-killing word. 'School.'

Should I bother to keep this up or sit in silence? Gen wondered. On top of the frustration of the one-sided effort, she was due back at the hospital to express some milk—this afternoon they were going to try Sam on breast milk.

'Perhaps you should come back to the hospital with me?' she suggested. 'You can wait in my room until your father or Elsie can come and get you.'

But at that moment heavy footsteps on the front steps suggested someone had arrived.

'Ah, Louise! Time you and I had a talk.'

Zeke's stern face softened as he turned to Gen.

'You all right?'

She nodded. 'But I've got to go. I've a date with an expressing machine.'

She walked quickly away, neatly avoiding moving close to Zeke, so the hand he put out to touch her arm missed and he was left with only a wave by way of goodbye.

Let him sort out Louise's problems, Gen thought, as she strode back down the hill.

Not that Gen didn't feel for the little girl. She understood how confusing it must be for her.

She'd just finished expressing milk, and had handed her still small donation to one of the waiting nurses when, like the whisper of a wind building up in trees, the news of a disaster filtered through the unit.

Overheard words in the corridors—accident, bus, schoolchildren—and nurses moving more swiftly. The echoing voice of the hospital call system grew more insistent. Doctors wanted in A and E, all available staff. Calls for Dr Elliot, Dr Jackson, Dr Wilson.

Was Dr Wilson still at home with his wayward daughter, or had he been paged?

Gen asked at the desk, but the woman there had little information.

'An accident—apparently a bus carrying schoolchildren ran off the road near the dam. Disaster plans are in place—the injured will go to the major hospitals, although most will come here as we're closest and have the best children's specialists and facilities.'

'I'm a paediatrician. I can help,' Gen told her. 'Where do I go?'

The woman hesitated a moment, then explained to Gen she'd have to go up a floor, then across a bridge to the building on the other side of the road, then down again and ask directions there.

Gen went.

The scene in the ER when she eventually arrived was like something out of a horror movie. Blood covered children screamed on trolleys, others sat silent, their frozen white faces showing deep shock. Parents were arriving—some anxious, some hysterical—pushing their way through the crowd in search of their children.

'I'm a paediatrician. Zeke Wilson or Lauren Cardwell will vouch for me,' Gen told the woman organising triage in the frantic room. 'What can I do?'

'Cubicle two. Suspected torn artery in the upper arm.'

Gen's mind clicked out of dazed motherhood mode

and into doctor mode so quickly she was sorry she hadn't had work to do earlier. She found cubicle two and introduced herself to a pale-faced little boy and an attendant nurse who was hanging a bag of fluid above him on a stand.

Gen checked his admission sheet and saw he'd been given fluid and pain relief at the site of the accident, and a tourniquet had been applied to his arm.

'I've loosened it once,' the nurse told her. 'He's still bleeding so I tightened it again.'

Gen looked at the wound—an open break of the child's humerus. The sharpness of the broken bone could have cut through his brachial artery.

'He needs to go to Theatre. What's the wait? What's the plan? Are some procedures being done down here? Ideally you need an orthopod to do an open reduction of the break, and he could stitch up the artery at the same time, but if they're all busy any competent surgeon could do it.'

'I'll let the manager know,' the nurse said. 'By now they'll have someone listing patients in order of importance—and, yes, there are facilities for some of the operations to be done down here.'

She went off while Gen checked the little boy over, feeling for other injuries, talking quietly to him all the time, although the drugs had made him so sleepy he was hardly aware of her presence.

The nurse returned with an orderly to move the boy up to the theatre floor, where he'd wait—probably in the passageway—until a theatre and a specialist were available.

'You'll be okay,' Gen told him, squeezing his hand as he was wheeled away.

Patients came and went. She moved from cubicle to cubicle while the atmosphere in the ER grew more chaotic, as more and more parents arrived in search of their children. There were policemen there as well, but Gen took little notice of what was going on around her. Her whole mind was focussed on patient after patient—patching up, setting up drips, easing pain, stitching, splinting, even wrapping limbs in casts—things she hadn't done since she'd begun to specialise.

But skills came back to her, and knowledge was never lost. Somehow, for every injury, an answer bobbed up in her head.

Several times during that hectic afternoon and evening she saw Zeke, said hello in passing, nodded, even, but her relationship with Zeke—what there was or had been of it—was the furthest thing from her mind.

'Okay, out of here now,' a voice said, and Gen turned to see Lauren standing behind her. 'Doctor's orders,' Lauren added. 'And I'm sending Zeke home as well. Paediatric ER is more my department than his, so I can tell him what to do.'

Zeke appeared at that moment, just as Gen's knees, unaccustomed to holding her up for so long, began to weaken. He hitched an arm around her shoulders and let her lean on him as he led her to the door.

'You didn't have to get involved,' he scolded, but half-heartedly.

'And you wouldn't have in my position?' she retorted, thinking how nice it was to have Zeke to lean on, and how impossible it was to think she could lean on him for ever.

'You're right,' he agreed, as he pushed through a pair of swing doors and into a dim corridor. 'What a day!'

He eased her towards a wall and slumped there, his arms around her, his head resting on her head—too tired, she imagined, for talk.

Which suited her just fine. Being here, in Zeke's arms, was quite enough for her for the moment, and given that there probably wouldn't be too many moments to be held like this she intended to make the most of it.

But eventually he straightened and looked at her, brushing her hair behind her ears, touching her face, tracing her profile.

'What a day in other ways too,' he said quietly. 'Although I feel bad thinking of my own problems when all those parents in there are suffering so much. But I do need to apologise to you for what you had to go through this morning. I had no idea Louise would listen in to other people's conversations—let alone that she'd heard Elsie and me talking.'

Gen tightened her arms around him.

'It's all right,' she said. 'My younger sister, Eloise, was always running away from home or ducking out of school, so I just handled the two of them as I handled her. And once I realised it was all so Louise could see Sam I thought it was the least I could do to take her in there. I thought—'

She couldn't go on—couldn't explain that she'd hoped, somewhere deep down in her heart, that seeing her baby brother might in some way warm Louise to that baby's mother. But who knew what Louise might have thought? The little girl was naturally reserved, so there was no way she'd tell a virtual stranger about her feelings.

'I can guess what you thought,' Zeke said, hugging her again. 'But don't despair. We'll work this out.'

Gen pushed away from him.

'Will we, Zeke?' she said, looking at his grey, exhausted face. This was not the moment, but she had to ask. 'And, really, why do we want to?'

He studied her for a moment, frowning, as if her words had a meaning he didn't understand, then he said, slowly and carefully, 'I don't know about you, Gen, but *I* want to. Quite desperately, in fact. Which worries me, because I've failed at one marriage and know little about marriage in general—even less about families. But it seems to me that's what we need to be—you and I, Louise and Sam—a family.'

Gen let the words percolate slowly through her head, but even brewed slowly they didn't make one hundred percent sense.

She latched onto the bit that, being so family-orientated, she'd heard loudest.

'Even less about families?' she asked, studying him in turn. 'I hadn't realised it, but all the time I babbled on about my family you barely told me anything about yours.'

'I told you I didn't really have one—not after I was six.'

For a moment she thought he would stop there. Then,

as if he realised that loving someone meant sharing with them, he took a deep breath and let the words come flowing out.

'When my parents died, the welfare people tried to trace family, but no one came forward to claim me. I was slotted into the adoption system. But most people want a new baby, not a six-year-old, so I got shuffled around in foster care places—some excellent, some not so good. Family, my very own family, is an unknown concept to me.'

He sighed.

'It was one of the reasons I was so devastated when Sharon and I broke up—I thought I'd found a family at long last, only to discover it was as insubstantial as a soap bubble.'

Gen's heart went out to him. She wanted nothing more than to take him in her arms and promise him *she'd* be his family—she and Louise and Sam—that somehow she, Gen, would make it work.

Even if he didn't love her?

The stumbling block that had risen in her path earlier popped up again.

Yes, her heart now whispered. *Even if he doesn't love me, I can still make it work!*

Or was she being foolishly optimistic? Loving him so much she wanted to give him the world?

'I don't know what to say,' she managed, shaking her head, because she found it hard to believe she had no answers.

He smiled—a pitiful effort, but enough to start Gen's heart racing.

'You could start by telling me whether or not you love me,' he murmured, and Gen stared at him in disbelief.

'Telling you I love you? What will that solve?'

The smile grew a little more confident.

'Well, it would make me feel better about telling you,' he said, very carefully, as if tasting each word before it came out. 'I do love you, Gen. I think I knew that when we were on the island. But back then our getting together was such an impossibility I didn't want to mention it. But meeting you again, being with you, I know I want you with me for the rest of my life.'

'You love me?' Gen whispered, unable to believe the love she felt could be returned.

'Very much,' he said, and kissed her hard to confirm his words.

'And we'll work it out?' she asked, pushing far enough away from him to see his face again.

'Somehow,' he said. 'That is always providing *you* love *me*. I reckon if that's the case there'll be enough love between us to take in Sam and Louise and possibly the whole world. I reckon we'll work it out!'

Gen nestled against him, wondering if this was some kind of postnatal euphoria she was experiencing, or if Zeke had really said he loved her.

He kissed her again, then seemed to think of something, and in turn eased away.

'You do *want* to work it out?' he asked, and Gen kissed him by way of an answer—kissed him hard and definitely, and held on to him very tightly while she told him all the reasons why she loved him.

'Let's get you back to your room,' Zeke said eventually.

'Sam first,' Gen told him. 'Poor baby will think he's been orphaned.'

They walked together, arms around each other's backs, through the hospital, trying not to think of the other parents sitting anxiously beside the beds of children, trying not to think of anything beyond the happiness of being together.

Entering the special care unit, holding hands now, they stopped to wash, then went on through—coming up short when they saw Sam's crib and the two people beside it.

Elsie was sitting on the chair, and beside her Louise stood, her hand resting on Sam's head.

'They gave him an injection and he didn't even cry,' she said, as if her presence there was the most natural thing in the world.

'He's very brave,' Gen told her, then she smiled. 'Maybe he gets it from his big sister?'

But Zeke couldn't handle this second shock in one day from his daughter.

'And what are you doing here?' he demanded, and though Louise looked a little apprehensive at her father's tone of voice she stood her ground, removing her hand from the Isolette and clasping her hands in front of her, shoulders straight, back erect.

'Elsie and I saw about the accident on television, and Elsie said Genevieve was a children's doctor and she'd probably have to help. And you'd gone back to help, which meant there was no one here with Sam, so Elsie and I came down.'

Her lips were quivering as she finished the explanation, and Gen couldn't help herself. She stepped forward and put her arms around the little girl and held her tightly.

'Thank you so much, Louise,' she said, dropping kisses on her head. 'You're going to make the best sister in the world, thinking about your little brother like that and coming to be with him.'

Then, very slowly, Louise's arms came around her and returned her hug, and the two of them stood there, locked together—the little boy responsible for this first step sleeping on oblivious beside them.

Gen woke late and lay in bed, staring at the ceiling—thinking. She wasn't optimistic enough to think that Louise was won over just because they'd shared a hug. Zeke had taken her and Elsie home not long after they'd all met up in the special care unit, and, suddenly exhausted, Gen had fallen asleep in the chair by Sam's crib, waking in the early hours of the morning to return to her room.

Now she was in another day—another day closer to when she'd have to leave the hospital—and no closer to working out what effect her moving in with Zeke immediately would have on Louise.

The ceiling wasn't much help, but remembering that Zeke loved her filled Gen not only with joy but with hope.

Gen was dozing beside Sam's crib late that afternoon when a nurse came in to tell her there was a little girl outside asking for her.

Louise was in full school uniform today. Gen greeted her uncertainly, smiling, wanting to give her a hug—if ever a kid needed hugging, this one did—but not wanting to go too far too fast.

'You've come to see Sam? Come on in.'

They went through the hand-washing routine and into the unit, where Louise again pressed her face against the Plexiglas.

'He doesn't look as if he's getting any bigger,' she said, and Gen had to agree.

'Although he is, because he's weighing more each time they weigh him. It's because we see him every day we can't see the difference.'

Louise washed her hands again and then reached in to touch him, talking to him at the same time.

'I saw the accident on the television again this morning,' she said, not looking at Gen but evidently addressing her. 'Will all the children on the bus get better?'

Gen moved closer and put her arm around Louise's waist.

'Yes, they will. Although some of them will take a long time,' she said. 'But no matter how careful we are, we can't stop bad things happening sometimes. That's one reason why we should try to make each day the best and happiest we possibly can.'

'Just in case something bad happens the next day?'

Gen thought about it.

'I suppose so. But mainly because we're alive, and we should be happy just because of that. When my little sister was eight our mother got sick, and my sister got very angry about it. She didn't know who she was angry at, because no one had *made* our mother sick, she was just very angry. Now she's grown up, with children of her own, and she's sorry she wasted all those days being angry—she's sorry she didn't get on with things and make her days happier.'

'Sometimes it's hard to make the days happier.'

The words were little more than a whisper, but Gen caught them, and caught the little girl too, lifting her in her arms and sitting down so Louise was snuggled on her lap.

'Only if we don't let people help us. That's what adults are for—to help kids be happy. Especially when they're feeling sad. You must be sad about your parents not living together, but if they aren't happy when they're together then it's better for them to be apart—especially for your sake, because if they're not happy how can they make *you* happy? It must be hard to have the two people you love best in the world in different places, but when you're with your dad you should talk and laugh and play with him—be happy with him—and when you're with your mother the same.'

'She doesn't need me to make her happy.'

Gen hugged Louise more tightly, her heart aching for the little girl.

'Of course she needs you. It's just that sometimes grown-ups get busy with their own lives and forget to tell their children how much they need them. Without you, your mum wouldn't be a mother, now, would she?'

'And she wouldn't get Mothers' Day presents!'

Louise pointed out, and though Gen thought that wasn't quite the point she was trying to make, she agreed.

Although she knew she had to try again.

'Even without the Mothers' Day presents you're still special to your mother. You're her first-born child—that's very special.'

'Will Sam always be special to you?'

'He will. But his brothers and sisters, if he has more, will also be special in their own way. Look at you—I didn't know you before, but already you're special to me because you're Sam's big sister, and no matter what happens you'll always be his sister.'

Louise snuggled closer to Gen, lying against her—perhaps thinking about the conversation or perhaps thinking, in the way of children, of something entirely different.

'I'd better go now. Elsie might be worrying.'

She stood up suddenly, and was halfway to the door by the time Gen got to her feet.

'I'll make sure you find your way out,' she said, wondering if her relationship with this formal child was better or worse for the cuddle.

'I can follow the signs,' Miss Independent told her, but Gen trailed along anyway, then stood outside the hospital entrance and watched the small girl in her school uniform trudge home up the hill.

Were they any closer to an understanding?

Gen didn't know.

But nor did she know what she could do to make things easier for Louise.

The only thing she did know was that without

Louise's acceptance of Gen as her father's partner no relationship between her and Zeke could work—no matter how much in love they were.

'Louise tells me she's going to be happy every day for the rest of her life,' Zeke announced, much later that evening. Their hello kisses had threatened to become too hot to handle, and they'd broken apart and were sitting on Gen's bed, doing nothing more sexy than holding hands.

'That's great—and does this happiness still come in a household made up of four? Louise, Daddy, Sam and Elsie?' Gen said, wondering why happiness should be so difficult.

Zeke smiled, but it was such a poor effort Gen was forced to give him a hug—which led to kisses, and a little fondling. So he was a trifle breathless when he said, 'Yes, that did seem to be the picture she was painting—I'm sorry, her trust is a little broken where a mother figure is concerned.'

'Not to worry,' Gen soothed, not hugging this time, because she knew where hugs led. 'I'll go into the serviced rooms, she and I will get to know each other when she visits Sam, and eventually—'

She stopped, because she had no idea where 'eventually' would lead.

'No,' Zeke said, not smiling now. 'That's wrong. I don't want you moving out into some cold, anonymous room. I want you home—in my home.'

Gen wrapped her arms around him and rested against him, wanting so much what he wanted, but with no idea how to go about getting it—so aware of Louise's insecurity that she knew the wrong move could have serious consequences.

In the end it was Sam who solved the problem. Louise was visiting after school, as she did most days, standing by his crib, holding his hand, when he opened his eyes and looked at her. His dark blue newborn eyes were not able to focus, but as far as Louise was concerned that was it.

'He knows me,' she said in delight, turning to Gen, who was slumped in the chair, wondering for the thousandth time just how she could win the confidence of this young girl.

'I think he would certainly know your voice by now,' Gen answered, then gave an involuntary, 'Oof!' as Louise dropped down onto her lap.

'Elsie says you'll have to breastfeed him. She says that's especially important for premmie babies.'

Gen nodded cautiously, expecting Louise to come up with a timetable for her to visit the house on the hill and feed her son.

'It'd be hard to do without you being there in the house, wouldn't it?'

Was Louise sounding uncertain?

Gen put her arms around her just in case—they often sat this way in the afternoons.

'I guess,' she said.

'But Sam should live with us, because he's Daddy's son and my brother.'

'Two against one,' Gen agreed.

Louise's head rested back against Gen's shoulder.

'And because you're Daddy's girlfriend you *could* share his room,' the little girl whispered, and Gen's arms tightened even further.

'Oh, sweetheart,' she said, 'there's nothing in the whole wide world I'd like more. But I don't want to do that, and your Dad certainly doesn't want it to happen if it's going to make you unhappy. Unhappiness is like a virus, and once it gets into a house then everyone can catch it. So if you were unhappy then so would I be—and your dad and Sam and Elsie, and your budgie and the guinea pig, and there'd be so many unhappy people up the hill the house would be horrible to live in, wouldn't it?'

'I wouldn't be unhappy *all* the time,' came the breathy whisper.

'Then if you can promise me one thing, maybe I could come,' Gen said.

Louise straightened so she could look into Gen's face.

'What one thing?' she asked, her face flushed, as if all the emotion in the room had settled there.

'When you are unhappy, you tell me and we talk about it,' Gen said. 'Could you promise that?'

'Just tell you when I'm unhappy? Is that all?'

Gen nodded, and watched as Louise thought it through again.

'I guess I could,' she said, but guessing wasn't good enough.

'Promise me?' Gen persisted, and Louise smiled.

'Promise,' she said, then she leaned forward and pressed a quick shy kiss on Gen's cheek.

'Well, look at this,' a deep voice said, and Gen looked over Louise's shoulder to see Zeke standing there. 'My three favourite people all in one place,' he added, coming closer and scooping his daughter off Gen's knee to give her a kiss and a hug.

'Have you been skiving off school again today, miss?' he demanded, but the affection in his voice killed any accusation in the question.

'Of course not,' Louise told him. 'I came up after school and Gen and I talked.'

And hearing the little girl say her name for the first time filled Gen with even more joy than her promise had. She smiled at Zeke, and saw his answering smile, and knew that everything was going to be all right…

* * * * *

Claiming the Ashbrooke Heir

MARY NICHOLS

Born in Singapore, Mary Nichols came to England when she was three, and has spent most of her life in different parts of East Anglia. She has been a radiographer, school secretary, information officer and industrial editor, as well as a writer. She has three grown-up children and four grandchildren.

Dear Reader,

Claiming the Ashbrooke Heir is a shorter story than I usually write and presented me with a challenge. The story is set in Regency times when being an unmarried mother was a terrible disgrace; her reputation would be in tatters and marriage out of the question, no matter how mitigating the circumstances, so my heroine is in trouble from the start, ostracised and penniless. But she adores her tiny son and is determined to make a good life for them, despite all the obstacles. I hope you enjoy finding out how she overcomes these obstacles to find true love in the end. I certainly enjoyed writing it for you.

Mary Nichols

CHAPTER ONE

July 1813

ANNETTE, carrying a brown paper parcel which contained the mending she had been given to do, dashed along the road so fast she was almost running. It was a hot day; the sun beat down mercilessly, reflecting the heat from the streets, and her chemise and underskirt were sticking to her.

She hated leaving Timmy in the care of her slatternly landlady but she had no choice; she had to work to earn enough to pay their rent and buy food. Every minute she was away from him felt like an hour, and she imagined all manner of terrible things happening while she was absent. He might be taken ill, with Mrs Grosse not realising or even caring that something was wrong, or one of the woman's brood of children might pick him up and drop him. He was only six weeks old, and very tiny, which was hardly surprising after all that had happened to her.

His birth had not been easy, and she had been

prepared not to take to him, but when he had been put into her arms by the woman who had been fetched in to help she had loved him at once. He was so small and helpless, with a little screwed-up face, a tuft of golden hair and tiny fingers that had a surprisingly firm grip. She had cried over him, knowing he had been born into a hostile world, and that she would have a struggle on her hands to keep them from starving, but do it she would. She had to make the best of the situation for both their sakes.

The pavement was crowded with pedestrians, most of them in a hurry to go somewhere, though a few hawkers stood by their barrows, selling vegetables and fruit. She was dodging between them when she looked up and saw a man walking towards her and her heart missed a beat. It was Jeremy; she was sure of it. What was he doing in Norwich? Surely he had not come looking for her? She put her head down, hoping he had not seen her.

She knew she had changed. Since her son's birth the weight had dropped off her. Her once thick hair had become thinner and there were dark rings round her eyes from lack of sleep, because Timmy cried a lot. He was not thriving as he ought to be, and she supposed it was because she had been husbanding the little money she had very carefully and she did not get enough to eat, so that her milk held little sustenance.

The man was almost level with her now. She slowed down to risk a glance at him from beneath the rim of her chip bonnet and realised it was not Jeremy, after all, but someone who looked like him. He was wearing a black frock coat with black velvet facings, black pantaloons and a double-breasted waistcoat. It was not his sombre clothes that reminded her of Jeremy, who favoured bright colours, it was his face. He had beautifully chiselled features, blue eyes and curly brown hair so like Jeremy's it was uncanny. But this man was taller and broader than Jeremy, and his complexion was darker—as if he spent long hours out of doors; he was altogether a more mature man, though probably only a few years older.

Her relief was so profound she smiled. The smile took him by surprise. Not because she had smiled; after all there were plenty of doxies on the streets of Norwich who habitually approached men with a smile in the hope of attracting their custom. No, it was the fact that it lit her face. It was like sunshine after rain. His own fanciful imagery made him smile too, and he found himself doffing his hat to her.

Taken aback, she stumbled, and a man hurrying along behind her bumped into her. The parcel flew from her hands. She reached out to grab it and lost her balance. The gentleman moved so quickly she was not even aware of it until his strong hands steadied her. Miraculously he managed to catch her parcel at the same time.

'Are you hurt, ma'am?' His voice was deep and mellifluous.

'No, not at all. Thanks to your swift action. And you saved my parcel too. I am indebted to you.'

Once again she surprised him. Her clothes, though clean, were well-worn, but her voice was cultured, the voice of someone educated, someone who could express herself among gentlefolk. He returned her package and bowed. 'My pleasure, ma'am.'

She took it, thanked him, and then hurried on, faster than ever now. She had to get back to Timmy. The encounter with the man who had looked so much like Jeremy had shaken her and made her realise how fragile was the life she had built around herself, how easily it could fall about her ears.

She left the busy streets behind and turned down an alley close to the river. Here the houses were huddled drunkenly together, and the air was filled with the stench of the river and the brewery close by. Ragged children played in the gutter and a couple of stray dogs fought over something loathsome. Annette hurried past them, in at one of the doors, and up the uncarpeted stairs to a room at the top of the house. She could hear Timmy crying.

'Mama's back,' she said, dropping her parcel on the table and crossing the room to pick him up. He was soaked. 'Oh, you poor thing. We shall soon have you dry and smelling sweet again.'

She sat on her bed to change him, annoyed with Mrs Grosse for not seeing to him when she was being paid to do so. When he was once more clean and dry, she fed him and sat cuddling him, staring at the filthy walls of her room and musing on how she had come to such a pass. This was the second home she had had since leaving Riseborough Hall, if you could call this hovel a home, but while she had her son she would do anything, put up with anything. He was the be all and end all of her existence.

If only Mama were still alive! But if she had been Annette would not have been working at Riseborough Hall, and she certainly would not be where she was now. They would still be in their cosy little home in Islington, running a school for young ladies, readying them for Society. There had been one or two younger children too, and it had been Annette's task to teach them the rudiments of reading and writing and how to enjoy themselves in play.

It was that ability to relate to young children that had led Lady Somers, the mother of one of the pupils, to recommend her to Lady Ashbrooke, who had been looking for a nursery maid for her two young children. It had been the week after Mama's funeral, and Annette had been sitting in the parlour after they had all gone, knowing that without an income she could not hope to stay in the house. Her plight had been brought home to her very forcefully when the landlord had given her notice to quit. A young girl of fifteen could not possibly live alone, he had told her, and if she had no one to take her in then she had best make her way to the workhouse. Lady Somers' intervention had been a godsend.

At Riseborough Hall she had been given two grey cotton dresses and several white aprons and a cap which constituted her uniform. Nearly four years she had been there, helping Miss Burnley, the children's governess, to look after Isabelle, who had been four years old when she first arrived and Harriet who was two. She had grown to love them, fitting into the regime of the household, glad to have a roof over her head and a small wage, and to learn a little of the ways of the aristocracy, for whom money meant very little and family reputation everything. She had sullied that, so her ladyship had said. No, she had not, she told herself. It had been Jeremy who had done that, but she was the one being punished.

She went to the table and opened the parcel she had brought in with her. If it had not been for the gentleman rescuing it, it would have been trampled in the dirt and then she would have been in trouble. It contained two sheets, petticoats, stockings, underclothes—all of which needed mending. The work had to be done and returned the next day, when she would be paid two shillings and sixpence.

'Do a good job and we might find more for you to do,' the housekeeper at one of the grand houses on St Stephen's Street had told her.

Thankful to find something after knocking on doors for the best part of the morning, she had been almost triumphant as she'd carried the parcel away and hurried home to Timmy. She had work of a sort and they would not starve. Not today at any rate. She took the first sheet and her workbox to the window, where the light was better, and set to work. Her fingers were busy, but it left her brain with nothing to do but reflect on the past.

Had Jeremy really condoned what had happened to her at the hands of his autocratic mother? 'You may have that,' she had said, pushing five gold coins along the table towards her, as if she could not bear to put them directly into her hand. 'That does not mean I believe your story, not for a minute. I do not. You are nothing but a harlot and not fit to have contact with my innocent children.' Annette had known it was no good expecting Jeremy to back her story because, according to Miss Burnley, he had been packed off to join his elder brother who was in Spain, fighting the war against Napoleon Bonaparte. To keep him out of her clutches, she supposed.

Oh, how she had longed to fling the coins back at the woman. But fortunately her good sense had come to her aid and she had pocketed it, telling herself it would be repaid in full one day. One day she would make Lady Ashbrooke eat her words.

Her ladyship had known perfectly well that she had no family, that there was not a soul in the world to whom she could turn, and yet she had given her only half an hour to pack and leave—and that in the middle of one of the harshest winters anyone could remember. Now, in the stifling heat of a July afternoon, with her child sleeping the sleep of the innocent and her hands busy with her needle, she could almost feel the cold.

She had left the house on foot, carrying her portmanteau which, except for a few books which had been too heavy to carry, contained the sum of her possessions—including the four gowns she had taken to Riseborough with her and not been allowed to wear. 'Too grand for a nursery maid,' Miss Burnley had said. What had lain before her was unknown and terrifying, and she had hardly noticed the snow seeping into her shoes, or that her toes and fingers were numb.

She had been passing Becky Musgrove's cottage on the edge of the village when the woman herself had opened her door and called out to her. 'Annie! Annie Ryston, where are you off to in this weather?'

Becky was elderly and tiny, with a mop of almost white hair, cornflower-blue eyes and a rosy complexion. She had once been nurse to Charles and Jeremy, the two older Ashbrooke boys by his lordship's first wife, and now lived a simple but comfortable life in the cottage, on a pension provided by Lord Ashbrooke.

'I am going to catch the carrier's wagon.'

'You'll not do that today, m'dear, the roads are impassable. Didn't you know that?'

'Oh, no. Now what am I to do?'

'Best come in and sit by the fire; you look frozen.'

She turned and followed the old lady into the cottage. It was a very tiny dwelling, but sparkling clean, and a good fire burned in the grate of the living room. The table had been laid for one and a delicious smell was coming from a pot suspended over the flames. She moved towards the warmth and held out her frozen hands.

'Sit down, child,' Becky invited. 'And take off those shoes and stockings or you will catch your death of cold.' Taking Annette's cloak, she hung it over the back of a chair close to the fire. 'Whatever possessed you to come out on a day like this? I cannot imagine what her ladyship was thinking of to allow it.'

'It was her ladyship sent me out,' she said, divesting herself of her wet footwear.

Becky looked towards the portmanteau, which had been dropped by the door. 'You've never been turned off?'

'Yes.'

'Goodness me, whatever have you done to deserve that?'

She looked up at the sympathetic woman and blinked back tears. 'Been a gullible fool.'

'Oh.' The old lady digested this with apparent understanding, then she said, 'It was Jeremy, I suppose?'

'I'm not saying.'

'You do not have to. I have seen him about the estate with you and the children and I can guess. Of the two boys in my care, he was by far the biggest handful. Not that Charles was an angel, far from it, but he was always the more thoughtful and responsible of the two. But I am surprised at you being taken in.'

Looking back, so was she, but it had begun so slowly she had been lulled into feeling easy with him. Back from university, and because of the war unable to go on a Grand Tour, which most young men of his rank usually did, he had been kicking his heels about the estate, ripe for mischief. He would make excuses to join her when she was out with the children, and then he would make himself agreeable, talking of nothing in particular, strolling along beside her, being charming and helpful. Then it had progressed to compliments on her good looks and her cleverness, and later he would send the children on ahead so that he could take her hand and flirt with her. And she, fool that she was, had soaked it up, believing him to be sincere.

She had been too naïve to see where it was all leading until the night he had come to her room and sat on the bed, saying he could not sleep for thinking about her. It had not been until he'd started to touch her through her nightclothes, murmuring endearments the whole time, that the alarm bells had begun to ring in her brain and she'd thrust his hand away and told him to go back to bed. If he had really loved her, as he'd said he did, he would have stopped then, but he took no notice, hardly seemed to hear her. She had not dared cry out for fear of waking the children, who slept in the rooms adjoining hers. Instead she had struggled silently and ineffectually.

He had been a bit sheepish afterwards, grinning while he dressed himself and kissing her lightly before he left her room, as if he had done nothing untoward. 'Part of your education,' he had told her. It had certainly been that. If it had taught her one thing it had taught her not to trust anyone—especially not young men with bright gold hair, mischievous blue eyes and winning smiles.

'What are you going to do?' the old lady asked.

'I don't know. I must find work where I can live in until—' She stopped suddenly, unable to contemplate the future. The prospect of the birth itself was frightening enough without the added worry of not knowing how they were both to live. The thought came to her that perhaps they would not live, either of them. Many women died in childbirth. Wealthy women as well as poor ones. It had happened to the wife of Mr Charles, so she had heard from servants' gossip. She had never met him, but if he was anything like his brother then it was as well she had not.

'When is it due?'

'Her ladyship called their physician in and he said about the beginning of June.'

'Some time yet, then...' Becky paused, then added, 'I have been thinking. My sister Martha takes in boarders and might be able to help. She is a widow and lives in Norwich. You will need to pay her; she is not a wealthy woman.'

'Oh, do you think she would? I would be so very grateful. I am sure I can find work even if it is only sewing.'

It had been easy to say that, sitting in a cosy room by a warm fire, with the bowl of soup Becky had just handed her in front of her. Since then she had discovered just how hard it was for a mother with a child and no man to support her.

Becky had offered her a bed for the night, saying she couldn't turn a dog out in that weather, and she had accepted gratefully. It was more than she could have hoped for when she had left the Hall, but she had been well aware it was only a temporary reprieve, that the future had to be faced. Shunned by society, spat upon, refused work and lodgings, all because of a child and the lack of a wedding band.

She had kept out of sight while she was with Becky, afraid that someone might see her and report her presence to the Hall, but three days later the roads had been cleared and she had set out on the carrier's cart to Bury St Edmunds, where she had boarded the stage to Norwich. Inside her bag was a letter to Mrs Porter, Becky's widowed sister, who lived in St Ann's Lane.

Mrs Porter was not at all like her motherly sibling. She was thin and hard-faced, but while Annette had been able to pay for lodgings she had been prepared to tolerate her, believing her to be Mrs Annie Anstey, the widow of a soldier killed in Portugal. It was there that her son had been born and put into her arms, and in that moment she had known that, whatever had brought him into life, she would nurture him and love him with every ounce of her strength. That was what had been missing ever since her mother had died: someone she could truly love and who might love her.

Lady Ashbrooke's five guineas, along with the proceeds from selling her mother's wedding ring and a small pendant which had been all that was left of her jewellery, had kept her going through her pregnancy, but a week ago all but a few shillings had gone, and she had been obliged to admit she did not have the rent money.

'I cannot keep beggars,' Mrs Porter had said, ignoring the fact that Annette had been helping with the housework and cooking for the other lodgers in return for a rebate on her rent. 'There are others ready and willing to pay well for a room as good as this. I only took you in because Becky asked me to.'

'I know. I'll find work. If you would be so good as to keep an eye on Timothy while I go out, I am sure I can earn the money for our keep.'

'No. I am not a children's nurse. I don't like children—especially when they cry all the time…'

'He can't help that, poor lamb.'

'No, but my other lodgers don't like it. I am sorry, Mrs Anstey, I have told a young couple they shall have this room. He is in work and there will be no trouble with the rent. I will give you to the end of the week…'

'But that's only four days away!'

'Then the sooner you start looking, the better, wouldn't you say?'

In despair she had packed her few things, picked up her child, wrapped in a shawl, and ventured out onto the street. And had ended up here, in this terrible hole. Mrs Grosse, who had a large family and had said it would be no trouble to keep an eye on Timmy while Annette worked, had demanded rent in advance, and so she had given the woman her last two shillings. Until she was paid for the work she was doing she had nothing. Nothing at all.

The sewing dropped into her lap and she looked across the room at her sleeping child and felt a tug at her heart. He was so beautiful and so helpless. Whatever happened she must not fail him. Sighing heavily, she bent once more to her needle.

CHAPTER TWO

CHARLES walked on, ruminating on the encounter with the young woman with the parcel. It reminded him of something his brother had said. 'Out of the ordinary,' he had told him, describing their stepmother's nursery maid. 'If she were dressed up a bit you could take her out and about in Society and no one the wiser. She has—what do you call it?—presence. Yes, that's it. Presence. She speaks as well as we do and she holds her head up, and she has the most lustrous dark brown hair and wonderful greeny grey eyes…'

He had smiled at the time, putting it down to Jeremy's fancifulness, but it exactly described the young lady he had just seen—except for the hair which, though dark brown, could hardly be called lustrous. She was too thin to be beautiful, but the rest fitted. He had almost spoken to her, accused her of being Annette Ryston, but had desisted, unwilling to make a fool of himself. If she was not the nursery maid then she would have laughed in his face or, worse, thought he was seeking an hour or so of pleasure. After all, Norwich was a large city, teeming with life, and there must be thousands of girls fitting the maid's description. It did not matter anyway, because he had the girl's direction and would see the real Annie Ryston there.

He stopped outside the boarding house on the corner of St Ann's Lane and King Street, hesitating whether to go in or not. It looked respectable enough: the windows gleamed, the curtains were clean, the step scrubbed and the brass knocker on the door shone with much polishing. If she was staying here then she was not doing too badly and perhaps it would be best to leave well alone. There was no proof of anything, and Jeremy had denied he had got the girl with child. Jeremy, his brother. Was he his brother's keeper?

The answer to that was that, in the absence of the brother himself, he was certainly his offspring's keeper—if such a child existed. He went up the steps and knocked.

A skinny little maid opened the door, and then left him on the step while she went to speak to her mistress. He did not have long to wait. Mrs Porter arrived, tying a fresh apron about her waist. He doffed his beaver. 'Good afternoon, ma'am. I am looking for Mrs Anstey—Mrs Annie Anstey. I am told she resides here.'

'No more, she don't.'

'Oh, do you know where she has gone?'

'No.' She was eyeing him up and down, probably coming to the conclusion he was the child's father. 'You've come a bit late in the day, hen't you?' she went on. 'She could ha' done with you a couple of months since.'

'She had a child, then?'

'Don't you know?'

'No. I met her husband out in Spain and I have a message for her from him.'

'Hmph,' she muttered, evidently not believing a word. 'I still don' know where she's gone. Try the work'us.'

He took his leave and went to the workhouse. She was not there, had never been there, and he was thankful for that; it was a dreadful place. Men separated from their families, mothers from their children, brothers from sisters, and they all looked listless and downbeat. He left and returned to the street, glad that he would never have to enter such a place, but wondering where to go next.

Standing on the pavement with his back to that forbidding building, with the sun beating down on him, he was transported back to Spain, to the last time he had seen his brother. When the command had come to move out of their winter quarters and pursue the enemy, the troops had marched with a will. None more so than himself. He hadn't been able to wait to get at the enemy. His quarrel with them was more than a soldier's duty, it was personal. He blamed them for the death of his wife and baby son nearly four years before, notwithstanding they had been safe home in England at the time. He had convinced himself that if he had been with them, if he had been at home and not waging war hundreds of miles away, they might have lived. He had been so ridden with guilt over it the burden had become intolerable. It had eased it to take his venom out on the enemy, and Napoleon Bonaparte in particular, who had started the conflict. He had vowed he would not rest or go home until he had seen him beaten.

It was a vow he had been obliged to retract when Jeremy had been mortally wounded at the Battle of Vittoria. His brother should never have been sent to war; he had not been soldier material and he cursed the unknown girl who had made it happen. He had known his father and stepmother would take the news very hard, and he could not let them learn it from an impersonal letter. He had seen his brother decently buried and come home.

He had been right; his father was wretched and his stepmother could do nothing to help him. Jeremy, the golden boy, had been his father's favourite, and he was dead. Charles knew he ought to go to Brookside, the country house he had shared with Arabella, but he could not bring himself to do so. It was not only that he could not bear to be reminded of her, but because he did not like to leave his father, who went about the estate with hardly a civil word to anyone and, when at home, sat in his chair in the library and brooded.

'I wish I could do something for him,' he had told his stepmother. 'He needs something to occupy him and take his mind off it.'

'You could furnish him with a legitimate grandson.'

'I could, but to do that I must marry again.' He remembered pausing, because her use of the word legitimate had made him think. 'I am hardly likely to come up with an illegitimate one, Mama.'

'No, but I think Jeremy has.'

They had been breakfasting together at the time, and he had put down the piece of toast he'd been buttering and stared at her. 'Tell me about it.'

And so she had told him about Annie, the nursery maid. He'd listened, remembering his conversation with Jeremy. 'He told me about her,' he said when she finished. 'But he said it was only a romp and he had not got her with child.'

'He did not know. I sent him away. I feel dreadful about it now. Not about the girl—because Jeremy was only doing what hundreds of other young men have done, trying out his manhood. It is up to the girls to stop them if they do not like it—but because I sent him to his death.'

Charles did not agree with her about the girls. Her attitude, and that of his brother and other aristocratic youths like him, was careless in the extreme, but he did not say so. Instead he asked what had become of the nursery maid.

'I have no idea. Does it matter?'

'I think it does. I think I should try and find her.'

'You never mean to bring her back here?' She was horrified at the idea.

'No, of course not. It would not do. But I can at least make sure she is not in want. If there is a child, she is not going to find life easy, is she? She might need help.'

'She should have thought of that before…'

'Mama, can you not find it in your heart to be charitable? After all, Jeremy must share some of the blame. If he had lived, I am sure he would not have let her starve.'

The trouble was that no one at Riseborough Hall knew where Annie had gone. She had not mixed with the other servants and had kept herself to herself. 'Too high and mighty for her own good,' Miss Burnley had told him.

He had found out quite by chance when he'd visited Becky, something he always did when he was at Riseborough. After their mother had died, giving birth to Jeremy, she had been the only mother they had known until his father had married again, and by that time they'd been grown up. Becky had always been a safe haven whenever they needed one.

She had been distressed on learning of Jeremy's death, and had spent several minutes talking about him and the mischief he'd used to get into. 'When you were at home you would always haul him out of his pickles,' she said, dabbing at her tears. 'But you weren't here that last time.'

'You mean the business over the nursery maid?'

'Yes.'

It was then, after a little hesitation, that she told him of Annette's stay with her and gave him the direction of her sister. And after all that Annette had moved on and his journey had been in vain. He turned on his heel and went back to his room at The Maid's Head. He had tried and there was little else he could do; the girl had gone, obviously intent on not being found.

And then he thought of the woman with the parcel. *Could* it have been Annette? She had had no child with her, but she could have left it somewhere—farmed it out, had it adopted. The idea did not sit well with him at all, and he knew he had to find her if only to confirm she was not the woman he sought.

Annette, taking the sewing back the following day, had the uncomfortable feeling she was being followed. She tried dodging down side streets, but still she felt that shadow behind her. She could not think who would want anything from her. Her purse was empty and the parcel she was carrying contained nothing of any value, though she knew people had been attacked and even murdered for less.

She hurried on, turning left before she reached the castle. It was a forbidding building which housed the city's prison population, and she always passed it as quickly as she could, as if afraid that she might be drawn into it for some misdemeanour she was not even aware of. It was then she saw him—the man she had stumbled into the day before. If he was her follower, he must have turned down a side street to come at her from a different direction.

She put her head up and made to pass him, but he barred her way and doffed his hat. 'Good morning, ma'am,' he said cheerfully. 'We meet again.'

Could it be coincidence? Why would he remember meeting her, of all the hundreds of people that thronged the city's streets? 'Good morning, sir,' she said, wishing he did not look so much like Jeremy. It was unnerving—more so when she carried on walking and he dropped into step beside her.

'I was hoping you might help me,' he said.

'Help you? If you are looking for directions, then you

have asked the wrong person. I have not long lived in Norwich…'

'Did you, by any chance, once live in Riseborough in Suffolk?'

The shock made her stumble, but she quickly recovered her balance and began walking again, faster than ever.

He was easily able to keep up with her. 'I think from your reaction I might be right. Is your name Annette Ryston?'

She had been expecting the next question and was ready for it. 'My name is Mrs Anstey.'

'Ah, then I am right. Becky said that was the name you intended to use.'

'Becky? I do not think I know the lady.'

'Oh, Annie, you know her very well, and so do I.'

She stopped suddenly and turned towards him. 'Who are you?'

'I am Major Charles Ashbrooke.'

She should have known; his likeness to Jeremy was uncanny. It was a likeness that had been passed on to her son. She saw it every day when she nursed him: Jeremy's golden hair and blue eyes, the squarish line of his jaw—a stubborn jaw even in one so young—but it did not fill her with any desire to see the young man again. She could not, would not forgive him.

'What do you want with me? If Jeremy has sent you…'

'No, my brother did not send me—unless it be from the grave. He is dead.'

'Dead?' The stark word shocked her, but being in

mourning probably accounted for his dark clothes. 'How?'

'I could explain if you would listen.'

'Why should I? He is…was…nothing to me.'

'Really? Now, do you know, I rather thought you had once been close?'

'Close. That's a funny way of putting it.'

'Putting what?'

'What he did to me. I did not ask for it. He came to my room and forced himself on me. Did he tell you that?' Her voice betrayed her bitterness.

'No, he did not.' He was shaken to the core. He knew his brother had been a rakeshame, who had loved and laughed without a thought for the morrow, but he had never thought him capable of such a despicable act. A tumble, he had said, adding that he did not know what the girl had to complain of. Had she complained? 'I find that impossible to believe.'

'I care not whether you believe it or not, sir, it is the truth.'

'Not something said to make you feel less guilty?'

'I do not feel guilty. I never have. I feel hurt and…angry.'

'Then all I can do is offer a heartfelt and humble apology on behalf of my brother.'

'It was not your fault,' she conceded.

'You did not stay at Mrs Porter's lodging house?'

'It did not suit me.'

'So you have moved on. Are you going to tell me where?'

'No. I cannot for the life of me think what you want

with me. Lady Ashbrooke turned me off in a snow-storm without a character. I have no business with anyone from Riseborough Hall. If, as you say, Jeremy is dead, then I am sorry for you, but it is nothing to do with me.'

'You are sorry for me?' He frowned. 'I think perhaps the shoe is on the other foot.'

'I do not need or want your pity, Major Ashbrooke.'

She was too proud for her own good. 'Then I will not offer it. Where are you going?'

'I am going to deliver this parcel.'

'It looks heavy. Please let me carry it for you.' He reached out and took it from her fingers. 'That's better.'

They walked side by side in silence, making their way round the cattle market, noisy with farmers selling and buying the Highland cattle which had been driven down from Scotland to be fattened up before being sent to London. He stuck to her side, one hand on her elbow to guide her through the throng as a gentleman would a lady. She should have thrown him off and left him, but he had her parcel, and that represented money and food she could not afford to lose.

'Where are we bound?' he asked.

'*We* are bound nowhere, Major. I am going to St Stephen's Street, and as we are nearly there I bid you good day.' She held out her hand for the parcel.

Reluctantly he relinquished it and bowed to her. He watched as she hurried along the road, and then followed her to see her turning in at the gate to one of the large houses that lined the road. Did she live there? He did not think so, because she had said she was delivering the package. He hadn't done with her. He could not get out of his head her accusation that Jeremy had forced himself on her. He could not believe it of his brother, but if she was telling the truth then it was his responsibility to try and make amends, if such a thing were possible. One thing Jeremy had been right about: she was definitely not the usual run of domestic servant.

He stood, idly leaning against a tree trunk, watching the house for her to emerge, wondering what it was that made her so different. She was clean, for a start. Her face shone with cleanliness, as did her hands and fingernails. Her gingham day dress, which had once been smart and modish, was now sadly dated, but that, too, was clean. It was not that. Jeremy had called her a pretty little thing, but she was more than that: she was beautiful. She had classic oval features, large luminous soft green eyes, neat brows and a firm mouth—a kissable mouth, he realised with a sudden start. No wonder Jeremy had been attracted to her.

He watched her come out of the house, still bearing the brown paper parcel—or perhaps it was another one. He wondered what was in it. Her step was light and she carried herself like a lady, back straight and head up. Again Jeremy's description came to his aid. Presence. She made everyone and everything about her look drab. He marvelled, considering she must be living in very poor circumstances. Unless she had a wealthy lover, of course; perhaps Jeremy had not been the only one? But a wealthy lover would surely have dressed her better than that.

He pushed himself off the tree and walked towards

her, admitting he did not like that idea at all. He had to know.

'Major Ashbrooke,' she said, trying hard not to let his continuing presence disconcert her. 'I should have thought you had something more important to do than hang about here.'

'At the moment, no. Allow me to escort you.' Again he took her burden from her.

'You do not know where I am going.' She was going to buy food and then hurry home. She had to rid herself of him before that, because it was important he did not see her son. It was the child that had brought him to Norwich; she was sure of it. Lady Ashbrooke had told her never to come back, and Annette did not doubt she had meant it, but perhaps she had had a twinge of conscience about the baby. Or had the Major come of his own accord? He struck her as a man who would follow his own path, never mind what others thought. He was so handsome and so very…very masculine. A strong man—not only physically, but in every other sense. Stronger than Jeremy, who had had little difficulty in overpowering her.

'Perhaps you would be so good as to tell me.'

'No, it is none of your business. I have left Riseborough. I am no longer employed there. So you cannot dictate to me.'

He smiled at her outspokenness as he fell into step beside her. 'I would not dream of doing so, but I think we should talk, don't you?'

'What about?'

'I want to hear what happened…'

'Between Jeremy and me? I told you. I have no wish to repeat it.'

'I find it hard to credit my brother would harm you, and am more inclined to think there was some misunderstanding.'

'There was no misunderstanding, Major. Do you know what it is like to have someone force themselves on you—someone you thought was honourable, someone you trusted? No, of course you do not. Nor do you know what it is like to be blamed…'

'No, but you could tell me. Look here, Annie…'

'I did not give you permission to address me by that name.' It was said with all the hauteur she could muster.

He smiled. He knew he had a battle on his hands. 'Miss Ryston, then. Or Mrs Anstey—whichever you prefer. All I was going to suggest was that you join me in a cup of tea somewhere we can talk quietly. The last thing I want is to upset you, or rake up matters that are distasteful to you…'

He was walking beside her for a reason, and though she wanted to be rid of him she had to admit a certain curiosity. 'What do you want to talk about?'

'What you have been doing since you left Riseborough. I am sure it has not been easy, and if you need help…' In the face of her antagonism he did not know why he was persisting. He did want to help her, he felt it was his duty, but it was more than that. He wanted to get to know her, to find out how someone so obviously educated and well spoken had come to be working at Riseborough Hall in the first place. Becky had told him that she would not be at all surprised to learn there was more to the girl's background than anyone knew. She could, of course, have learned her ladylike ways from being in the households of aristocratic employers, but he did not think poise like that could be learned that way.

Annette, unaware of his thoughts, gave a wry smile. 'Help. Now that's something I could have used six months ago, but no longer.' She held out her hand for the parcel. 'Go home, Major Ashbrooke. Go home. Your conscience need not trouble you.' They were making their way towards the river and soon she would have to turn along the towpath to reach her lodgings. She certainly did not want him to accompany her there.

He gave her the package and bowed. 'Can I persuade you to meet me again? I shall be in the cathedral tomorrow at noon. We could talk there uninterrupted...' His request was accompanied by a smile which lit his eyes and took away the somewhat sombre expression he had hitherto shown. That was another difference between him and Jeremy. Jeremy's eyes had always been full of mischief; the Major's were deeper and darker and in some way sorrowful, as if he had forgotten how to laugh. But he was in mourning, so perhaps that accounted for it. 'I promise I will not detain you a moment longer than you wish.'

'I do not think so,' she said.

For the second time that day he watched her hurry away from him. Had he done all he could? Should he have offered her money? If he'd read her character aright, she would have thrown it in his face.

He waited until she had turned the corner and then

followed her. He was just in time to see her picking her way along a street whose gutters ran with filth and stank to heaven. She stopped to make some purchases at a corner shop, before walking on and turning in at the door of a miserable-looking dwelling. His dogs were better housed.

Resisting the impulse to bang on the door and drag her away, he turned and went back to his hotel. If she did not turn up at the cathedral he knew where to find her again. In hell, by the look of it.

CHAPTER THREE

STOPPING only to buy a few provisions, Annette hurried back to Timmy. She had been more shaken up by her encounter with Major Ashbrooke than she cared to admit. He had seemed sympathetic to her plight, and had treated her courteously, but that could all have been a charade to get his hands on her son. His nephew. Help, he had said. But help came in many guises. His concern was not for her but for the boy. Could he legally take him from her? She had no idea. But she did know that money could buy most things, not least a good lawyer, and that was something *she* could not afford.

She must keep Major Charles Ashbrooke from finding out about Timothy. If he ever accosted her again, she would have to say she had no child. But Becky must have told him the state she was in when she befriended her, and he had spoken to Mrs Porter. That lady certainly knew Timothy had been born, and had been alive only the week before. She was almost in a panic by the time she reached home, and once again Timothy was crying. Oh, how she wished she did not have to leave him with that slatternly woman! She ought to find other lodgings, but where could she go that was as cheap?

She changed him, then rocked him in her arms, her tears mingling with his until his heartbroken sobs turned to the occasional hiccup. She pulled herself together and fed him, but when she had nothing left in her to give he was still hungry. Wondering if he might take bread and milk, she put him down, poured a little milk from the can she had bought into a pan and took it downstairs to Mrs Grosse's kitchen, intending to ask if she might heat it on her fire.

As soon as she opened the door she wished she could retreat. Except for Mr Grosse, who was working on the wherries that plied on the river and broads, the whole scruffy family were crowded into the small room, and there was one she had not seen before. He was a young man in his twensties, sitting at the table and apparently entertaining the company with a tale of his adventures while he ate an enormous dinner which made her empty stomach rumble.

He looked up as she entered. 'Why, who've we got here?' he said, eyeing her from top to toe appreciatively.

'This here's Mrs Anstey,' his mother told him. 'She hev took the attic room.'

'Is that so?' He stood up and walked all round Annette. He was a big man, dressed in cord trousers and a fustian jacket. A spotted handkerchief was tied about his throat. He had gingery hair and a freckled, weatherbeaten face.

'Cecil is my eldest,' Mrs Grosse told her. 'He's a drover, just down from Scotland with a herd of cattle.'

'How do you do?' Annette said, wishing she could turn and run.

'How do you do?' he mimicked, laughing at her refined accent, so very different from the broad Norfolk vowels of his family. 'Why, I do very well. How about yew?'

'I am sorry to intrude, ma'am.' She ignored him to address Mrs Grosse. 'I'll come back later.'

'Not so fast,' Cecil said. 'We hen't got to know one another yet.'

Annette felt a frisson of fear. His steady gaze was more than appreciative; it was lascivious. She wanted to escape, but the thought of her hungry child kept her where she was. She held out the pan of milk. 'I wonder if you would be kind enough to heat this up for me, Mrs Grosse?'

The woman took it and set it on the fire. 'Sit down. We was all hearin' on Cecil's tale of Scotland. It's a mighty long way, did yer know that?'

'Yes, I believe it is.'

'Walked all the way with two hundred head o' cattle,' the young man said. 'I'll wager you never met anyone doin' that afore.'

'No, I haven't.' She did not like the look he was giving her, and was glad when the milk bubbled up and Mrs Grosse took the pan off the stove.

Before Annette could reach for it Cecil had taken it. 'I'll carry it up for you.'

'There's no need. I can manage.'

Like someone else she had known, he would not take no for an answer and followed her up the stairs to her room. She turned at the door to thank him, but he walked in and put the pan down on the table. Then he saw Timmy.

'Oh, you've a babby.'

'Yes.'

'Where's his pa?'

'Dead. Please excuse me, I must feed him.' She ushered him towards the door.

He laughed, and reached out to touch her cheek, making her flinch. 'Later, then. I'll look forward to it.' He left, still laughing.

As soon as he had gone she locked the door and propped a chair against it. Then she broke up a slice of bread in a basin and poured the milk on it. Picking Timmy up, she sat at the table and spooned a little into his mouth. He spat it out at first, but she persevered and in the end he ate quite a bit of it. She finished the rest herself and put him to bed. And then it was back to her sewing.

But she was worried. Cecil Grosse was a threat to her peace of mind—certainly more worrying than Major Ashbrooke. Unlike the Major, he would not treat her with courtesy. He was strong enough to take her by force, and then... The prospect of his dirty hands on her and the possible consequences could not be borne. Tomorrow, after she had returned the mending and been paid, she must find somewhere else to live. Somewhere safe. Perhaps with a few shillings in her pocket she could find somewhere more wholesome.

She slept badly that night, because half her mind was on her dilemma and half was listening for footsteps outside her room. Once she heard someone rattling her doorknob and a soft laugh, and she knew her fears were not unfounded. She rose early the next morning, knowing she had a busy and trying day ahead of her. She could not carry her belongings, her child and the heavy parcel of sewing all at once, so she left Timmy with her landlady and returned the sewing.

With two shillings and sixpence in her pocket, she returned to her lodgings at a run, where she packed her belongings, wrapped Timmy in a shawl and told the astonished Mrs Grosse she was leaving.

'I have decided to go to my husband's family,' she told her. Then, weighed down with her baggage and her child, she walked out, not knowing where she was going. She must find lodgings and more work. She must not give any of the Ashbrooke family cause to accuse her of not being able to look after her son. They were wealthy enough and influential enough to take him from her. That they might not want to do that did not occur to her. He was beautiful and adorable; who would not want him?

Charles sat in the cool of the cathedral and wondered if she would come. He wanted her to come. She intrigued him. His head was full of questions. Where had she come from when she'd arrived at Riseborough? What was her background? Who were her parents? Did she really have a child? And, if she did, was it Jeremy's or did it belong to someone else? She might be the harlot his mother had called her, but if she was she was being very clever about it—clever enough to disdain his help to begin with, perhaps in the hope of getting more out of him. Why did he not want to believe that? She had, after all, been at pains not to let him know the dreadful conditions under which she lived. The child could not possibly thrive there.

It was nearly half past twelve, and he was about to leave when he saw her. She was carrying a large bag and a bundle. He realised the bundle was a baby wrapped in a shawl when she dropped into the pew beside him. She looked exhausted. Her face was white with strain, and her lovely eyes looked even more troubled than they had the day before.

'What has happened?' he asked, not bothering with a greeting.

She looked up at him and a tear rolled down her cheek. He reached out and wiped it with the back of his finger. His gentleness seemed to open a dam inside her and she gave way to sobs.

He was in no hurry. He waited, not daring to touch her, though he was sorely tempted to take her into his arms to try and comfort her. He could imagine her reaction if he tried that. Instead he offered her his handkerchief.

'I am sorry,' she said at last, wiping away her tears.

'No need to be sorry. Tell me how I can help?'

She gulped. 'I have had to leave my lodgings…'

'Why?'

She gave a bitter laugh. 'History was about to repeat itself. The young man of the house…'

'Oh, I am sorry for that. What can I do to help?'

'Would you...?' She gulped, swallowing her pride. 'Would you lend me some money? All the rooms I have looked at are beyond my means at present. I can get work. I will be able to repay you.'

It had taken all her courage to ask him, but after a morning of trudging about the city she was exhausted. Either the rooms she'd looked at were too expensive, or they were even filthier than Mrs Grosse's hovel—and even then the landladies would not countenance the baby. In the end, it had been the workhouse or the Major. No choice at all.

'Certainly I will. You should have come to me before. Shall we go to my hotel for some refreshment? Later we will see about decent lodgings for you.'

'I did not mean... Oh, dear... I do not want to put you to that trouble. Two or three guineas will suffice, then I will be on my way.'

He was not going to let her go again. 'Nonsense!' he said. 'You are done in.'

That was true. A sleepless night and the burdens she carried—not only in her arms but in her head—had ensured she could hardly put one foot in front of the other, and she had been glad to sink into the pew beside him. But there was still some spirit left in her. Enough to question his motives.

'Just what do you want with me, Major? If you think that because your brother had his way you can follow his example...'

'Do you imagine every man you meet is after your body?' he demanded sharply. 'It is a very lovely body, but I have no use for it.'

She gave a cracked laugh. 'Well, that has put me in my place and no mistake.'

Even *in extremis* she could find a light-hearted retort, he noted. 'Shall we stop sparring with each other and decide to be friends?' He reached forward and drew the shawl away from the baby's face. There was no doubt in his mind the child was Jeremy's. The shape of the face, the slightly square jaw, the tuft of very fair hair and the wide blue eyes that looked up at him unblinkingly proclaimed it. He was sorry he had ever doubted it. But it did not answer her accusation that she had been taken against her will. 'A boy?' he queried.

'Yes. His name is Timothy.'

'You did not name him for his papa, then?'

'No, I did not. Why should I do that after what he did to me?'

He ignored that. 'Come back to my hotel and take some refreshment. Then we can decide what to do.'

'*We* do not decide anything, sir. *I* decide.'

He laughed. 'Then do you think you could decide to humour me, just this once? I give you my word that after we have spoken together you may walk away, if you wish, and I will not attempt to follow you.'

She had a feeling the loan depended on her complying, and she desperately needed it. Without it she had nowhere to sleep that night and no food either. The dreaded workhouse loomed. She looked up into his face, a lean, bronzed face, with fine lines at each side of the eyes. The eyes themselves were gazing back at her, studying her, reading her hesitation in her expression. It was all about pride and independence and motherly love. She adored her son. Should she not do all she could for him? And if that meant being beholden to this man, then should she not take what he offered? After all, Timothy was his brother's baby. And perhaps he was sincere.

'Very well.'

He did not attempt to take the child from her, but picked up her bag and led the way. The Maid's Head was only just across the road from the cathedral, and he was soon ushering her through the door. He left her while he spoke to the proprietor, and a few minutes later they were shown upstairs to a large sitting room with an adjoining bedroom.

'These are not my rooms,' he hastened to assure her. 'So sit down and make yourself comfortable. There is food on the way. What does the baby take?'

'He takes his mother's milk,' she said. 'Unlike the aristocracy, I do not farm my child out to a wet nurse, and would not even if I could afford it.'

'Good for you. You will need some privacy. I shall go downstairs and hurry that waiter up.' And with that he left the room.

She stood looking about her for a moment, lost in a kind of trance. Was he just being kind or was there more to it? She could not make up her mind. Experience had told her to be wary, but instinct told her she could trust him. But how far? She could not answer that, and decided her priority was to feed Timothy and leave the questions until later.

With the baby fed and changed, she took him into the bedroom and put him in the middle of the bed, piling the pillows round him to stop him rolling off. Then she took advantage of the water and towels on the wash-stand to clean and tidy herself. She had just finished when there was a tap at the door, and she opened it to Charles, who came into the room followed by two waiters carrying plates and cutlery, a bottle of wine, two glasses and an array of food which they set out on the table before bowing their way out.

'What have you done with Timothy?' he asked.

She nodded towards the bedroom. He walked over to the bed and stood looking down at the child. It brought a lump to his throat, remembering the child he had lost, the son he had never seen. He and Bella had both loved children, and they had hoped the child would be the first of four or five. But it was not to be. The nursery suite they had made ready was, like the rest of the house, empty and shut up. He reached out and stroked the little one's cheek with a gentle finger. How soft his skin was!

'He is a contented child,' he said to Annette, who had come to stand beside him.

She laughed. 'He has just been fed. You should hear him when he is hungry.'

'I should not like to think he was hungry,' he murmured. 'Nor you, come to that. Let us go and eat.'

They returned to the table and sat down opposite each other. 'Now, let us be civilised,' he said. 'May I help you to meat pie? I can vouch for its goodness; I had some yesterday.'

Bemused, she sat and watched him heaping her plate with pie and vegetables. The delicious smell was inviting and she pulled herself together to tuck in with a will. She would have been a fool to turn her nose up at it when she had no idea where her next meal was coming from.

'Tell me about yourself,' he said.

'What do you want to know?'

'Everything. Who your parents were, where you were born, how you were educated, how you came to be working at Riseborough Hall.'

'Goodness, that is a tall order.'

'We are not in a hurry, are we?'

'I need to look for lodgings…'

'There is plenty of time for that. Is there some secret about your past you do not wish to divulge?'

'Certainly not!'

'Fire away, then.'

'I was born in India nineteen years ago…'

'India!'

'Yes, is that so very strange? My father was a Captain in the East India Company…'

'And his name was Timothy.'

'Yes, but how did you guess?'

'You would not name the infant after his papa, but his grandfather is another matter.'

'Yes. Captain Timothy Ryston. He died of a fever when I was eight and my mother brought me home to England. She set up a school for young ladies and we managed very well.'

Along with a love of literature, embroidery and drawing, her mama had taught the girls how to make polite conversation, how to curtsey and to dance, how to rebuke a too-ardent swain and how to avoid the pitfalls of indecorous behaviour. But it had all been very superficial, and had told them nothing at all about men and their desires. The subject would have been considered far too delicate for young ladies, but it might have helped *her* to know.

'What about the rest of your family?'

'I know of none. I had no siblings, and my father said he did not remember his parents. He was brought up in an orphanage until he was old enough to work. I am not sure about my mother's parents. From hints she let drop I gathered they did not approve of her choice of husband. That was why Papa took Mama to India. He expected to make his fortune out there and vindicate himself, but it was not to be.'

'So you never met your grandparents? Your mama did not take you to see them when you came back?'

'No, but I remember her taking me to see a big house. I have no idea where it was. We went there on the stage. We did not go up the drive and I assumed she had once worked there. She did not say.'

'But your mother must have been educated if she could set up a school?'

'Yes, she was.'

'And she educated you?'

'Yes. Then, when I was old enough, I began teaching the younger children.'

'So what happened?'

'Mama…' She paused and gulped, unwilling to remember that dreadful day when her contented life had been shattered. 'She was hit by a runaway horse and a high-perch phaeton when she was out shopping.' The horror of it came back to her as if it was only the day before, and she struggled with her emotions. 'Mama had just left the house, saying she was going to buy material for the young ladies' embroidery class and would not be gone long.' She shuddered. 'I heard the crash from indoors, and then horses neighing and someone screaming, and I ran outside. She was…she was…lying in the road under the wheels of the phaeton…'

'Do not distress yourself, my dear,' he said gently, reaching across and putting his hand over hers on the table—though he made no attempt to grip it, and she was easily able to withdraw it. 'You do not need to go on if you would rather not.'

'There isn't much more. She never regained consciousness and died later that day. The school had to close. I could not stay in the house alone, so I had to find work where I could live in. Lady Somers, whose daughter came to the school, recommended me to Lady Ashbrooke. You know the rest.' She took a gulp of her wine.

'Thank you. Tell me, what was your mother's maiden name?'

'I do not know. She never said.'

'You must have sorted out her belongings when she died. Did you find nothing to give you a clue?'

'No.' She paused. 'But I remember I did find a piece of paper with a name on it. Goodness, what was it? Fettle-something. I forget.'

'Not Anstey?'

'No, not Anstey. I made that up. It suddenly came into my head when I was trying to think of something to call myself.'

'I see. Was there an address on the paper?'

'No, it was a piece torn off the top of a letter, I think. It was probably someone Mama had done business with. She had used it as a bookmark, so perhaps it meant nothing at all…'

'Were you never curious? About your mother's parents, I mean?'

'No. If they could not see what a fine man my father was, and how much he and Mama adored each other, then they were not worth knowing.'

She did not want to say any more on the subject and he did not press her. They stopped talking to eat, then he put down his cutlery and pushed his plate away. 'Tell me about Jeremy.'

'I did tell you. If you do not believe me…'

'I did not say that. I want to try and understand. He was my brother, after all.'

So she told him, and he listened. 'I did not want it to happen, Major. I tried to push him off, tried to appeal to his sense of right and wrong, but he was in no mood to listen. He had always been good company, and had gone out of his way to be helpful and charming, and I suppose I was too trusting. I was never so mistaken in anyone. Afterwards I was so angry. What he did deprived me of a job and a home and left me destitute.' She paused. 'But you could say there is a brighter side. I have my son, and I will love him and look after him to my last breath.'

'Of course. Does that mean you have given up hating his papa?'

She gave a little smile. 'Perhaps.'

'I am glad,' he said. 'Hate is such a destructive emotion…' He stopped speaking, wondering why he had said that. There had been hate enough in his heart after Bella had died, and Jeremy too. He remembered how he had cursed the woman who had caused his brother to be sent to war—the woman who sat opposite him now. He could not hate her, could not even blame her.

'I can't believe he is dead,' she said. 'How did it happen?'

'Do you really want to hear about that?'

'Yes, if it is not too painful for you. People at home just read about the battles in the newspapers. They are told whether it was a setback, which I think is probably a euphemism for a defeat, or whether it was a victory, but not much detail.'

He had ceased to be surprised at the way she expressed herself. It was the way she had been brought up, and he suspected she had an innate breeding that even she did not know about. 'Probably because it would be too unpleasant,' he said. 'The newspapers like to glorify war. It is not glorious, though many of the young men who go out to fight go with the idea that it is. They are soon disillusioned.'

'There speaks the veteran.' Her laugh was a pleasant sound, easy on the ear, and it made him smile. 'I imagine your brother was like that?'

'Yes. He came out to Spain while we were in winter

quarters. I wasn't expecting him. Our father always said one son risking life and limb was enough and refused to obtain colours for Jeremy.' He smiled suddenly, as he remembered. 'There wasn't a speck of dirt on his uniform, and the epaulettes, buttons and gold braid gleamed. He looked as though he had just come from the Riseborough Hall drawing room, while I looked more like a scarecrow.'

Annette looked across the table at him and could not believe he had ever looked anything but impeccable. His eyes had a distant look, as if he were not in the room with her, but back in Spain with his brother—the brother he had loved and whom she despised.

'Come to join you,' Jeremy had said, grinning at Charles. 'Thought I'd have a crack at old Boney. Aren't you pleased to see me?'

'Of course. But I wonder at Papa allowing it.'

'It was his idea. Said it would make a man of me…'

'Oh? What have you done?' Only some scrape or scandal would have made their father change his mind about allowing Jeremy to come.

'Nothing, brother, nothing.' He had looked sheepish. 'Well, it was only a mild flirtation, a bit of a romp. Don't know what she had to complain of…'

'No, you wouldn't.'

Sadly this was true. Jeremy had never considered the consequences of what he did. If a fancy had come into his head to do something he'd done it without thinking, be it swimming a river, climbing a tree, riding hell for leather, making outrageous wagers, flirting with any pretty girl who crossed his path. Though he had been sensible enough not to choose the daughters of their father's friends. And somehow he'd always got away with it.

It was then he had described the nursery maid, his face becoming animated as he spoke. 'She's a little peach. Pity she's so toplofty.'

'Oh, Jeremy, you fool!'

'No worse than anyone else. A little flirtation does no harm. You should try it some time. You can't mourn Bella for the rest of your life, you know. You are the heir, and need to start another family.'

Jeremy had only been repeating what his father and stepmother had said the last time he had been home on leave, just after Bella had died, but he had no intention of subjecting any other woman to the kind of life he led. He had not been fair to her.

'I don't see the necessity when you are around to supply the deficiency—although it ought not to be a nursery maid.'

'Good God! I never thought of *marrying* her. What do you take me for?'

He realised with a start that Annette had stopped eating and was looking at him, waiting for him to go on. He did not think it was wise to tell her everything; it would hurt her. And the last thing he wanted was to distress her; she had had enough of that already. Suddenly he realised that it mattered to him what happened to her; it mattered very much. In the last couple of hours he had come to admire her for her courage, for the very pride he had been doing his best to conquer, for her determination to keep her child. If he had had any idea of taking the infant from her and carrying him off to Riseborough he dismissed it now. He could not do it. In fact he would not even tell his stepmother he had found her.

'We had been idle all winter,' he went on. 'But when the snow began to disappear preparations were made to continue the fight, and by then the odds were in favour of the allies. We had been receiving reinforcements for some time—not only men, but guns and ammunition, food, horses and fodder. The men had not been behaving well while they were in winter quarters, but as soon as the order came to move they were as keen as mustard.' He gave a quirky grin, but Annette was not sure if he was smiling at her or his own memories. 'They had heard there was untold treasure in the French baggage train, and it put a spring in their step as they marched. Jeremy was laughing and making jokes, as he always did. If he was worried about what lay ahead he did not show it.'

'But you were worried?'

'Not for myself. I am an old hand. But I worried about the raw recruits, and especially about Jeremy. When the battle began I was too busy with my own bit of the action to wonder where he was, but after it was all over, when the French retreat had turned into a rout and they had abandoned the town and all their baggage, I went looking for him. I found him mortally wounded. He died in my arms.'

'I am sorry for your loss,' she said softly.

He fell silent and she waited, hoping he would remember he had promised her a loan and would give her the two or three guineas she had asked for. She could not leave until she had it. But he had settled back in his seat, his chin on his chest, apparently deep in thought.

CHAPTER FOUR

'I THINK perhaps you have always looked after your brother,' she said, to break the silence. 'Miss Musgrove told me you were always pulling him out of scrapes when you were boys.'

'Did she? He was three years younger than me, you see, and as we had no mother when we were boys I had to look after him. He was always into mischief, but there was never a malicious bone in his body. And I think he was genuinely fond of you.'

'What makes you say that?'

He smiled, wondering how much to tell her. 'He was speaking about you just before he died.' The little lie was worth it if it made her feel less angry. 'It is why I set out to find you.'

'Did you know who I was when you saved me from falling down in the street three days ago?'

'No. I was on my way to Mrs Porter's lodging house and expected to find you there. When I called I was told you had moved. It was then I remembered meeting you.'

'Goodness—why should you remember that and connect the girl with the parcel to your stepmother's one-time nursery maid?'

'I really do not know. There was something about you—something Jeremy said about the way you held yourself. Anyway, I thought it was worth trying to find you again and glad I am that I did.'

'Why? You surely do not feel responsible for me?'

He did not know how to answer that. He could hardly be held to account for his brother's misdeeds, although as a boy he had often taken Jeremy's punishment on his own shoulders. Perhaps if he had not done that Jeremy would have grown up a more responsible adult. 'In a way, I suppose I do.'

'None of it was your fault,' she said slowly. 'I am grateful for a delicious meal in comfortable surroundings, but I still have to find somewhere to live, to earn my living and bring up my son.'

Right on cue, Timothy stirred and began to whimper. Annette rose to go to him, but Charles was quicker. He went into the bedroom and picked the child up. 'Were you feeling neglected, my little cherub?' he queried, cradling him and rocking him in his arms.

The incongruous sight of the aristocratic soldier holding her son against an impeccable black superfine coat and murmuring nonsense struck Annette as both funny and very moving—as well as worrying. He would make some lucky child a wonderful papa. It was then she remembered that he had lost a child of his own; surely he did not mean to replace him with Timothy?

She reached out and almost snatched the infant from

him. 'Major, I must go. The afternoon is well advanced and I have yet to find lodgings. You said you would make me a loan. If you would be so good as to do so, I will be off. Rest assured I will repay it as soon as I can manage it.'

'How do you propose to do that?'

'Earn it. I have been taking in sewing.'

'Oh, so that was what was in the parcel?'

'Yes. I have been promised more. All I need is to find lodgings.'

'I think I can do better than that.'

'What do you mean?' She was extremely wary.

'You need a proper home…'

Her unease increased. 'Major Ashbrooke, if you think I would be prepared to—' she began angrily, gathering up her belongings one-handed as she spoke; her other arm was supporting her son, who was grizzling at being ignored.

He held up his hands as if to ward off a blow. 'Hold hard. Don't fly into the boughs. I never meant anything like that. I simply want to make sure you are comfortable, and that Timothy is healthy and growing strong. And you too. You are a little pale. I should like to see more roses in your cheeks.'

It was the first personal comment he had made, except to say he was not interested in her body, and she felt the heat come into her face. He saw it and smiled. 'That's better. I know you have had your faith in people severely shaken, but you must learn to trust again. I am not an ogre. After what you have told me I realise you have been badly treated, and I want only to make amends.'

'Make amends! No one can do that. Your brother made a fallen woman of me, a pariah not fit for respectable company. It is something I have to live with every day of my life. Only Timothy makes it easier to bear.'

'You do not have to bear it alone. Sit down again and listen, please.'

Slowly she obeyed, still wary, rocking her son to quieten him. He watched her a moment, wondering if he was doing the right thing. But, having found her and seen the conditions under which she was struggling to live, he could not leave her to it. She had tugged at his heartstrings in a way no woman had since he had lost Bella. He admired her pluck and independence, but he could not let her bring up his nephew on the pittance she could earn sewing. She needed a family to care for her. It was in his mind to try and find her mother's people, but in the meantime she needed protection. It was up to him to provide it.

He had spent the time earlier that afternoon while she was feeding Timothy wondering what to do. He could pay for lodgings for her, but he knew instinctively she would not accept that. He had been right, considering her reaction to his suggestion that she needed a home, and that was before he had even explained what he had in mind. He had thought of taking her to Brookside. It was time the house was opened up again, but on reflection he realised that installing her and her child there would certainly give the gabblegrinders something to get their teeth into. And if he were to restore her to her family there must be no hint of scandal or they might reject her. It was then he'd thought of the gate house.

'I own a small estate,' he said now. 'It is in the village of Brookley, just to the north of here.'

'I know. Jeremy told me. He said it was shut up after…'

'After my wife died. Yes it was. I was away at war and did not need it.' His voice was level but she detected the hurt in his eyes. It was not only his brother's death that had put it there.

'But you are home now,' she said softly.

'Yes, I have been thinking it is time the house was lived in once more. At present there is a very small skeleton staff, headed by Mrs Hurst. She is the widow of one of my sergeants, a brave and resourceful man I was proud to fight alongside.'

'What has that to do with me?'

'I think we could help each other. If you agree, that is.'

'Major, what are you suggesting? You know I could not live under the same roof as you without causing a great deal of gossip. Your good name would be ruined, and as for me I would be branded the harlot your step-mother called me, a kept woman…'

Timmy had fallen asleep in her arms and she looked down at him with loving tenderness. Carefully she put him down on the hearth rug, where he could come to no harm; there was no fire in the grate on such a warm day, though it was not as hot as it had been. For him she would make any sacrifice, so had she any right to be so particular?

'I thought you would say that, and I must agree with you.'

'Then what?' she asked in surprise, straightening up to look at him.

'There is a gate house which is presently unoccupied. You are welcome to live there.'

'On what terms? If it is in the country, how am I to earn my living?'

'By helping Mrs Hurst open up Brookside and make it habitable again. I am afraid it has been sadly neglected for more than four years, and is in want of a lady's touch.'

She laughed suddenly. 'How do you know I would be any good at that? Apart from Riseborough Hall, I know nothing of grand houses.'

'I will take a chance on that. So, what do you say we give it a try? A home and a small wage for the work you do. Would it not be better that struggling on here?'

She thought about it long and hard. The idea seemed attractive, but if she and Mrs Hurst did not get on she would be back where she started—worse, for she would have lost the customers she had. And how much would he try to interfere in the bringing up of her child? But she was strong enough to resist that, wasn't she? And when his house was once more the home he wanted it to be he would surely give her a reference so that she could find somewhere else? Could she afford to turn down what was, after all, a godsend?

She had been looking down at her son, but now she looked up into his face. He was smiling at her, the expression in his eyes softly appealing, as if he truly needed her help. It was nonsense, of course, but she found herself nodding. 'Very well. A trial. Provided it is convenient to Mrs Hurst.'

'Good.'

'There is a condition. If I accept your help, I want a promise from you.'

'Oh?'

'Do not tell anyone at Riseborough you have found me. Especially do not mention Timothy.'

'Why? Do you think they will try and take him from you?' He knew as he spoke that it was exactly what she thought.

'Let them try!' It was said defiantly. 'I have made a life for myself as a widow and that is what I must remain.'

'Very well. I give you my word. I will say nothing unless you give me leave. I will arrange for you to stay here tonight, then we can go tomorrow—after we have been shopping.'

'Shopping?'

'Yes, shopping. You will need a cradle and a basket, and no doubt other things for young Timothy's well-being. We shall buy those tomorrow. I have arranged for one of the inn's servants to look after the child while we are out.' Seeing her about to object, he held up his hand. 'Now, do not put obstacles in the way for I am determined.'

He squatted down beside the baby, who had kicked off all his covering and was working his legs like a turtle thrown on its back. He tickled the child's stomach. 'Why, he smiled at me!'

'It is only wind.'

'I am sure it was a smile.' He stood up. 'I will leave you now, but I shall return tomorrow morning. Shall we